**Don't miss a single book
in the Broken Destiny series
from Jeaniene Frost and HQN Books**

JEANIENE FROST

THE BRIGHTEST EMBERS

Recycling programs for this product may not exist in your area.

ISBN-13: 978-0-373-78942-9

The Brightest Embers

This edition published by arrangement with Harlequin Books S.A.

For questions and comments about the quality of this book, please contact us at CustomerService@Harlequin.com.

® and TM are trademarks of Harlequin Enterprises Limited or its corporate affiliates. Trademarks indicated with ® are registered in the United States Patent and Trademark Office, the Canadian Intellectual Property Office and in other countries.

www.HQNBooks.com

Printed in U.S.A.

To everyone who has faced long odds,
and kept fighting anyway.

CHAPTER ONE

I WALKED INTO the museum with a half demon holding my hand and a gargoyle waiting for me back at our car. As a history major, I'd often dreamed about going museum hopping throughout Europe, but not once had I pictured doing it like this.

"We're here for the four p.m. tour," Adrian, my new husband and the aforementioned half demon, told the museum attendant.

"The four p.m. tour group is over there," she said, pointing toward a small cluster of people about a dozen feet away.

As we walked off, Adrian traced the braided rope tattoo on my right hand. My sleeve hid the rest of it, just like my high-necked blouse and long pants hid the remains of the other hallowed weapon that had supernaturally merged with my flesh. If the hallowed weapon we were looking for was here, I'd no doubt end up with a third supernatural tattoo.

Of course, that tattoo might one day end up decorating my cold dead corpse.

"Feel anything, Ivy?" Adrian asked in a low voice.

I directed my senses outward and felt the distinct vibes that meant this was hallowed ground, as well as extra brushes of power from the various religious relics in this museum. But I didn't feel anything potent enough to punch a hole through every demon realm in existence, and that was the specific ancient relic we were after.

"No," I said, frustration coloring my tone.

I hadn't felt the power we were seeking when we were at Saint Peter's Basilica in Rome last week, or the Hofburg Palace in Vienna earlier this week. Now we were at the Mother See of Holy Etchmiadzin complex in Vagharshapat, Armenia. This was the third place in the world claiming possession of the spearhead of Longinus, aka the Holy Lance, aka the final hallowed weapon that I was supposedly fated to wield. The third time was, unfortunately, not the charm according to my lineage-derived radar. I could sense hallowed objects, and the famed spearhead wasn't here, unless wards were messing with my ability to feel it.

I wasn't optimistic about our chances. "I suppose if the real spearhead was at one of the places it was supposed to be at, demons would've stolen it centuries ago," I said.

Someone close enough to overhear that gave me a startled look. I just waved at her. I wasn't worried about shocking her with the truth about demons, demons' minions, Archons—better known as angels— or any of the other supernatural creatures I now knew were real. I could spend the next twenty minutes telling everyone here that all these things existed, and no one would believe me even if a bunch of demons were breathing down their necks while I spoke. I knew that from experience.

Adrian drew me closer, brushing back my dark brown hair. "We had to check out this museum to be sure the spearhead wasn't hiding in plain sight. Besides," he murmured, leaning down until his mouth nearly touched mine, "this might not be a successful relic hunt, but it's turning into a great honeymoon."

My cheeks weren't the only parts of me to grow warm at his statement, yet instead of leaning into his lips, I pushed him back. The look in his eyes said he was about to kiss me in a way more suited to our bedroom than a museum located on the headquarters of the Armenian Apostolic Church.

Still, Adrian was right. We might have struck out at finding the third hallowed weapon, but other than that, this had been the best month of my life. I'd used the second hallowed weapon to close the gateways between the demon realms and our world, effectively locking the demons out. That made it a thousand times safer for me, Adrian, my sister, our friend Costa and every other person in the world. Only demons' minions were left on this side of the realms, and with their demon masters locked up, the minions seemed to be running scared instead of terrorizing anyone.

"Kiss me later. Let's do the tour now," I told Adrian. "I might not feel anything, but the last weapon's power was blocked by wards. Maybe the spearhead is here, and I just can't feel it yet."

"Maybe," Adrian said, his light tone belying the sudden darkening of his sapphire-colored gaze.

Then he straightened, and just like that, the teasing, passionate man I loved was replaced by a hardened fighter who'd been raised by demons to be the world's most effective killer. I took in a deep breath, reminding myself that the demons' efforts had backfired. Now Adrian used all of his amazing abilities to fight against them instead of for them.

Besides, he was only gearing up in case the spearhead *was* here. If so, its incredible power would compel me into attempting to use it on the spot, and I wasn't ready to do that. Not yet. That was why Adrian would fight to the last ounce of his demonically fueled, destiny-enhanced strength to stop me.

Because if I did use the spearhead now, it would kill me.

AS IT TURNED OUT, neither one of us had anything to worry about. One glance at the relic should've been enough to prove that it wasn't the real deal. Touching the glass around it to make sure it hadn't been protected by wards had almost been redundant. A first-century Roman spearhead wasn't a short, flat, ornamental object that looked better suited to be a necklace than an ancient tool of war. It was a nasty, two-foot iron shank crowned with a sharp, pyramid-shaped point designed to impale someone even through protective armor.

No, this was another replica, and now we had no idea where to look for the real spearhead. Adrian wasn't nearly as upset about that as I was, and he wasn't even trying to pretend otherwise.

"You could at least fake some disappointment," I said as we left the museum and walked toward our rental van.

He gave me a sideways glance. "Then I'd be lying, and I thought we agreed there would be no more lies between us."

We had, but he didn't need to rub in how he'd much rather that I never found, let alone wielded, the spearhead. I could understand his reasons, but if I gave this up, then the demons would win and thousands of innocent people would die.

"And I thought *you* agreed to support me," I said, the weight of all those lives making my tone sharper.

Adrian stopped and turned to face me. The sun was starting to set, casting artificial shades of red across his golden hair. His towering height, impressive physique and gorgeous features had turned countless heads as we walked, but he didn't seem to notice anyone else. Adrian stared at me as if I was the only person on this massive complex.

"I do support you." The smoothness in his tone didn't fool me. Unbreakable ties could also be made of finest silk. "My every action is driven by my undying love for you, in fact. What more do you want?"

Put that way, what more could I want? Yet something still felt…off, as if what Adrian *wasn't* saying was more important than his words.

Underneath my joy this past month, I'd also had a nagging feeling that I was missing something important. Of course, it could be that I just didn't know how to truly be happy. I'd never had a real relationship before. Plus, until six months ago, I and everyone else who knew me had believed I was crazy.

"I know you're not chomping at the bit to find the spearhead because using it is dangerous for me," I said, exploring that nagging feeling. "But I've survived lots of risks before, remember? I'll come out on top this time, too."

Adrian opened his mouth as if to argue, then closed it. "I know you will," he said, still in that smooth, easygoing tone. "You're just not ready to wield it yet. That's why I'm glad none of these relics have been real. Later, when you've had more time to train, you'll be prepared to handle it."

"Yeah, well, later better end up being sooner," I muttered. All the people still trapped in the demon realms couldn't wait years for me to bulk up on my supernatural fortitude.

"Don't worry," Adrian said, intensity deepening his voice this time. "I'll keep you safe. I promise."

I gave him a lopsided smile. Yes, between Adrian and our good friend Costa training me, my stamina, strength and skills had grown by leaps and bounds. Eventually, with more training, I was counting on it being enough to keep me alive when I attempted to wield the final hallowed weapon—assuming we ever found it.

I shook off that nagging feeling. It had to be me projecting my own paranoia onto Adrian. After all, aside from our fight when I'd decided to go after the spearhead, Adrian hadn't argued with me about it. He'd arranged these trips, helped me train and been nothing but supportive. So, even though I felt like I'd grown an inner "trouble brewing" sensor in addition to my hallowed one, it had to be in my head.

"Fine," I said, my tone brightening. "Since the spearhead is a bust, do you know any good restaurants around here?"

I stopped speaking when Adrian flung me forward. He'd shoved me so hard that I would have hit the pavement facefirst if not for all the training I'd undergone. Instead, I rolled, muscle memory taking over. Several loud pops sounded in quick succession above me, as rapid as fireworks, yet when they were followed by screams, I knew what they really were. Gunfire.

"Ivy, run!" Adrian shouted.

I darted toward the nearest car for coverage. I didn't have to worry about Adrian—bullets weren't lethal to him. He hadn't joined me behind the car, but he'd run in the direction of the shots. That would be suicidal for anyone else, but his half-demon bloodline meant that only another demon could kill Adrian.

"I'm good!" I shouted so Adrian wouldn't worry about me.

The car window above me shattered from another round of gunfire. Worse, the angle from that shot had been completely different. That meant we were being attacked by *two* shooters.

I hit the ground and began to crawl toward another car, shredding my knees on the concrete, but not caring about the pain. Another shot hit the ground only an inch away, and I lurched forward to avoid the next one.

"Larastra!" I shouted to Brutus, using the Demonish command Adrian had taught me. I hoped the gargoyle could hear me. Our rental van was on the other side of the parking lot.

A familiar roar responded to my shouted command, followed by a much louder crashing sound. I fervently hoped it was my pet who'd caused that noise instead of a third attacker joining the mix, but I didn't dare pick my head up to look. I stayed as low as I could, hunkered behind a truck that should be wide enough to protect me.

New screams jerked my head around. A blonde girl knelt next to a nearby car. She was shaking all over, yet her gaze appeared almost blank when she looked at me. She also wasn't crouched low enough to be safe.

"Get down," I hissed.

Her eyes widened, but she didn't move. Maybe she couldn't. I'd seen shock freeze people before, but she needed to get down or—

"Dammit!" I shouted when blood bloomed on her shoulder after another burst of gunfire. She shook harder yet still didn't drop down low enough to avoid another hit. I glanced in the direction where the shots were coming from. I was no expert, but from the angle, the shooter was probably on a roof. That would give him a great view of the parking lot and me, if I came out from behind the truck to help her.

I'd get shot if I did that. That was probably the gunman's plan: wing the blonde in order to lure me out. Well, I had news for him. I was staying right here.

"Help me," the blonde girl whispered.

She had blue eyes like my sister. She looked to be about Jasmine's age, too. And she was caught up in a war she didn't even know existed.

Stay where you are! a dark sense of self-preservation urged me. *If this girl can't duck, that's her problem, not yours!*

Don't you dare! my conscience snapped back. *She doesn't deserve this. These shooters are here for* you, *not her!*

This might be reckless, but I couldn't leave her out in the open. If the gunman had winged her once to get my attention, he'd do it again, and she might not survive the next one. I rose from my crouch to get better traction, then stared at her.

Here I come, I mouthed.

CHAPTER TWO

I LUNGED FORWARD with all the speed of my supernatural lineage. It still wasn't enough. Pain erupted in my calf and I heard another loud crack, but I was still able to tackle the girl and get her all the way behind the car. Then I placed her hand over her gunshot wound.

"Stay down and keep pressure on this."

She still looked like she was numb from shock, but her hand stayed where I'd put it, and she didn't try to get up. I gave her a firm nod for encouragement.

"Don't move. Help is on the way."

Another explosion of glass followed my promise, then another one, and another. The shooter was trying to blast his way through the car to get to us. We were sheltered now, but the car could only take so much before one of those rounds made it through.

I looked at my calf. Blood flowed freely from a nasty hole that hurt as bad as it looked. When I tried to put weight on it, I had to bite back a cry. I could walk on it, maybe even run, but not fast enough to avoid getting shot again.

I was weighing my options when a massive winged beast landed on the car behind us. The hood crumpled like a tin can under his weight, and I had only a second to hear the car alarm go off before the gargoyle's roar deafened me to everything else.

"Good boy!" I said to Brutus in relief. "Who's getting steak tonight?"

My pet gargoyle, Brutus, spread out his leathery wings as if he knew I needed the cover. I ran to him and scrambled onto his back, using the harness he always wore now.

More cracks of gunfire sounded. From the way Brutus jerked, they'd hit him. His scaly hide was too thick for the bullets to really injure him, but they must've stung. Brutus let out another roar, his talons shredding the car's hood in outrage. Then a beat of his mighty wings had us airborne. I didn't want him to merely fly us away, though. I wanted to stop this shooter before he hurt anyone else.

I pulled on the reins, directing Brutus to fly nearly straight up. Then I angled him downward toward the roof of the museum Adrian and I had recently left. There was a small structure on that roof, like a short turret, and I glimpsed the barrel from a long sniper rifle protruding from its open window.

I gave it a vengeful look, then patted Brutus's side. "Let's get him, boy!" I shouted, and steered Brutus right at that window. Then I hid behind the gargoyle's wide back.

Brutus knew what I wanted him to do. He drew in his massive wings at the last moment, leaving his body streamlined for maximum velocity. I braced when we burst through the window, his body taking out a lot of the wall, too. We landed with a thump that made all my bones rattle.

I forgot about that when I opened my eyes. Brutus had landed on someone hard enough to make the guy's guts burst out of his sides. I was worried until I saw the rifle in the dead guy's hands. When the shooter began to turn to ash, my suspicions proved correct.

Only minions and demons turned to ash after they died. Since demons were locked away in their realms, not to mention we were currently on hallowed ground that demons couldn't cross, the dead gunman had to be a minion.

Brutus spun in a half circle, his long, leathery wings shooting out. Until then, I hadn't noticed the second guy crouched on the far side of the room. He sprawled forward under the blow, looking stunned as well as terrified. Light rolled over his eyes, as if he were an animal caught in a car's headlights. That inhuman trait outed him as a minion, too.

"N-n-nice birdie," he stuttered at Brutus.

Thanks to Archon glamour, he didn't see a massive, nine-foot-tall gargoyle with dragon-like wings and grayish-blue reptilian skin. Instead, he and everyone else saw only a fluffy-feathered seagull. Granted, one that had somehow flown through a window and stomped his buddy to death, all while carrying a passenger on his back. No wonder the minion looked as if he didn't know whether to scream or to faint.

"Davidian," the minion said. "Have mercy."

"Mercy?" I repeated in disbelief. "You mean like the mercy minions show humans when you enslave them for your demon masters? Or the mercy demons showed my adoptive parents when they murdered them and pinned their deaths on me? Or maybe you mean the mercy demons showed my sister when they used her as bait in one of their countless attempts to kill me?"

He glared at me almost sullenly. "Who are you to judge? You've murdered hundreds of people."

"No, I've killed hundreds of *demons*," I corrected him, waving my tattooed right hand at him. "King David's ancient slingshot turned out to pack quite a punch, but I'll tell you what. I'll show you the same mercy you just showed me when you watched your friend use me as target practice."

His look became hopeful. "You'll let me run for it?"

"Make it to the door and you're a free man," I told him, loosening Brutus's reins. "I promise I won't stop you."

He whirled around—and Brutus lunged forward, biting him in half with one vicious snap of his huge jaws.

"Details matter," I said under my breath. "You should've made me promise not to let *him* stop you, either."

Once, I would have been horrified by seeing a man bit in half, but that person was long gone now. She'd been replaced by the new me, and the new me had been hardened from grief, betrayal, survival and a whole lot of destiny and death.

Plus, if I'd let the minion go, he would have destroyed more peoples' lives. Now the only thing he was destroying was the carpet as his ashes stained and smoldered on it.

"Good boy," I said again to Brutus, holding on tighter when his instant, happy wiggles were enough to almost unseat me. Brutus loved praise more than he loved life itself. "Now you'll get *two* steaks for dinner tonight."

CHAPTER THREE

I HAD BRUTUS fly us down from the back of the roof, where there were the least amount of people. Sure, someone would still swear that they saw a woman and a seagull jump from the second story, but no one would believe them. Just like no one would believe that a seagull had carried a woman on its back up through the tower window in the first place. I wasn't being naive. I'd seen cell phone videos of a demon realm spilling onto a college campus be dismissed as "fake," let alone eyewitness testimony from hundreds of people be discredited as "mass hysteria."

The bottom line was, most people refused to believe whatever they didn't *want* to believe, and no one wanted to believe in demons, let alone demon realms existing alongside our world. I hadn't wanted to believe in that, either, and my lineage had caused me to see through demon glamour my whole life. I'd only accepted that I wasn't suffering from hallucinations, as doctors had long told me, after minions tried to kidnap me. Adrian had saved me, then had taken me to meet a powerful Archon named Zach, who told me I was the last descendant of King David's line and thus destiny-bound to fight demons with three hallowed weapons.

Even then, I'd still hoped that I was hallucinating. Especially then.

Still, I wasn't going to push things by having Brutus fly me back to the parking lot in full view of all the spectators there. Instead, we ran with me under the protective canopy of Brutus's wings. I didn't hear more gunfire, but the fight might not be over. Brutus and I had taken out one gunman and his henchman. Where was the other shooter?

And where was Adrian? Bullets might not be able to kill him, but they could injure him, and I couldn't risk him being carried off in an incapacitated state. If there was one person minions wanted to cart off to their demon masters more than me, it was Adrian. He was the last descendant of Judas who'd refused to fulfill his destiny by betraying me unto death.

More people were hiding behind the first couple rows of cars we ran past. They didn't know I'd taken care of the roof shooter. My heart began to pound when I found a blood trail that started at roughly the same point where Adrian and I had been standing when the first shots were fired. The splatter thickened as it led deeper into the parking lot. That wasn't my blood or the girl's blood. We'd been shot on the other side of the parking lot. *Please*, I found myself thinking. *Don't let Adrian be badly hurt!*

I burst around the next row of cars…and skidded to a stop in relief. Adrian had a blond-haired minion pinned beneath him, and while Adrian had a bullet wound hole in his shoulder, he must not be too injured. Not from how he was pounding the stuffing out of the minion he'd tackled.

"You tried to kill Ivy. Why?" I heard Adrian demand between brutal rib punches.

I would've thought the "why" was obvious. The

minion must've thought it was a stupid question, too. He let out a pained laugh and said something in Demonish, which was what I called the strange, harshly beautiful language that demons spoke. Whatever it was, it pissed Adrian off into a whole new level of outrage.

"Fuck you," he snarled. Then his fist slammed into the minion's face with such force, it went all the way through to the back of his skull. I winced, both at the instant gore splatter and at the impact as concrete finally stopped his blow. If Adrian's hand weren't broken after this, it would be a miracle.

"You *murdered* him!" a woman screamed, coming out from behind a nearby car. Then with shaking hands, she pulled out a Taser from her purse and pointed it at Adrian.

Brutus let out a warning chuff and squared off on her. He wouldn't tolerate anyone threatening us, human or otherwise.

Something about the noise he made caused the woman to blanch, as if on an instinctive level she sensed the predator he really was. If she could see Brutus's real form behind the seagull disguise, she wouldn't just pale. She'd piss herself.

"No," I told Brutus, yanking on his harness for emphasis. To the woman, I said, "You're in shock. He didn't kill anyone. There's no one else here but the three of us."

"There is!" she snapped. "He's right there—"

She stopped in midsentence when the minion crumbled into ashes before her eyes. Adrian got up, shaking the blood off his right hand while brushing the ashes from his jeans with his left. Soon, the blood on him turned to ashes, too, and all of those dark specks began to slowly blow away in the breeze.

"That's...that's not possible," the woman whispered.

"Like I said, you're in shock from the shooting," I went on. "The mind plays tricks on people when that happens. Go home, be with your family and don't think about this again."

More people were starting to peek around the cars they'd been hiding behind. It wouldn't be long before an ambulance showed up, which would be good for the wounded girl, but the police would soon follow, and that was a hassle we didn't need.

Adrian knew it, too. "Time to go," he said, taking my arm. Then he stopped, cursing when he saw my leg. "You've been hit."

"Flesh wound," I said, which was true, although it didn't help with how much it hurt.

Adrian picked me up. "There's manna in the van," he said, striding away from the onlookers. "We'll get you fixed up on the way to the hotel."

We'd parked the van at the back of the lot, where a big tree had shaded it from the sunlight Brutus hated so much. One look at it, though, and I knew we wouldn't be leaving in that.

"Brutus killed it, too," I said, sighing at the missing side door and the long, rending claw marks. No way were we getting our security deposit back.

Adrian set me down and pulled our duffel bag out of the ruined van, then emptied the glove box of our paperwork.

"Brutus can fly us back," he told me, taking the small plastic bag out of the duffel bag. It looked like it contained crumpled-up sugar cookies, but the substance that Adrian smeared on my leg wasn't baked goods. It was the famed bread of heaven that had sustained the Israelites for over forty years in the desert. Only, manna was good for a lot more than food. It could also heal anything except for a mortal wound.

I cast a dubious look at the not-quite-dark sky. "That's a lot of exposure. Why risk it when we can take a cab?"

"We need to get back before dark," he said, picking me up and carrying me even though the manna would heal me in another few moments. Brutus easily kept pace with Adrian's rapid strides, his big head swiveling around to check for danger.

"What's the rush? We don't have to worry about being outside after dark anymore. There are no more demons in our world, remember?"

"Maybe, maybe not," he responded, his pace increasing. "It's possible some of them managed to stay behind here."

"What?" I burst out. "How? You told me demons couldn't stand our realm for long. It's been over four weeks since the gateways slammed shut, so any demons stranded on our side should be dead by now!"

"Not if they're on cursed earth," he countered, heading for a cluster of trees. "You remember the demon I trapped beneath that old chapel? I cursed the ground he was on so he could stand being in our realm, even beneath a church. Demons had advance warning that you were going after Moses's staff, and they knew it could close the gateways. Some of them could've cursed sections of ground in this world as safe places in case you succeeded, which you did."

This was the first I was hearing about the possibility

of demons still being in our world. Why hadn't he told me before?

I didn't have a chance to ask that, let alone any of the other questions that sprang to mind. Adrian hoisted me onto Brutus's back with a muttered "Damn, sun's almost down." Then he jumped behind me, grabbing the reins and shouting, *"Tarate!"*

The gargoyle took off, leaving the Mother See's complex of buildings, churches and museums below us. The sky stretched out in front of us, the few remaining dusky shades of sunset darkening into the bluish-black haze of night.

I told myself it looked nothing like when a demon realm swallowed a place in our world, and mostly, I was right. Still, I couldn't shake my feeling of foreboding as the darkness spread until it snuffed out the last remains of the light. Something bad was coming with that darkness, I could feel it.

And if Adrian was right, that something might be demons.

CHAPTER FOUR

OUR HOTEL HAD been more than thirty minutes away by car. By air, it took less than fifteen. Adrian used the GPS on his smartwatch to find it, since you couldn't see street signs from this height, then had Brutus land on the hotel's roof. That allowed us more privacy for our unusual arrival. Even though there were other buildings around, most people didn't spend their evenings staring up at the night sky.

"Did you try Jasmine and Costa again?" Adrian asked as one hard kick broke the lock on the roof's only door.

"Yes. Still no answer."

I tried to control my rising fear. Maybe they'd gone out on a date. My sister and Costa thought we didn't know that they'd started seeing each other, but we did. We were just waiting for them to admit it to us.

"Wait here with Brutus," Adrian said curtly. "I'll be back in ten minutes. Any sign of danger, have him fly you away."

"No way," I snapped. "If a demon *is* somehow here, I'm not leaving you, Jasmine and Costa alone to deal with it."

"If one is, *you're* in the most danger," he shot back. "If nothing's wrong, you only waste ten minutes up here while I make sure that Costa and Jasmine are ignoring their phones because they're too busy having fun."

"But I'm the only one who has this," I said, pointing at the slingshot embedded in my right arm. "This can kill demons, so I'm going with you. End of discussion."

His features hardened in a way that said he wasn't listening. I started to shove past him, but he pushed me back and said a word in Demonish I'd never heard before.

Brutus snatched me around the waist and pulled me back against him. His arms crossed around my midsection when I tried to wrest away, and pounding against them was as effective as trying to chop down trees with my bare hands.

"Ten minutes," Adrian said over my furious demands to be released. "If I'm not back by then, leave."

With that, he disappeared into the staircase. I continued my struggles while cursing both Adrian and Brutus. The gargoyle whined as if in apology, but his unbreakable grip didn't loosen. After a few minutes, I realized that all my struggles were doing was giving me a nice set of bruises.

Still, I wasn't about to give up. I was destiny-bound to save people, dammit! Not to stand by and let others do the fighting for me. Brutus apparently couldn't be berated into releasing me, but maybe there was another way.

"Who's a good boy?" I suddenly asked, ceasing my struggles.

Brutus's whine changed, sounding less sorry and more hopeful. I couldn't be sure, but I thought I also felt his back end start to shift from side to side. Over the past couple months, I'd found out that Brutus loved being praised, to the point where when he got lots of it, he fluttered his wings and shook his butt as if he were wagging an invisible tail. Sometimes, he did both things with such fervor, he nearly knocked himself over. Watching a huge, right-out-of-your-nightmares gargoyle do that was hilarious, yet now it might also be exactly what I needed.

"Whooooo's a goooooood boyyyy?" I said again, elongating my vowels and increasing my pitch to a baby-talk voice.

I *definitely* felt a wag this time, and his wings began to inch up as if he were a peacock about to display its feathers. I increased my compliments, telling Brutus that he was the cutest, smartest gargoyle who ever lived. That got me more butt-shakes and wing-fluffs, but not enough to do what I needed.

"You know what I'm going to do?" I crooned, adding in bribes. "I'm going to give you five, no, six, no, seven, yes, *seven* big pot roasts tonight! Because you're the bestest, most beautiful Brutus, yes you are, yes you are!"

His whole body began to shake with joyous anticipation. He might not understand tons of English, but he knew the words *pot roast*. It was his favorite raw meat. His wings began to flutter frantically and his butt wagged so hard, he almost knocked himself off his feet. Most important, his grip loosened.

I slithered beneath his arms and ran for the door as fast as I could. Brutus lunged, but it was too late. His overly delighted state had distracted him, costing him precious seconds, so his talons ended up grasping only air as he tried to grab me. The narrow space in the stairwell was too small for his wide body to fit through.

"Sorry, boy!" I called out as I ran down the staircase.

His betrayed-sounding howl chased after me, making me feel guilty, but I'd make this up to Brutus later. Now I had to make sure that Adrian, Jasmine and Costa were okay. Our rooms were on the fifth floor, only three floors down from where I was. It shouldn't take me long to get to them—

Pain erupted in my right hand. Then the braided brown rope of my tattoo began to change color, lightening to a beautiful golden shade. Seeing it, my heart began to pound.

Only one thing in the world caused my supernatural tattoo to change color and burn like it had suddenly caught fire, and that was the close proximity of a demon.

CHAPTER FIVE

I GRABBED THE glowing etching and pulled. More pain shot through me, but I came away with a loop of rope as the ancient tattoo became as real as the danger I was in. I kept pulling, ignoring the increasing pain. By the time I reached the fifth floor, my whole arm throbbed, yet the entire length of the famed sling that David had used to slay the giant Goliath was now a real, tangible weapon.

A feminine scream caused panic to bolt through me. That sounded like Jasmine. I burst through the door leading to the fifth floor. As I ran down the hallway, I saw a large mirror propped against the wall. It hadn't been there before, and since demons used mirrors as portals for travel, its presence was ominous.

In the short moment that I was distracted, a door opened and a guy pushed his room service cart right in front of me. I was running too fast to avoid it, and I hit it hard enough to knock it over. It fell with a crash, yet I barely registered that, or the startled yelp the hotel guest made. Something more important caught my eye.

The vase on the cart had been filled with decorative glass rocks, and those rocks were now scattered across the floor.

I snatched up as many as I could, not caring that I slashed my hands on the broken plates in my haste. I stuffed most of the rocks into my pockets, but I put one in the notch on my sling.

New crashing sounds and fresh screams turned my blood to ice. I ran toward the racket, wincing at how the other tattoo running along the length of my body now felt like it was burning, too. Moses's staff, the second hallowed weapon that had melded into my flesh, must react to the presence of demons, too, yet I had no idea if it would manifest like the sling did. This was the first time I'd been near demons since I'd wielded it to close the gates between their realm and mine.

Adrian crashed through the wall about thirty feet ahead, grappling with someone whose long mass of reddish-black hair hid her face. I started to spin my sling. The unknown woman had to be a demon. A human or minion wouldn't be able to take the punch he slammed into her, let alone to reciprocate with a block that knocked Adrian off his feet. She immediately jumped onto him, and I glimpsed a smile through her wild tangle of hair. Why did the demon look as if she were enjoying his fierce, bucking attempts to dislodge her...?

"Sonofabitch!" I spat, recognizing her.

I'd met this particular demon only once, but she was hard to forget, and that had more to do with how she'd been Adrian's longtime girlfriend than it did with her looks. Some demons looked like normal people. Some appeared animalistic, right down to the cliché horns and hooves, and some, like Obsidiana, were so beautiful that it actually hurt a little to look at them.

"Get off him, you bitch!" I shouted.

She finally noticed me, and Obsidiana shot me a single, malevolent glare before jumping off Adrian.

He seemed as surprised by her instant compliance as I was, but he leapt up just as fast, going right for her throat. He'd ripped it out the last time they'd fought, yet Obsidiana must've remembered that.

She dodged him with lightning-like swiftness, using his momentum to spin him into the wall. It dented from how hard he hit it, and before I could release the stone from my rapidly spinning sling, she had Adrian in front of her like a shield. Her blood-red nails shot out to the length of knives, and she jabbed them into Adrian's throat.

"One more step, Davidian, and I rip out his jugular," she said in a purr, her distinctive accent the same as Adrian's.

I tried not to think about everything else they had in common. She'd been Adrian's lover for longer than I'd been alive, and I wasn't too proud to admit that I was ragingly jealous of her. But not enough to risk Adrian's life. I lowered the sling and didn't move. Obsidiana raked her topaz-colored gaze over me, taking me in from head to feet.

"Is this the real you?" she asked, arching a brow.

"In the flesh," I said, arching my brow right back at her.

The other times Obsidiana had seen me, I'd been disguised by Archon glamour. I wasn't now, and as her expression turned contemptuous, you'd think I had morphed into a dead mouse that some alley cat had dropped at her feet. Well, screw her. As I'd told her once, beauty faded, but Evil Bitch was forever.

"I can't believe you left me for *that*," she finally said to Adrian. "Honestly, darling, you're punishing yourself."

I wanted to flip her off with both hands, but I didn't dare. If Obsidiana had harnessed enough dark energy to curse the ground in order to stay in our realm, she was a lot more powerful than I'd initially given her credit for. That made her even more dangerous to Adrian.

He didn't seem to share my concern. He laughed, a low, vicious sound. "I hadn't met Ivy when I left you, Obsidiana. I did it because I was happier alone than I had been with you."

Ooh, burn! I thought, but still said nothing. Hell hath no fury like a demoness scorned. Didn't Adrian realize that?

"I remember you being happy," she said, her voice deepening into a seductive caress. "Many, many times."

I stiffened, and from her smirk, she'd caught it even though she acted as if Adrian had her full attention.

"Too many times to count," she continued, her other hand starting to play with his hair. "You hurl cruel words at me now, *benhoven*, but your cruelty only confirms the whispers I've heard. The man I love is still inside you. That is why I risked so much to see you. The little Davidian tried to turn you into something you are not, but she failed." Obsidiana shot another hostile glance my way. "She just doesn't know how badly she failed yet—"

Adrian grabbed her wrists, yanking them forward and bending over at the same time. The force he used flipped her over his head as if he were a professional wrestler. I let out a horrified gasp at the instant spurt of blood as her nails tore into his throat. Then I couldn't see anything through her dark mass of hair and the tangle of limbs as he landed on top of her.

CHAPTER SIX

"ADRIAN!" I SHOUTED, running over to them.

Obsidiana screamed as my sling touched her, but I couldn't even relish her pain. I was too frantic as a red gush flowed from Adrian's throat. I tried to stem that flow, but unbelievably, Adrian shoved me away. Obsidiana lunged at me as much as she could while trapped under his body. Her daggerlike nails raked over my stomach, cutting through my clothes and into my flesh, then Adrian grabbed her by the throat and pulled. Hard.

Her body went limp, but blood didn't gush out. Her jugular vein wasn't in her throat. Demon physiology was different. Adrian had just ripped out her version of a heart, yet that would render her only temporarily unconscious. Not kill her the way her attack on his throat might kill him.

"Adrian, stop!" I cried, flinging myself at him when it was obvious that he intended to keep tearing at Obsidiana.

He swayed, then looked down at the curtain of red streaming from his neck as if only now realizing that it was there. I kicked Obsidiana's limp body aside and set down my sling, then covered that gushing wound with my hands. I couldn't risk touching Adrian with the sling. He was half-demon, so when it was tangible like this, it would hurt him, too, and he was already too injured as it was.

"Lie back," I said, panic rising at how much blood he'd lost. "Don't move—it'll make it worse. Stay very still."

"Oh, shit!" a male voice said, then Costa, our best friend, came out of a nearby hotel room.

Some part of me was glad to see that Costa was okay, but I was too worried about Adrian to feel any real relief. "Where's Adrian's bag?" I said urgently. "He brought it with him, and it has manna in it. Bring it to me. Now!"

I couldn't get up to get it. If I didn't keep pressure on Adrian's neck, he'd bleed out right in front of me. With all the blood he'd lost, he still might. I tried not to burst into tears as I kept attempting to stem that horrible, pulsating flow. *Don't die, Adrian, please! I can't lose you now!*

Costa left, and I was vaguely aware of him cursing and overturning things in the nearby room. I also noticed that the fire safety sprinklers had activated, because water pelted me from seemingly all directions, yet I didn't move to wipe it away even when it hit me in the eyes. I kept all my attention on Adrian as I tried to close the gaping wound in his throat.

"You're going to be okay," I told him, smiling so he didn't know that I was terrified. *Don't die. Don't die. Don't die!* I mentally screamed. *You can't! I love you too much!*

"Ivy!" My sister knelt next to me. "What can I do?"

As if on autopilot, I answered, "Smash the mirror in the hallway." Otherwise, more powerful demons could use it to get here.

Jasmine ran off, and I heard the sound of glass breaking moments later. Then, so faintly I almost missed it, I heard Adrian's voice.

"Have to…kill her, Ivy."

I couldn't believe Adrian could talk with his throat half ripped out, and I tried not to panic at how more blood spurted through my fingers from his efforts.

"Don't talk," I urged him before yelling, "Where's the fucking manna, Costa?"

Adrian grabbed my wrist, his grip surprisingly strong. "Kill…'er," he repeated, jerking his head toward Obsidiana.

His movement sent another spurt of blood free. Now a strange wind began to blow my hair back, but I paid it no mind as I put more pressure on Adrian's neck.

"As soon as you're healed," I promised him.

Adrian grabbed his neck, blood making his hands slick enough to slide beneath mine despite the pressure I'd been applying. With his throat in a tighter grip than I'd dared, he stared at me, his sapphire-colored gaze seeming to burn.

"Now."

Didn't he know he was inches from death himself? Yes, Obsidiana would wake in an hour or so, but until then, she wasn't a threat.

Or was she? She'd been strong enough to survive on this side of the realms when the gateways had sealed. Maybe Adrian knew she'd wake a lot sooner than I expected her to.

"As soon as you get the manna," I said. I refused to endanger Adrian's life by killing Obsidiana now, even if it meant that waiting would endanger mine. I'd take that risk.

Adrian made a frustrated sound and tried to get up. I pushed him back, gasping, "Don't!" in horror. He only gestured angrily at Obsidiana. *Kill her now!* that wave demanded.

Costa finally came out of the hotel room, a heap of manna in his hand. I was so relieved; I couldn't tell if I started crying or if it was the water from the sprinklers.

"Move," he ordered, pushing me and Adrian's hands away.

I watched Costa smear the manna over Adrian's throat and found myself praying. That odd wind increased, until between that and the sprinklers increasing until they jetted out like fire hydrants, it was getting hard to see. If Adrian's injury was fatal, the manna would do nothing because it didn't work on mortal wounds. If he'd lost too much blood while waiting for Costa to find the manna, I'd have to watch him die.

The clump of manna over his throat immediately turned crimson, the flow of blood turning from paste into freely running liquid. I was shaking so hard, it felt like the whole hotel was shaking along with me.

"Ivy," Adrian whispered, his voice fainter as that merciless red flow continued down his throat. "Please…kill her."

Adrian *couldn't* be dying…but if he was and this was his final wish, I wouldn't fail him. The last thing he'd see was me killing the bitch who had done this to him.

I stood up and looked around almost blindly for the sling. Then my shaking hands caused me to miss it twice before I grabbed it. "I love you," I told Adrian, tears choking my voice.

I spun the sling as I kicked Obsidiana's body a safe

distance away from Adrian, then I hurled the glass stone it contained at her. Even with my vision blurry and my whole body shaking, the stone hit her right in the chest.

Her body burst into ashes as if I'd thrown a dozen supernatural grenades at her. The instant cloud of embers was caught by that strong breeze and rolled over us like a fog, coating me, Adrian and Costa in its dark wake.

For a moment, I stood there, not looking away from the ashes wetly falling to the carpet. I'd faced a realm full of demons and minions determined to kill me, yet I had never been more afraid than I was now. What if I turned around and saw that the manna hadn't worked? How could I bear it if the last seconds I'd spent with Adrian were the final ones we'd ever get?

I tried to breathe, but my chest ached too much. The wind picked up and the sprinklers began shooting out as if trying to douse a five-alarm fire. *Please don't let this be the end. Please, please, please!*

"Ivy."

A sob escaped me when I heard Adrian's voice. I whirled, my paralysis vanishing. I fell to my knees next to him, an incoherent sound escaping me as I saw him brush the remains of another clump of manna from his now-healed throat. Then hard arms pulled me to him, his lips found mine and I kissed him until I couldn't breathe for a different reason this time.

When he finally lifted his head, he was smiling. "I love you, too," he murmured. "More than you will ever know."

"I'm glad I get the chance to find out," I said, so overcome I wanted to laugh and cry at the same time.

I thought a shadow crossed his features, but it must be remains of the wet ashes. "One day, you might."

CHAPTER SEVEN

ADRIAN KISSED ME AGAIN. I could've stayed that way for the rest of the night, but Costa cleared his throat in a manner meant to get our attention. When Adrian and I both ignored him, he tapped us on the arms. Hard.

"Guys," Costa said through gritted teeth. "Security's here, and they look pissed."

I looked up to see three uniformed men glaring down at us. Then they looked around in a disbelieving way at the holes in the wall, the dark stains on the sodden carpet, the broken mirror farther down the hallway and, finally, the blood still staining Adrian's clothes.

"What in hell happened here?" one of the guards asked in heavily accented English.

From the other people peeking out of their hotel rooms, they weren't the only ones who wanted to know that. Adrian got up, bloody droplets accompanying his every move, and reached into his pants pocket.

"Don't worry—I'll pay for all of it," he said, pulling out a credit card with a ridiculously high charging limit.

That was one way out of this situation. The security staff no longer looked as if they were about to tackle us, but they were still clearly pissed.

"You'll pay on your way out," one of them growled

before giving another disgusted look around. "This flooding will take days to clean up!"

"Hey, that's from *your* sprinklers," I corrected him.

"What sprinklers?" the guard snapped.

I pointed at the ceiling, but the word "Those!" died on my lips. The hallway had several smoke alarms, but unbelievably, I didn't see any sprinkler heads. Now that I was thinking about it, the water had seemed to come from the sides, not just from the ceiling, and I still had no explanation as to where the strange, strong wind had come from.

"Don't say anything else," Adrian murmured, taking my hand.

I looked down at our clasped hands. I hadn't noticed the slingshot melding back into my flesh, but it now once again resembled a tattoo instead of the ancient supernatural weapon that it was. That awful burn running along the right half of my body had stopped, too, so the staff was no longer reacting to the presence of a demon.

Wait a minute. The staff... "Oh, shit," I whispered.

My sister, Jasmine, slicked her wet blond hair back before giving me a supportive, if somewhat pitying, smile. "Guess we now know what your other tattoo can do."

Guess we did. Then again, Moses's staff was famous for supernatural weather events, hence all those plagues against the Egyptians that resulted in the Israelites' exodus several thousand years ago. Next to that, a little indoor rain and wind was pretty ho-hum.

"Get the rest of our stuff," Adrian said to Costa and Jasmine. "We'll meet you downstairs." To the guards, he said, "Feel free to escort us to the front desk, if you're worried about our skipping out on the bill."

He received a barrage of Armenian for his reply. I was glad I didn't know the language, because I was sure I wouldn't have liked what was said. One of the guards stayed with Costa and Jasmine while the other two took Adrian up on his challenge and escorted us all the way to the front desk.

Once there, we waited while the manager checked out the fifth floor and returned to chew us out in very good English. When it was all said and done, Adrian paid the hotel an amount that could have also purchased a great used car.

"Once again, sorry for the mess," he told the manager. "The wife and I just love to play with Super Soakers."

"And paintball guns," I added, since Adrian's shirt was still stained with red.

"You forgot smashing mirrors and putting holes in the walls," the manager said sourly.

Adrian flashed a grin at him. For someone who had been inches away from death less than an hour ago, he looked like his usual cocky self now. "What can I say? It's our honeymoon."

The manager gave him an extremely unamused look. "Congratulations. Now, get out."

We met Costa and Jasmine at the front of the hotel. They'd brought our bags and were in the process of trying to hail a taxi, but the sight of those smaller sedans made me remember that not all of us were here.

"Brutus," I said with a gasp. "I left him on the roof!"

"I figured as much, so I went up there when I was getting the bags and told him to stand by," Costa said.

"But you're afraid of him," I blurted, then could've

kicked myself. No guy liked being called out on his fears, especially in front of his not-so-secret girlfriend.

A hard smile ghosted across Costa's lips. "If you'd been trapped in a demon realm with Brutus as its flying guard, you would be, too. But these past few months have shown me that Brutus isn't evil. He was just being directed by evil people."

Adrian looked away, and now Costa was the one who looked like he was mentally kicking himself. He might not have meant to bring up the fact that Adrian had been ruling the realm Costa had been trapped in, but now it hung in the air like a cloud of sulfur. Costa continued to shift uncomfortably, while Jasmine cleared her throat and found something fascinating to stare at.

I squeezed Adrian's hand. He rarely talked about the guilt he felt for all he'd done when he'd been brainwashed by demons into believing *they* were good and people were monsters, but I knew it still cut deeply.

"Brutus wasn't the only one being directed by evil people," I said, addressing the unspoken tension. "All of us have our reasons for being in this fight."

"Damn straight," Costa said quickly.

A humorless smile played on Adrian's lips. "Don't ever feel bad for bringing up the past, Costa. You're not the only one who isn't able to forget it."

"Yes, but none of us are going to let it define us anymore," I said, then tried to change the subject. "I didn't get a chance to say this before, but I'm so glad you and Jasmine are okay. I freaked when I heard those screams."

"Oh, that was me," Jasmine said, shooting a quick glance at Adrian. "I don't know how that demon found us, but she burst into my hotel room and went right at me. She must've thought I was you, because she kept calling me Ivy. If Adrian hadn't plowed into her before she could reach me, I might not be here."

I gave Adrian a grateful glance as I remembered Obsidiana asking, *Is this the real you?* "I'd been disguised by glamour the other times she saw me. That's why she thought you might be me."

"Yeah, well, I'm glad the bitch is dead," Jasmine said shortly. "Scared me shitless to see a demon again. I thought they couldn't get to our world anymore."

I'd thought that, too, and I intended to find out more about the ramifications of cursed earth allowing some to stay behind in our world as soon as I had Adrian alone.

"Apparently, there's a loophole," I said. "Either way, it's not safe for us here anymore. We weren't just attacked at the hotel. Minions tried to take us out at the museum, too."

"Oh no!" Jasmine said, running her hands over my shoulders as if belatedly checking me for injuries. "That's—"

"Why we have to leave now," Adrian interrupted, stepping out into the middle of the road. The taxi that had been about to sail by us was forced to slam on its brakes or hit him. The driver chose slamming on his brakes.

"Thanks," Adrian told him, ignoring the driver's angry sputters as he opened the passenger door. Costa flashed a wry smile at Adrian and grabbed our luggage.

"You should call Brutus down so you can tell him to follow us by air. Otherwise, he might get restless and eat a hole through the roof looking for you."

Adrian snorted. "He only eats meat."

"That reminds me!" I said, smacking my head. "Wherever we're going, we have to stop at a grocery store first."

Adrian arched a brow. "What for?"

"Pot roasts," I said succinctly. "I owe Brutus seven of them."

CHAPTER EIGHT

WE ENDED UP taking a train from Yerevan back toward Europe. Flying would have been faster, but that was impossible to do with Brutus, and our former tour bus was back in the United States. It would take days, with lots of stops along the way, but I intended to enjoy the long trip through countries I'd never seen before. Most important, since the train was in near-continuous motion, we didn't have to worry about demons popping up. We would be much harder to track when we were never in the same place.

Brutus was in one of the luggage cars, since he was far too bulky to fit in one of the small first-class passenger cabins. Costa and Jasmine were a few doors down in their own cabins, so after the attendants checked our tickets, Adrian and I finally had some privacy. Ever since the hotel attack, we'd been careful to go from plot of hallowed ground to plot of hallowed ground while waiting for the train that would take us out of here. Now that we were all finally safe, I intended to find out why Adrian hadn't warned me that demons were still in our world.

Adrian, however, had other intentions.

He pulled me to him before I could speak, his mouth slanting across mine while his hands ran over me as if this was the last chance he'd ever get to touch me. My urge to talk died away and another urge rose, fueled by the knowledge that a short time ago, I thought I'd lost him. I hadn't, and the taste of him, the feel of him, was a larger-than-life reminder.

He kissed me, hot and desperate. I kissed him back with the same feverish desperation, tugging at his bloodstained shirt and pants in wordless demand for him to take them off.

He pulled his shirt over his head and tossed it aside. My ruined blouse and bra followed suit, as did our pants and underwear. When he laid me against one of the cabins two narrow bunks, I let out a sound of unabashed need at the feel of his hard, naked body on top of mine.

He kissed me while his large, skillful hands teased my nipples until they were tingling. Then his hot, seeking mouth replaced his hands and turned those tingles into throbs. I was already breathing in gasps by the time he left my breasts to slide lower down my body. When his mouth found my center, I gave up all attempts to keep my voice down despite the cabin's thin walls.

After several mind-blowing minutes, I was gripping his head as tightly as he held my hips. He didn't stop until I was panting from a rapidly approaching climax, then he abruptly pulled me up and lifted me until I was straddling him. I gasped at the suddenness of his movements, then that small sound turned into a shout as he thrust deeply inside me.

If I hadn't been so wet, taking all of his long, thick length at once might have hurt. Instead, my overstimulated nerves clenched with such rapture that I came. I clutched him as those inner tremors shook me, lasting longer from how he hit all the right spots as he moved against me.

"I love feeling you come," he growled against my neck, moving his arms under my hips until he was supporting me. Good thing, too, because my body felt like it was turning into warm caramel.

"That makes two of us," I said, the words breathless, since I was still panting.

His low laugh teased my neck, then he tightened his grip and began to move with toe-curling intensity. The pleasant lethargy that had followed my orgasm began to change, turning back to desire with each deep thrust. I was still on top, but he was the one in control, using everything from the angle of our bodies to the rocking of the train to maximize each sensation.

Soon, I was back in a state of mindless, passionate need, crying out against his mouth when he kissed me, or his neck when I pulled away to breathe. I don't know when he switched position and got on top, but when I came the second time, I raked my nails down his back from his shoulders to his ass. When Adrian finally came, he gripped me to him so hard that I felt every spasm as it shook him. Even when his grip eventually loosened, he didn't let me go.

A THUNDEROUS BOOM woke the woman and her baby. They'd both been sleeping in the backseat, but at that sudden noise, her baby began to wail. The crashing sounds that followed only made it worse. She tucked the blanket around her baby, gently shushing her before leaving her in the backseat to investigate. Something awful had to have happened, and though it was daylight, she had to make sure it was a natural awful and not something else.

The brush she walked through was tall and thick, which was why she'd chosen this spot when she'd stopped late last night. Not only did it hide her car from prying eyes, at some point, it had also been a cemetery, though the headstones were long gone.

As soon as she glimpsed the highway, the source of the loud commotion was obvious. A tractor-trailer was turned over on its side in the middle of the road, with multiple cars piled up behind it and around it. Each passing second brought a new screech of tires and screams. She winced as she watched more cars slide helplessly into the wreck. The suddenness of the accident combined with rush hour traffic resulted in a horrible domino effect as people were unable to stop in time.

Then the back of the trailer burst open, and people scrambled out. Some disappeared into the tall grass that lined the road, while others limped a few feet before collapsing, clearly too injured to run like their companions had.

The tractor-trailer must have been smuggling undocumented immigrants over the border. She started forward to help the ones who were hurt, then forced herself to stop. The police would be here soon, and she couldn't afford to be questioned. No one could know where she was. The creatures who hunted her were relentless, and if they found out about her baby...

She hurried back to her car, not caring that the tall, prickly brush tore into her from how fast she ran through it. She needed to get out of here before the police showed up. Quickly, she opened the backseat door and began to strap her baby into the car seat. She was halfway finished when a familiar voice seemed to whisper across her mind.

You cannot take the child with you.

She stopped and spun around. The entire sky was thick with clouds that looked ready to burst from rain, but in the middle, a brilliant ray of sunshine broke through. It streamed down to touch the side of the road where she'd been standing before, and though the implication was clear, she shook her head.

"No. No, I can't leave her."

If you want her to live, you must, *that voice whispered while the light grew brighter. Then another sunbeam appeared, and another, all illuminating the same spot, until the brightness was so intense, she could barely stand to look at it.*

No! *she screamed in her mind. Tears began to stream down her face. She couldn't leave her baby alone here! She was too young, too small, too fragile, too helpless, too...too* hers!

I've done everything else you asked, but I won't leave my little girl. I can't!

You must, *that whisper repeated. No sunbeams touched her, but she suddenly felt enveloped in soothing warmth that spread from the top of her hair all the way down to her feet.*

She stood there, every maternal instinct fighting against that voice. How could abandoning her daughter be the right thing to do? How could she bear it if she never saw her again? How could she live with herself if she walked away without even knowing if her child was safe?

Trust me, *that voice whispered insistently.*

Heaving back a sob, she took her baby out of the car seat and began walking toward that stream of light.

"Promise me she'll be safe," she choked out when she laid down the child in the illuminated section of grass alongside the road.

I promise, whispered across her mind.

She kissed her baby on her soft, velvety cheek, saying, "Te quiero, hija mia," before grief made it impossible for her to speak. As if she knew she was being abandoned, her baby started to wail again. The sound made that burning in her chest worse, and she turned and ran back toward her car. If she didn't leave now, this second, *she wouldn't be able to at all.*

She tore up the brush from how fast she spun the tires when she peeled out of her former hiding spot. When she made it onto the highway, she cut across all the lanes in a dangerously reckless move that nevertheless put her ahead of the jackknifed tractor-trailer and the cars piled up behind it. Once she was clear of the accident, she looked back, craning her neck to see, since her rearview mirror was gone.

A blond-haired woman rushed out of her car, heading toward the small, precious bundle she'd left alongside the road. The last thing she saw was the fair-haired stranger bending down to pick up her daughter, then tears stole her vision away...

I woke up with my heart pounding. I'd had this dream before, too many times to count, yet never so vividly. The other times, I could only see what the pretty Latina woman had been doing. I hadn't known what she'd been thinking, let alone feeling, and the intensity of her emotions had me fighting back tears.

It would be silly to be so affected, except I had it on

good authority that this was no ordinary dream. Zach, the Archon who at turns both helped us and hindered us, had told me my recurring dream was an actual account of what happened when my birth mother abandoned me. I'd always thought she'd done so because she'd been one of the undocumented immigrants who'd fled the scene after the accident, and I'd understood that making a run for it with a baby would have been impossible.

Yet the day I'd met him, Zach had said I was wrong and my birth mother hadn't wanted to leave me. If this far-more-detailed dream was true, he was right. I fought another shiver as I remembered the strange voice telling the woman—*my mother?*—that she had to do it or I wouldn't survive. Was that true?

I only knew one thing about my birth mother: that she was dead. Otherwise, I wouldn't be the last Davidian. Yet this new, possible insight left me with a thousand questions I hadn't allowed myself to wonder before. Had she been hunted by demons, too? If the dream was real, the lack of a rearview mirror would indicate that, as would her choice to stay on hallowed ground. And who—or what—was the voice in her head? Delusion? Angelic interference? Something else?

"Hey, sleepyhead," Adrian murmured.

"Hey," I said almost distractedly. He was sitting on the small berth across from mine, and I blinked at the curtains behind him. They looked much darker than when I'd seen them before, and it took me a second to realize why. The sun was no longer shining through them. I must have slept the day away.

"Why didn't you wake me?" I asked in surprise.

He smiled. "Why? You're so beautiful when you sleep."

Liar, I thought, but smiled back. Then my smile faded as I glanced again at the darkened windows. Somewhere out there, demons were still prowling around. We were safe now, but eventually, we'd get off, and we couldn't just park ourselves on hallowed ground forever.

Thoughts of hallowed ground brought me back to the dream, which wasn't hard. I still ached inside due to the loss she'd felt. For years, I'd tried never to think about my biological mother because it hurt me too much. Now I was feeling all of her pain, and it left mine in the dust.

But I couldn't focus on that right now. There were other, more important things than the past to dwell on.

"Adrian, why didn't you tell me some demons could've stayed behind in our world after the realm gateways were sealed off?"

CHAPTER NINE

HE STARED AT ME, and I realized the emotions the dream had brought up had sharpened my tone, until my question was more accusation than query. I faked a cough to lessen the tension.

"Granted, that should have occurred to me because I met the demon you held captive on cursed earth beneath the church, but for some reason, it didn't. You had to have noticed that, yet you never corrected me about it. Why?"

He sighed, getting up and pulling down one of our suitcases from a small, overhead bin. I hadn't seen him put them up there, but from his change of clothes and freshly showered, damp hair, he'd been awake and getting stuff done while I slumbered.

"I didn't think it would be a problem," he said, setting the suitcase on the end of the futon. It was mine, and yes, I would need it soon so I could change, but I wasn't putting off this conversation any longer. Adrian had a very disturbing tendency not to tell me important things if he thought I couldn't handle them, and that had to stop. Now.

"How could you *not* think that?" Demons being loose in our world was always a problem, and I had the entirety of human history as my Exhibit A on that point.

He sighed again. "Only very powerful demons would have access to relics strong enough to curse large patches of earth, and what were the chances of lots of them being on this side of the realms when the gateways closed? Yeah, I knew a few might, but I thought they'd be stuck in a small spot, unable to move or be a threat, like Blinky when I had him trapped. I certainly didn't expect Obsidiana to rally minions to attack you, or to use mirrors to come after you herself."

Mirrors might not be the same as the now-closed demon realm gateways, since they *didn't* act as a bridge from one realm to another, but with demons still in our world, they were dangerous. No wonder Adrian still smashed the mirrors in our hotel rooms. I'd thought he'd done it solely out of habit.

"I hadn't expected that, either," I said. "And you should have told me it was possible."

"I'm sorry," he said softly, closing the distance between us. "If I'd thought for a second that you would get hurt—"

"*You* got hurt," I interrupted, the memory of him nearly bleeding to death hardening my voice. "And Jasmine and Costa almost did, too. It's always made things worse when you keep things to yourself. You know that, so why did you do it again?"

He looked away in obvious guilt. "Not that the attacks were your fault," I hastily added. "Whether you had told us or not, we still would have gone looking for the spearhead. I just hate that you're still keeping secrets. I might have had a hard time dealing with things when we first met, but I'm not that same girl anymore."

A muscle ticked in his jaw, and it took several seconds before he met my eyes again. When he did, his jaw was set in granite, yet flashes of pain skipped over his expression.

"Fine. Then there's something else you need to know, and you're not going to like it."

"Tell me," I breathed, my breath hitching. This had to be the unspoken issue I'd been feeling between us. It wasn't just paranoia—he *had* been holding something back!

Adrian stared at me, his fists clenching and unclenching as if he were fighting a terrible inner battle.

"The truth is…" He stopped, took a deep breath, then said the next part in a rush. "You can't beat the demons, Ivy, no matter what. You closed their realms off for now, but demons don't age or die of natural causes, so they'll just wait until the realm walls eventually weaken and the gateways reopen. When that happens, they'll go back to enslaving humans and making more minions, so even if you find and wield the spearhead, they still win."

I stared at him, my jaw feeling like it had dropped into my chest. "You can't believe that."

His gaze hardened until his eyes resembled silver-encrusted sapphires. "I lived with demons for over a hundred years. Yeah, some want to kill you because you murdered hundreds of their kind, but most demons aren't sentimental. Hunting you puts them at risk, since you have a weapon that can kill them. But leaving you alone only costs them their current slaves if you succeed with the spearhead, and none of them think you will."

He didn't say it, but I could hear, *And neither do I*, in the silence that followed. I'd always known that my chances weren't good, but I hadn't given up hope that somehow I'd pull off saving those trapped people. Had I only been fooling myself by training to build up my strength? Had it all been a waste of time because I never stood a chance? And was it pointless anyway because, no matter what, the demons would win in the end?

"Thanks for telling me this," I said in a very calm tone. "Now, I'm going to get dressed and check on Brutus." I'd been intending to do that anyway, and after these revelations, I needed to be by myself.

Adrian's hands closed over my shoulders. "Ivy, wait—"

"It's okay," I said, shaking him off. "You told me the truth, and I'm glad. I just need a little time to let it sink in. Come on, we're on a train, so you know I'm not going anywhere. Besides, you're not the only one who's allowed to storm off to be brooding and moody."

He didn't smile at my halfhearted attempt at humor. "Fine," he said, moving so he no longer blocked the small door. "Take as long as you need."

CHAPTER TEN

BRUTUS SEEMED TO love being in the luggage car of the train. It had no windows, so he wouldn't have had to hide from the sun during the day, and he'd perched himself on top of a pile of soft-sided luggage like a king on a throne. Add that to the large cooler full of raw meat that Adrian had left for him, and I could see trains becoming the gargoyle's preferred mode of travel.

I spent about fifteen minutes with Brutus, petting him and praising him while my mind was a million miles away. Then I left the luggage car, but I didn't head back to my cabin. I was still too upset. My new, overwhelming sense of futility was now matched by an anger darker than I'd ever felt.

What was the point in my bio mother going through all that pain to give me up, if I wouldn't be safe like she'd been promised? What was the point in breaking Adrian's heart by dying trying to wield a weapon that would probably kill me long before I was able to free the trapped humans? Worse, what was the point in *anything* I'd done? I'd closed the realms, but as I now knew, that only amounted to a "pause" button for the demons in those worlds. As for the ones in this world, thanks to cursed earth, they could wait it out. Then they'd be right back to enslaving and killing humans, and everything I'd done to stop them would be no more than a punch line on my deluded, very short life.

Perhaps worst of all, I was endangering everyone I loved to keep looking for a weapon I might never find. It was one thing when I thought we were searching for the spearhead in a demon-free world. Now I knew that demons could pounce around any corner. How could I do that to my sister and Costa, who'd already suffered too much at demons' hands? How could I do that to Adrian, who'd nearly died more times than I could count in these quests? I wasn't risking only my life by searching for the spearhead—I was risking all of theirs, and the deck was more stacked against us than I'd realized.

Besides, if anything happened to Adrian or my sister, it would break me. Then I wouldn't be able to keep looking for the spearhead anyway. But would I really not stop until one or both of them were dead? How could I do that to people I loved?

I was so engrossed in my thoughts, I didn't think anything of the young man I passed on my way through the dining car until he touched my hand. Startled, I jerked away, only then registering the familiar faded blue hoodie he wore. He tipped it back, revealing close-cropped black hair, dark brown skin, handsome features and brown eyes. Nothing remarkable, unless you looked into his eyes. Then you'd feel what it was like to have a real-life celestial being see past all your defenses and stare straight into your soul.

"Hi, Zach," I said, wondering why I was surprised to see him. Didn't he always show up at pivotal points in my life? If I'd been thinking things through, I would have expected him.

"Ivy," he greeted me, glancing at the seat across from him. "Won't you have a seat?"

"Ooh, asking me to do something instead of ordering me," I remarked, sounding flippant even though I felt anything but. "What's with the new niceness?"

The faintest twitch touched his mouth, his version of a full-fledged grin. "You must have grown on me," he said dryly.

I batted my lashes. Being a smartass was better than what I was feeling now. "Stop with the compliments. You're making me blush."

There was the look I was used to: half censure, half annoyance. "I am not here for meaningless banter. I've come to see if you've chosen to abandon your pursuit of the spearhead."

That was right to the point. Normally, Zach was as cryptic as the day was long. "You've been here long enough to read my mind, haven't you?" Mind reading was one of his talents as an Archon, and he had never shied away from doing it before. "Or did your 'boss' tell you that I was reconsidering this quest?"

His shoulder lifted in a half shrug. "Does it matter?"

"Not really," I said, and sat down. I hadn't wanted to finalize such a momentous decision right now, but when had life ever waited until I was ready? "Is Adrian right?" I asked, meeting Zach's piercing gaze. "Will demons just reopen shop again eventually?"

"Of course." Not only was there no sympathy in his tone, it actually had a faint tinge of amusement. "Did you really believe that you, a human, could defeat all the dark legions of the underworld permanently?"

Put like that, it did sound delusional, but I hadn't thought I'd be able to kill them all or anything grandiose like that. My big hope had been to save the humans still trapped in the demon realms while also keeping others from ever being enslaved or killed by demons again. That had been worth dying for, but this?

"So what's the point of me risking everyone's lives to hunt for a spearhead that—in all likelihood—will kill me, if everything is only going to go back to horrible demonic normal one day anyway?"

Zach leaned forward. Tiny lights seemed to glow in the dark depths of his gaze as he stared at me. "Your best-case scenario was only ever to possibly free the thousands still trapped in the demon realms, if you found the final hallowed weapon. Not to defeat the demons or keep them from ever harming people again. That is a fight for Archons, not humans."

"Let's talk about that, too," I said, gripping the side of the table so hard, my hands hurt. Still, better to feel physical pain than the hurt frothing inside me. "No one thinks I'll be able to free the humans even if I *do* find and wield the spearhead. They think I'll drop over dead as soon as I touch it. You just said 'possibly' free them, so you sound doubtful, too. Well? Am I strong enough to do it or not?"

Zach didn't say anything. My anger grew, a welcoming balm over the pain.

"I'm going to die for nothing, aren't I?" I said sharply. "And you don't care, because you're an Archon and humans are like ants to you, but Adrian cares. It ripped my heart out when I thought he was dying earlier, yet you want me to rip *his* out by dying in this quest because Davidians are *supposed* to die for their destinies, right?"

Again Zach said nothing. He wasn't denying any of

this, and since Archons couldn't lie, not denying it was the same as admitting it.

A toddler suddenly scrambled out of her chair and darted over, tugging on my pants and saying, "Up!" with adorable demand. Almost as quickly, her mother ran over and swept her up.

"So sorry," she said, then grabbed those chubby little hands before they could snatch at my hair.

I stared at the little girl. Her eyes were brown, not hazel like mine, but for a moment, I could see myself as this child. Except by the time I'd been her age, my mother had been forced to abandon me.

The dream with all its agony roared to the forefront. I barely noticed the woman leaving with her little girl. All my attention was on Zach. He hadn't moved. Neither had I, except for my hands. They felt like they'd left indentions in the table that I was gripping as if my life depended on it.

"What about my mother?" My voice was thick with everything she'd felt that day. "Did this destiny kill her, too? Or what about my bio father? Did he have to watch her die the way you expect Adrian to watch me die?"

"Your biological father was murdered by minions years before your mother's death," Zach replied with infuriating coolness. "And your mother took her own life."

I closed my eyes, my breath hitching between a gasp and a sob. I'd known that she and all her blood relatives must be dead, but I'd hoped…what? That somewhere in this world, I still had family? How naive of me. Anyone close to a Davidian was a demon target. It should come as no surprise that my bio father had been murdered. My adoptive parents had been murdered, too. Now I had no one left except for Adrian, Jasmine and Costa, yet if I continued on this quest in a world still filled with demons, they might get murdered, too.

"Tell me it's not all for nothing," I said, opening my eyes and staring at Zach. "Tell me that if I use the spearhead, I *will* save those people. Tell me, or I am walking away from this. I refuse to sacrifice one more person for a destiny I didn't ask for, or a quest I have no chance at succeeding at."

"I will not tell you," Zach said, his brown gaze turning hard. "You do not get to demand answers in advance of efforts. Either continue without knowing your quest's resolution, or do not. The choice, as always, is yours."

I let go of the table to bang my fists on it. "You call that a choice?"

"It is," he said, steel coating his words now. "In fact, it is a choice at its most unbiased."

My anger rose again, dark and deep. Did he really think I was like him? That I'd blindly obey "orders" without question or care about how it affected those I loved? "Then I choose to take my chances living instead of dying," I said, rising from the table. "That means this is goodbye."

He said nothing for so long, I thought he was waiting for me to leave. I started to, then I felt his hand on my arm. When I looked down at him, I expected to see anger, condemnation or his usual Archon smugness in his gaze. Instead, I saw pity, disappointment and an utter lack of surprise.

"Then this is goodbye," Zach agreed softly.

I nodded, looking away to swipe at a tear that appeared for no reason. When I glanced back, Zach had disappeared. No one else in the dining car seemed to notice that a passenger had suddenly vanished into thin air, either. They were all too busy living their own lives, as I'd decided to do.

More tears escaped. Why did I suddenly feel bad about this? No matter Zach's claims, he'd left me no real choice. Hadn't I saved enough lives despite the risk to myself? It was thanks to me that most demons were locked out of our world now! Otherwise, the realm walls would have continued to crumble, and I'd seen firsthand how horrifying it was to have one of their worlds spill out into ours. Now no one would have to worry about that happening for a long, long time. Shouldn't that alone have earned me the right to a little happiness?

It did, I decided, brushing back my tears. In fact, I'd probably saved millions of lives by sealing off the realms. I would've kept trying to save more, too, if Zach hadn't arrogantly refused to tell me if I had a real chance at freeing those trapped in the realms. Why should I be the one feeling guilty? All I'd asked for was the knowledge that I wouldn't be risking my life and everyone else's for nothing—

Agony shot up my right arm, forcing a scream from me. *Demon!* I thought, expecting to see the tattoo turning a warning gold color. Yet aside from the awful burn that felt like it went straight through to my bones, the tattoo looked the same.

Then, to my shock, the braided rope etching began to fade. I grabbed it as if by doing so I could stop it from disappearing, but even as I snatched and pulled at my skin, the ancient, hallowed sling continued to dissipate, until finally, it vanished from sight. When another spine-deep pain ripped through me from shoulder to ankle, bringing me to my knees from the intensity of the invisible blow, I ripped open my blouse with a combination of agony and desperation.

The gnarled wooden outline of the staff that had marked the entire right side of my body since I'd wielded it was now fading, too. As I watched in disbelief, it disappeared until nothing but smooth skin remained. When it vanished, so did the pain, leaving me staring at my body with a stunned sort of understanding.

I'd chosen to renounce my destiny, so the hallowed weapons that had merged with my flesh had apparently chosen to renounce me.

CHAPTER ELEVEN

NO ONE ELSE around me cared that I'd experienced a supernatural and existential crisis. That was clear when the nearest train attendant grabbed me, keeping me on the floor while calling out for help. He probably thought I was having a psychotic breakdown. That would be the most logical explanation for someone suddenly screaming and tearing open her blouse in the middle of the dining car, and if he'd known my mental health history, he would have *really* believed that.

Since I didn't want to experience Europe's version of a padded cell, I quickly fabricated a story about being allergic to bees and saying I'd thought one had gotten inside my blouse. Not the most ingenious excuse, but luckily, the attendant spoke English, and my story was enough to stop them from continuing to restrain me. I was in the middle of getting up and apologizing to everyone when Adrian stormed into the dining car.

"I heard you scream. What happened?" he demanded.

I held my torn blouse together with one hand and patted him with the other. "Nothing. I thought I saw a bee, and I panicked. You know how allergic I am."

He pulled me close, his gaze flicking around in a predatory manner. He knew I was lying, so he was coiled and ready to attack.

I couldn't tell him what had really happened here,

so I tugged him toward the back of the dining car. "I'm so embarrassed. Let's just go back to our cabin now."

He glanced down—and froze. A hiss escaped him as he stared at the newly blank skin on my right hand. "Ivy—"

"Cabin. Please," I repeated, tugging him harder.

He grasped my hand and walked out of the dining car. I had to nearly run to keep up with his rapid strides, not that I minded. I wanted to get away from all the stares leveled my way.

We ran into Jasmine and Costa in the hallway of our train car. Costa's hand was in his jacket pocket, and I saw a very suspicious bulge protruding from the fabric. I realized he'd heard my scream and jumped to the wrong conclusion, too.

"Put that away," I hissed. All we needed was for someone to glimpse the outline of the gun and assume that he was about to commit a terrorist attack.

"What happened?" Costa said, eyeing me and Adrian.

Our cabin was small, but I waved everyone inside. It was standing room only once we shut the door, yet my decision affected everyone, so they all deserved to hear it.

"I have something to tell you," I began. "I've—"

"What the hell?" Jaz exclaimed, grabbing my right hand. "Ivy! Your tattoo is gone!"

Costa muttered something in Greek as he stared at my hand. Adrian didn't look away from my eyes, even when I pulled back my torn blouse to reveal that the staff tattoo was now gone, too.

"I know," I said, forcing the words out despite my throat closing off with a surge of unexpected shame.

"I've been thinking a lot about things since the attack yesterday, and I think…"

I stopped and dropped my eyes. Jasmine and Costa had both been terribly abused in demon realms, so my choice to bow out might come across like I was saying what happened to them didn't matter to me anymore. Oh God. What if they hated me for this?

"Think what?" my sister asked impatiently.

Adrian slipped behind me and drew me into his arms. Those thick, warm bands and the solidness of his body soothed my sudden case of trembles.

"I'm not going after the spearhead anymore," I said bluntly. "I've been kidding myself about being able to survive it long enough to save those people. I also learned that the realm walls will eventually weaken again, putting demons right back in business. So, I don't see a point in risking everyone's lives trying to find a weapon that'll kill me before I can help anyone anyway—"

Jasmine threw her arms around me, cutting off the rest of my explanation. Her hug was so welcome and unexpected; I didn't care that it was difficult to breathe between her tight frontal embrace and Adrian gripping me from behind.

"You're not mad?" I got out, wiggling to get more room.

"Why?" She drew back, showing that her face was now wet from tears. "I never wanted you to do it in the first place! Each time you left to look for the staff or the spearhead, I've been terrified that you'll never come back. It's all I've been able to do to hold myself together these past few months. Good God, Ives, I have a white streak in my hair and I'm not even twenty! *No*, I'm not mad that you're stopping. In fact, I'm so happy—" her voice broke "—I'm so happy I can't even stand it."

She dissolved into tears, and Adrian let me go so I could hold her. I stroked her hair and whispered reassurances that everything would be all right while, over her shoulder, I met Costa's eyes. They were shiny with tears that didn't hit his cheeks, yet his jaw was set in a hard line as he nodded at me.

I understand, that nod said. I didn't know if he agreed like Jasmine did, but right now, his understanding was enough.

"So, your tattoos vanished after you decided to stop looking for the spearhead?" Jasmine asked with a final, teary sniff. "Guess that's the supernatural version of having security throw you out after quitting."

I let out a breathy laugh even though I felt more conflicted than amused. "Guess so. I saw Zach right before they disappeared, so I'm guessing he had something to do with it."

"Zach was here?" Adrian sounded more surprised by that than by my decision to abandon my destiny.

"Yeah," I said, giving Jasmine a last pat as I turned toward him. "He was waiting for me in the dining car after I checked on Brutus. He somehow knew what I'd decided, too. Guess he'd gotten a cosmic heads-up or something."

Adrian's eyes narrowed. "And he had nothing to say to you?"

I glanced away. I didn't want to repeat what Zach had said. "Not much," I settled on. "And it ended with 'goodbye.'"

I could feel Adrian staring at me, measuring my words and locating the gaps between them. I tried to mentally erase the guilt, second-guessing and other emotions from my expression, but I must not have been that good at it.

"Give us a minute, guys," Adrian said, opening the cabin door. Jasmine and Costa filed out after Jaz gave me a final hug. Adrian locked the door behind them, then turned around to face me.

I waited for him to speak, but without a word, he drew me into his arms. For several minutes, he held me, his warm, strong hands caressing away the bone-deep tension I hadn't known was there until I finally felt it begin to loosen.

I closed my eyes as I rested my head against his chest. Oh, how I'd needed this! With every stroke of his hands, brush of his lips and tightening of his arms, Adrian was telling me that he loved me. *Me*, not the person other people wanted me to be, or what I was supposedly destined to be, or what I could be, if I only tried harder. Me: flaws, fears and all.

I took in a deep breath and let it out slowly. "Thank you."

His short laugh was muffled against my neck. "For what?"

"This," I said, drawing back to look at him. "I needed it."

He stared at me, his eyes appearing bluer from the intensity in his gaze. "And I need you. That's why I'm thrilled about your decision. I never thought the pay-off was worth the risk."

"It could have been," I said, thinking about all the people still trapped in the realms. As soon as I did, that deep-seated tension returned, as did my guilt. Quickly, I tried to brush both aside. "But it's not," I continued, reminding myself as well as saying it to Adrian. "Zach all but confirmed that I had no chance to survive the spearhead long enough to save them."

Adrian sighed, then rested his forehead against mine. "Don't beat yourself up. You saved lots of other people, and you tried to save them, too. You've done enough, Ivy."

I mustered up a shrug that looked far more laid-back than I felt. "The former hallowed weapons would seem to disagree. I abandoned my destiny, so they wasted no time in abandoning me."

He pulled me back into his arms, lifting me until my feet were off the floor and our faces were level.

"Screw Zach and screw them," he whispered fiercely. "They might have left you, but I never will."

I wrapped my arms around him and kissed him, needing his strength, his unconditional love and acceptance, and the passion that flowed between us, covering my guilt, doubt and second-guessing. Right now, all I needed to be was me. Right now, the only thing that mattered was the two of us. In his arms, everything was finally as it should be.

"I love you, Adrian," I told him between searing kisses. "You're my only destiny now."

CHAPTER TWELVE

WE ENDED UP going back to Vatican City, and not because I had fallen in love with it when we were here looking for the spearhead. The entire mini, walled city was on hallowed ground, and it had tight security due to its many famous treasures. I didn't think it was a coincidence that Obsidiana had waited until we were away from Vatican City to send her minions to attack us, let alone come after us herself.

The added safety of the enhanced security combined with extensive hallowed ground had Jasmine visibly relaxing, and she wasn't the only one. Adrian was as chill as I'd ever seen him, and I didn't know if that was because of our surroundings or his relief over my decision to abandon the spearhead quest.

They weren't the only ones basking in a newfound sense of relief. I didn't fear the coming of night anymore, and I'd even taken to going on solo walks during the day. I couldn't remember the last time I'd gone somewhere for the sheer, simple pleasure of it. Yet despite my newfound sense of security, all wasn't entirely well.

I tried to hide my lingering feelings of guilt from Adrian, Jasmine and Costa, telling myself that it would go away in time. In the interim, I'd focus on being grateful, which was easy to do with the man I loved, my sister and our best friend at my side. Adrian had rented a lovely little villa inside the city walls for all of us. Everyone enjoyed it so much that our stay stretched from one week into two, and then two weeks into three. Even Brutus seemed to love it, staying inside during the day and then using his seagull disguise to fish from the nearby Mediterranean Sea at night.

By our fifth week, I was starting to feel good enough to confront one of my guilt-ridden phobias. "I'm going for a walk," I told Adrian.

Both golden brows rose. "A little overdressed for that, aren't you?"

I looked down at my lavender silk dress and my high-heeled sandals as if just now realizing I was wearing them. "Eh, maybe," I said with as much vagueness as I could muster.

Adrian got up, and his gaze raked over me with a lot more suspicion now. "What are you trying to hide?"

I almost said, "Nothing!" but then I stopped myself. Why wasn't I telling him what I was really going to do?

"I've been avoiding churches," I explained, beating back my inexplicable urge to lie. "Abandoning my destiny made the paranoid part of me wonder if I'd be smote on the spot if I entered one, but I know that's ridiculous. So, I want to prove it to myself by going to one today."

"Oh," Adrian said. Then his lips began to twitch as if he were fighting not to laugh over my smiting fears. "I'll go with you."

"You don't have to. This whole thing is silly."

"Ivy." The smile wiped from his face as he came over to me. "It doesn't matter," he said, taking my

JEANIENE FROST   73

hands. "Silly or serious, if something is bothering you, I want to be there. Whatever it is, we'll face it together."

I squeezed his hands, once again wondering why I'd tried to hide this from him in the first place. "You're right."

Now he smiled, and it warmed me more than the bright day outside. "Let's see, we didn't spend much time in Saint Peter's Basilica before, and it *is* one of the main attractions here."

"Not there," I said. The basilica felt more like an incredibly elaborate museum than a church. "Saint Stephen's of the Abyssinians."

That reminded me of a more antique version of the church my parents had occasionally taken Jasmine and me to when we were kids. After everything that had happened, I longed to feel the same sort of normalcy I'd felt back then.

"I don't think that's open to the public," Adrian pointed out. "Unless you want to break in, you might have to pick another one."

I gave him an arch look. "I have a way around that. You'll have to dress up to make it work, though."

He chuckled and went to get dressed. When he came out ten minutes later, he wore cream-colored pants, a matching open jacket and a pale blue shirt that made his eyes appear an even more vivid shade of sapphire. Combined with his golden hair, six-six height and face that looked half-angel instead of half-demon, he was so stunning, there was no chance of him going unnoticed.

"I might have to make you wait outside, or you'll ruin my plans to blend in," I said, giving him an admiring stare.

He came over and tipped the brim of my hat back.

"You're the one everyone will look at," he said, and bent to give me a deep kiss.

I broke it off when I found myself thinking about abandoning my plan in favor of spending the day in bed with him. "Behave," I told him, wiping a smear of my lipstick from his mouth even as it curled into a smirk.

"Who, me?" he asked with mock innocence. "Always."

Right. Behaving wasn't in his DNA, let alone his personality. Still, he could be incentivized. "You'll be glad later if you do," I said in my most suggestive voice.

Now his grin was every shade of wicked.

It didn't take long for us to reach the small chapel. Saint Stephen's of the Abyssinians might be closed to regular public foot traffic, but it could be rented out for private weddings. Late summer in Rome was apparently a popular time for them, and today had more than one nuptial on the docket. My plan was simple: pretend to be one of the many guests so I could sneak in. When a thick cluster of guests approached the chapel, I grabbed Adrian's arm, pasted a smile on my face and followed them inside.

Adrian let me choose our seats, and I picked ones in the back. As I sat down, I found myself tensing. If any of my fears were founded, now would be the time for something awful to happen. Yet as the minutes ticked by, nothing did.

"See?" Adrian murmured, gently squeezing my hand. "You're fine, Ivy."

Now I felt even sillier for letting my lingering guilt make me so paranoid. "Let's go, before someone notices that we don't belong here," I whispered.

We left the church. It had been a sunny, beautiful day

ten minutes ago, and now that I'd left my irrational fears behind, it seemed even brighter and lovelier. Adrian and I were enjoying a leisurely stroll back toward our villa when I realized that I'd have to find a bathroom sooner rather than later. My previously bunched-up nerves must have given me an upset stomach.

"I need a bathroom," I told Adrian. "Have you seen one?"

Thankfully, he had, and I almost ran inside it. A short time later, I was washing my hands when the bathroom mirror began to ripple in a frightening way.

I hadn't broken the mirror when I'd entered because we were on hallowed ground, but it wasn't too late to fix my mistake. I grabbed the nearest trash can, about to bash it into the mirror, when an all-too-familiar voice said, "Don't!" Then it went on to say, "I believe we're long overdue for a chat, Davidian."

I paused in midswing. Demetrius, Adrian's biological father and my arch nemesis, had never wanted to *chat* before. He'd tried to kill me more times than I could count and held my sister hostage as bait, but one-on-one conversation? That was new. Still, it was daylight and I was on holy ground, so if Demetrius did try to cross over in another attempt to kill me, he would fry as soon as he left the mirror. The thought of seeing him burning and screaming appealed to me so much, I lowered the trash can.

"What did you want to talk about, Daddy-in-law?"

CHAPTER THIRTEEN

DEMETRIUS'S FULL APPEARANCE became visible in the mirror, so I caught it when he winced, as if being reminded of our new familial tie had caused him actual pain. I'd hoped it would. It certainly stung me a lot.

"*Never* call me that again," he bit out.

"Believe me," I said, glaring at him. "I find it mutually repellant."

Demetrius was one of those demons who looked like a regular person. He had unremarkable features, black hair, pale skin and a wide mouth, so Adrian must have gotten his gorgeous golden looks from his mother. A closer inspection revealed that a writhing mass of darkness clung to Demetrius's outline. His shadows had once been far larger and more impressive, and they weren't Demetrius's only trick. He was also a shape-shifter.

The first time I'd seen him, Demetrius had morphed into a huge dark cloud with flesh-ripping claws and teeth. That form had been beyond terrifying, which was why he'd chosen it. Demetrius was as cruel as he was inventive.

"What, no congratulations on the happy news?" I continued to needle him. "It's a shame you missed the wedding. It was thrown together last-minute, but still, it was beautiful—"

"Speak softer, before Adrian hears you and storms in here," Demetrius snarled.

He'd revealed a lot with that statement. While Demetrius could have guessed that Adrian was with me *in general*, he shouldn't have known that Adrian was close enough to possibly overhear us. Unless...

"You have minions watching us right now, don't you?" I said, trying not to show how much that freaked me out.

Demetrius rolled his coal-black eyes. "Of course I do."

I casually crossed my arms behind my back so my hands were hidden from his view. Demetrius had never seen my staff tattoo, but he was well acquainted with my slingshot. I'd decimated his formerly immense shadows with it, and the last thing I wanted was Demetrius seeing that it was missing. Then he'd know that I'd lost my only deadly form of defense against him.

"If you've got minions tailing us, why haven't you used them to try to kill me?" The danger I'd unknowingly put everyone in made my stomach roil, but I managed to ask the question as if the answer only mildly interested me.

Demetrius smiled, and the sight of it sent chills rippling over my skin. I'd never known that a smile could be a messenger of evil before I'd met Demetrius.

"Because at this particular moment in time, I'm *not* trying to kill you."

"You're not, huh?" I said while getting my rattled nerves back under control. It couldn't be because he'd had a change of heart—Demetrius hated me. That was clear in his burning ebony gaze. But he must have something else up his sleeve. "I don't imagine we have long before Adrian figures out that something else is going on besides me having digestive issues, so if you don't want me dead, what do you want?"

"You've been here too long to still be searching Vatican City for the spearhead, so why haven't you left?"

His arrogance was astounding. He thought I owed him an explanation for my recent activities?

"Yeah, this has been nice, but you can go fuck off now," I said, heading for the door.

"Wait!" The command in his tone didn't make me pause, but his next words did. "It's because you've given up looking for the spearhead, haven't you?"

If I didn't know better, I'd swear he sounded *disappointed.* I swung around in disbelief. "What's it to you, demon?"

"More than you realize, Davidian," he said, giving the same insulting emphasis to my lineage as I'd given to his species.

Why? Demetrius had pulled out all the stops to prevent me from finding the first two hallowed weapons. How could he suddenly have something invested in my finding the final one? "How so? I know you don't care about freeing the trapped humans, and that's all the third weapon's good for."

"Simple. Twit," Demetrius said, sounding out each insult as if I wouldn't understand them otherwise. "Did you truly believe that was the spearhead's only power?"

I bristled. "Zach never said it could do anything else—"

Demetrius's laughter cut me off. The demon even bent over, as if his spine couldn't bear the weight of his mirth.

"What's so funny?" I asked acidly.

He held out a hand as if too overcome to audibly ask me to wait while he attempted to control his mirth. Well, screw him! I was more than halfway to the door when Demetrius, still chuckling, said, "You can leave now, but Adrian's life depends on you staying to hear me out."

I stopped, still fuming, but unwilling to let my pride cause me to miss out on possibly useful information just because I hated its source. Demetrius was evil, but in his own twisted way, he loved Adrian. He'd even let me escape once after he'd gotten the drop on me because Adrian had been dying, and I'd had access to the manna that could save him. If Demetrius said that refusing to hear him out could cost Adrian his life… then there was a fifty-fifty chance that he might be telling the truth.

Besides, he knew where I'd been these past several weeks. Hallowed ground might stop him, but it was no barrier to minions, as the attack at the Mother See in Armenia reminded me.

"Make it quick," I said shortly.

"Zach didn't tell you that the spearhead has another, equally powerful function, but is that a shock?" Demetrius asked, his voice a taunting purr. "Archons might not lie, but even you can't be so obtuse as to believe that one would tell you, a mere human, the entire truth if he didn't want to."

Zach did have an infuriating tendency to leave out a lot of important details. Case in point—Demetrius being Adrian's father. Zach had kept *that* bombshell a secret for years.

"Fine. What else can the spearhead do, if I were to find it and wield it?"

Demetrius's eye roll was contemptuous. "You? *No one* believes you could wield it long enough to do anything other than turn into a pile of bones."

His continued insults had me tapping my foot to keep from hurling curses at him. "Don't draw out the drama, Demetrius."

He smiled, showing all of his teeth. "Let's pretend a miracle happened and you didn't die wielding it. You know that the spearhead would cause special, human-only gateways to open in all the realms, thus providing a way for those miserable meat bags to escape. But if a *demon* harnessed the spearhead's power, another type of gateway would open in all the realms, and this one would allow *my* kind free passage back and forth again."

I stared at him. Yes, I knew every hallowed item could be turned dark. That was why demons had wanted David's sling. In my hands, it killed demons, but in their hands, it could kill Archons. Likewise, Moses's staff had sealed up the realm walls when I used it, but if demons had wielded it, it would have sent them crashing down. In context, I don't know why it hadn't occurred to me that if the spearhead were turned dark, its other purpose would be the exact opposite of its hallowed one.

And if that happened, everything I'd done to help people would get undone. It would be hell on earth in no time, and here I was, without any hallowed weapons to fight it because they had disappeared when I'd renounced my destiny.

I was reeling from horror and guilt, but one question roared to the surface. "Why are you telling me this?"

"Because I don't want that to happen." After my instant scoff, he said, "Yes, under other circumstances, I would love nothing more than to have the realm gateways reopen. Aside from the obvious, I'm sick of being stuck in a small slice of your rotten world. However, whoever wields the spearhead would have complete control over the gateways, and that, my dear despised Davidian, I cannot abide."

Now his concern made sense, and of course, his own selfishness was at its core. "That would make the spearhead-wielding demon top dog over you, wouldn't it?"

He shrugged, but there was nothing casual in his gaze. "I'm not the only demon who doesn't want a king. We had one once, and it did *not* suit. We might have minor power struggles, but no demon since Lucifer has ever had the chance to rule all of us. This would change that."

I couldn't care less if Demetrius chafed at the thought of being ruled. In fact, his misery would make my day, if it didn't come at such a high cost. I couldn't stand the thought of the demon realms reopening, and the demon staring at me knew it.

"So you want me to find the spearhead to stop another demon from finding and using it."

"Yes," he said, a nasty gleam appearing in his eyes. "And do try to wield it if you do. Having you implode from its power while simultaneously saving me from being under a king's rule would be—what does your race call it?—a win-win."

I almost flipped him off, but I stopped myself because I didn't want to flash my non-tattooed right hand at him. "Yeah, well, I'm not going to do that," I said shortly.

He cocked his head. "Which, go after the spearhead, or attempt to wield it?"

I glared at him. "Guess."

He shrugged. "Could be either after your soul-tying to Adrian." At my confused look, he said in an almost kindly tone, "You do realize that's the reason for your newfound apathy toward the humans trapped in my realms, don't you? Otherwise, you would have never abandoned those mortal meat bags to certain death just to ensure your own happiness."

"I didn't abandon them. I couldn't have saved them, anyway!" I snapped, fighting a wave of familiar guilt.

"Oh, you are correct," Demetrius said, coming forward until another inch would have caused him to breach the mirror. "You never stood a chance because you are weak, Davidian, and this only proves it. When you and my son wrapped your souls around the deepest parts of each other in that tethering ritual, his didn't come away lighter, but yours came away darker, and that darkness only continues to grow."

CHAPTER FOURTEEN

I STARED AT HIM, my mouth opening and closing because I couldn't think up a strong enough denial. That couldn't be! If it were true, then I wouldn't have decided to look for the spearhead *after* the soul-tying ceremony! But I had, so tethering my soul to Adrian's couldn't have had this kind of drastic, "darkening" effect on me.

"You're wrong," I said in a furious whisper. "For starters, I am *not* going dark side, and more importantly, Adrian might have half your blood and all of Judas's remaining legacy, but he is *nothing* like either of you."

Demetrius's laugh sounded like a low roll of thunder. "The fact that you have no idea who Adrian is and what he is capable of only proves me correct. And you might not yet manifest the full effects of having your soul tainted with the essence of both demons and Judians, but give it more time, and you will."

Was he implying that it was like an incubating virus? That was ridiculous! Yes, I hadn't been thrilled about going after the spearhead even after I'd decided to do it, but hey, I hadn't wanted to hunt down the slingshot and the staff at first, either.

Still…I hadn't given up while searching for either of those, and doing so had been just as dangerous to me and Adrian as looking for the spearhead. Yet I *had* given up on that. I was also catching myself lying for no reason, and several weeks ago, I'd let that poor girl get shot before I finally helped her.

Could Demetrius be right? Could tying myself to Adrian's admittedly darker soul have, well, tainted something in me?

Adrian had worried himself about that happening, saying he never would have done it if he'd known that he was half-demon at the time. Doing so had also cost me access to the light realms that were the beautiful, sunny counterparts to demon realms. What if— partially—Demetrius was right? What if… What if I was kinda evil now?

The thought was too upsetting to ponder more in front of Demetrius, so I moved on. "You said Adrian's life depended on me hearing you out," I said, abruptly changing the subject. "So far, I haven't heard how yet."

"Demons are naturally rebellious," Demetrius said with a quick, feral smile. "And Judians betray. That's why Adrian joining the Archons against us wasn't a complete surprise. I'd expected him to do something terrible and backstabbing eventually." He sighed. "I didn't expect it to last this long. I was convinced he'd quickly grow bored with the endless rules and restrictions 'good' people are expected to keep."

"Get to the point," I said through gritted teeth.

He stared at me without blinking. "Adrian is my son, so I love him despite his murderous, extended treachery and rebellion. Oh, I'll torture him for it— what self-respecting father wouldn't?—but I *won't* kill him, and that makes me in the extreme minority among my kind."

I closed my eyes. "And if another demon is crowned king by controlling access to all the demon realms through the spearhead, he'll likely rally demons to kill Adrian, both for his fighting against your people and for his refusal to fulfill his destiny by betraying me to my death."

"Not entirely stupid, are you?" Demetrius said mockingly.

I did flip him off then, left-handed. He returned the gesture, with an added throat-slitting mime from the remains of his shadows that was a lot more ominous. I'd seen him cut someone's throat for real with one of those dark, lethal wisps, and it was nothing I wanted to experience for myself.

"But the spearhead's been lost for two thousand years," I said, trying to find a silver lining in the choking darkness Demetrius had described. "Who's to say it won't be lost for another two thousand?"

Demetrius's snort was scathing. "Hasn't anyone told you about the countdown?"

Countdown? "What countdown?"

He chuckled, low and contemptuous. "You don't know? Well, Davidian, then I'll give you the respect that my son and that Archon obviously felt you weren't deserving of. As soon as you wielded David's sling, the prophesied countdown began. Do you want to know what it is?"

Demetrius was too smug to be lying, so once again, I'd had critical information about my destiny withheld by the people I trusted most. Anger burned a hole into my guilt and fear. Time and again, Adrian had had the chance to tell me this, yet he hadn't. Had he also realized what would happen if the spearhead fell into demon hands? Did he simply not care if the realms opened again? And more frightening—would I end up having that same sort of darkness in me, as time went on?

"Yes, I want to know," I said in a stony voice.

"Prophecy says once the first hallowed weapon is wielded, the others will be found within a year," Demetrius said with gleeful malice. "That doesn't leave much time, does it?"

No, it didn't. Only a few months, and here I'd spent weeks lazing about in Vatican City. If not for Demetrius, I might have spent several more weeks doing that, and all while Adrian knew that the spearhead would soon be found by someone else.

I heard the bathroom door open. "Ivy, are you okay?" Adrian called out from the other side of the privacy wall.

"I'm fine!" I yelled while Demetrius immediately started to fade from the mirror. "Just finishing up!" I'd have it out with him, but not in front of Demetrius. I'd given the demon too much to gloat about already.

"Okay," Adrian said after a slight pause, probably surprised by the anger in my tone.

I turned back to the mirror, which now showed no demon staring back at me, but I knew that Demetrius was still there.

"Since you want me to find it, got any idea where the spearhead is?" I asked, not really expecting a response.

His voice was faint, as if he was much farther away, yet his disdain came through loud and clear. "At one of Adrian's former favorite places in your world, of course."

He knew that Adrian was the metaphorical "map"?

Oh, *shit*! We thought we were the only ones who'd figured that out!

I left the bathroom feeling overwhelmed, angry and grimly determined. I might have given up looking for the spearhead before—and thanks to Demetrius, I wondered if that was me, or my new, festering darkness's influence—but now I was going after it with everything I had. I couldn't let another demon find it first. I would *not* let the realms reopen for human slavery sooner rather than much, much later. Plus, I might want to kill Adrian myself now, but I'd be damned if I'd let demons do that, either.

"Demetrius and I just had a chat," I announced as soon as I left the bathroom.

He ran into the bathroom before I had a chance to say anything else. Several crashing sounds later, I knew he'd smashed the mirror. *Too late now*, I thought bitterly.

"If he found us, then we need to leave," Adrian said moments later, wiping his bloody knuckles on his jacket. That was how rattled he was. He'd smashed the mirror with his bare hands. "And why did you stay long enough to see which demon was using the mirror as a portal? You could have been killed, Ivy!"

I shook him off when he tried to take my arm. "I made sure I wasn't close enough to be pulled into the mirror, and no demon could come out of it or the hallowed ground would've fried them."

"Let's forget about the fact that Demetrius moves faster than you do, and probably could have pulled you into the mirror with him. What about if he threw a spear at you and impaled you?" he asked harshly.

"Or hurled acid into your face? Or threw a powdered, inhalable poison at you? Are you getting the picture?"

I was, and while his high-handed tone added to my already-simmering anger, it also made me believe that Demetrius had been telling the truth. Well, the part about why he didn't want me dead. Otherwise, he could have killed me in all the ways Adrian had described, and knowing Demetrius, probably a few more that Adrian hadn't thought of, too.

"You know what really would help?" I asked, my roiling emotions causing my tone to turn withering. "If you'd quit waiting to tell me important stuff like that until *after* the danger has passed."

His hands clenched into fists. "You knew that mirrors plus demons equaled danger. I didn't think I had to spell out all the different ways that this was true."

"Of course you didn't!" I snapped. "In your mind, I *never* need to know everything that you do, even when it's my life at stake. How many times do I have to tell you to stop? I don't treat *you* that way. If I did, I wouldn't have told you about my talk with Demetrius in the first place!"

He flinched, something skipping across his features before he spun around and all I saw was his back. My jaw clenched. He'd done something similar countless times over the past several weeks, and now I knew why. He was giving himself a moment to school his features so his lies would be more believable.

Fine. I'd give myself a little time, too. But once I had Jasmine and Costa safe, I was letting Adrian have it. All of it.

After a couple seconds, Adrian sighed and ran a

hand through his hair as he turned around to face me again.

"You're right. I should have told you all the dangers of demons using mirrors back when I told you that demons could use them as portals, and I'm sorry."

That was the only thing he was admitting to? I continued to glare at him. "That's all you're sorry about?"

He pulled my anger-stiff body into his arms. "No, it's not," he whispered. "I might be over a hundred years old, but some things are still new to me. God, Ivy, the last thing I'm used to doing is telling the truth, the whole truth and nothing but the truth, even to someone I love."

Yeah, being raised by demons meant that Adrian's baseline sense of right and wrong had been completely skewed. Add that to being half-demon and the last Judian, and he must fight every day to turn from his lineage, his DNA and his upbringing.

But he had to keep fighting that battle, and more important, he had to win it, or we were doomed as a couple. I now knew I had to fight it, too. He wasn't the only one battling demonically fueled inner darkness, and that knowledge caused some of the fury to leak out of me.

What Adrian had done was worse. Far, far worse, but I wasn't innocent, and as he'd said earlier, we had to fight our battles, big or small, together.

"It has to stop," I said, my voice softer, yet still stern. "Even if we have to stay up all night tonight spilling our guts to each other, we need to tell each other the truth, all of it. No matter what."

"Okay," he said after the faintest pause.

If that pause was him still deciding what he would

and wouldn't tell me, I had bad news for him later. The jig was up. But as for now…now it was my turn to ante up.

"I'm going after the spearhead again."

He drew away with a horrified look on his face. "What?"

I began to walk back toward our villa. He followed, and I told Adrian what Demetrius had said about the dark, opposing powers of the spearhead if a demon wielded it instead of me.

"*Demetrius* told you that?" Adrian couldn't sound more incredulous if I'd said that a mermaid had shown up holding Aladdin's lamp to offer me three wishes.

"Yes, and as you pointed out, he could have killed me instead of sharing this information, so I believe him—"

"I don't," Adrian said sharply. "If it were true, he would have told me himself already."

I stopped walking to stare at him. "When would he have done that?"

Come to think about it, Adrian hadn't seemed surprised to hear that Demetrius was one of the demons who'd managed to stay in our world when the realm gateways had closed. Had he gotten a visit from the demon that he hadn't told me about?

"During one of the million times Demetrius told me to kill the last Davidian before she could find and wield any of the hallowed weapons," Adrian replied in a cool tone. "That was a recurring theme while I was growing up, remember?"

"Yeah, I'm aware," I said, but I was filing his reaction away as something to follow up on later, when all of us were safe. "But since Demetrius endlessly harped on the hallowed weapons and the importance of killing the last Davidian, why didn't he tell you about the opposing purpose of the spearhead back then, too?"

Adrian began to walk briskly again. "I guess I shouldn't be surprised. As I just said, demons don't rush to confide the whole truth about anything to anyone, even those they love."

I said nothing, keeping up with his rapid pace while I turned his words over in my mind. Adrian's hatred of demons had been the first thing I knew about him back when we met. Since then, that hatred had never wavered, and its relentlessness had hidden an important fact about him that I now realized. Adrian might have devoted the past several years of his life to their destruction, but deep down, he still thought of himself as a demon.

Oh, he'd deny it if I said it, but this last statement combined with a thousand other things confirmed it. In fact, now I didn't know why it had never occurred to me before. I'd known that I was adopted, yet I was still Thomas and Beth Jenkins's daughter and Jasmine's sister. Some ties went deeper than blood. Last Davidian I might be, but until my final breath, I would also be a Jenkins. In the same way, Adrian had spent over a hundred years as an accepted, loved and lauded member of demonkind. Hate them he might, fight them he might and kill them he might, but deep down, he still *felt* like one of them.

Was that also what Demetrius had meant when he was taunting me about how I didn't really know Adrian? If so, then the joke was on him. I hated demons, but regardless of Adrian's destiny, DNA or species identification, I loved him, and he loved me.

We had issues to work through—big ones—but they weren't insurmountable. Not unless we allowed them to be.

"So, you're determined to resume your search of the spearhead to keep it from falling into demon hands?"

Adrian asked the question as if the answer didn't mean much to him, but from the tight set of his shoulders and the muscle ticking in his jaw, he was struggling to remain calm.

"Yes," I said, waiting to see if he mentioned the countdown. When he didn't, I clenched my fists but kept walking. Demetrius might not be interested in killing me at the moment, but he was fully capable of doing something awful to Jasmine or Costa to incentivize me, and if he knew where I was, he knew where they were. "I still don't intend to use it, but I need to make sure it's safe from any demons who are hunting for it. That way, they can't use it to reopen the gateways, or rally the other demons to kill you."

"They already want to kill me," Adrian said with a grunt.

"Demetrius doesn't, and he's powerful enough to keep a lot of the rest of them from trying it," I said shortly. "But for many reasons, we can't let a demon end up controlling all the realm gateways through the spearhead."

"Is that *all* Demetrius said to you during your chat?"

My lips thinned. Only someone with something to hide would wonder what else Demetrius had told me.

"No," I said, and left it at that.

Adrian tugged on my hand when we reached the villa. "What else?" he asked, sounding wary.

I'd give him a tidbit, but I'd save the meal for later.

"He knows you're the 'map' for the hallowed weapons." At Adrian's shocked expression, I shrugged. "Guess their being found at two of your former homes in this world tipped him off. You told me yourself that he kept chasing you when you'd sneak out to go to this world, so if any demon would be able to figure that out, Demetrius should. That's why he suggested that we resume our search for the spearhead in places where you used to live."

Then I squared my shoulders as I stared at Adrian.

"But you've never lived in Vatican City, Hofburg Palace or the Mother See campus in Armenia, so why did we start our search for the spearhead there?"

CHAPTER FIFTEEN

SOMETHING SKIPPED ACROSS Adrian's features. Then his face became blank as a new sheet of paper and he gave a nonchalant shrug.

"Like I said, I doubted the spearhead would be in any of the places that claimed to have possession of it, but we had to rule them out just in case."

A plausible response, but now I doubted it was true. Could he be hiding something *else* from me? Demetrius had said I had no idea how deep Adrian's darkness ran. Even Obsidiana had hinted that there was a lot I still didn't know about him, and Adrian had nearly died making sure she couldn't say anything else. Then he'd insisted that I finish her off before he even found out if the manna would heal him. Last but not least, he'd just admitted in a roundabout way that he still held things back from me, even if he knew he shouldn't.

No, I hadn't been imagining the unspoken tension between us or the feeling that something was off. Adrian had been lying to me again, either outright or by omission. Despite all his promises, here we were again. Now all that was left was to find out how many different things he'd been lying about.

"You weren't surprised to hear that Demetrius was on this side of the realms," I said, giving him a chance to tell me the truth on his own about that, at least. "Why not?"

Adrian opened his mouth—and Costa flung the front door open so hard, it almost hit us. It did hit the side of the villa, the knob knocking off a chunk of plaster from the impact.

"Time to go!" Costa said, hauling a suitcase through the door. "Jasmine's almost packed. You two need to hurry."

Adrian pulled me behind him, putting the villa at my back while he blocked my front. "What's wrong?"

"Fucking minion made a house call," Costa snapped, gesturing to a pile of ashes near the entryway that I'd assumed was dirt from the nearby garden. "He just showed up and told me they knew where we were. Didn't even fight back or try to run when I jumped him, either. If I didn't know better, I'd swear the fucker *let* me snap his neck!"

That had to be one of Demetrius's minions. How he'd gotten him to go on a suicide mission, I didn't know, but it more than underscored how serious Demetrius was about my restarting the search. He must be *really* worried that another demon would beat us to it. Then again, since Demetrius had figured out that Adrian was "the map" to the hallowed weapons, maybe other demons had, too. Since Demetrius had found us weeks ago, it wasn't hard to imagine that other demons might have found us, too.

"Wish that was the craziest thing I've heard today," Adrian muttered, grabbing my hand and pulling me into the house.

Costa gave him a startled look as he popped the

trunk of our rental car and threw his suitcase into it. "If it isn't, what kind of day have *you* two had?"

"Tell you when we're out of here," Adrian said, giving me a light push toward our bedroom. "Start getting us packed. I'll wake Brutus. He'll have to fly to follow us."

I looked at the sunlight, imagining Brutus's horror when he found out that he'd be flying in this. Yeah, I'd much rather pack than be the one who broke *that* news to him.

I THOUGHT WE'D take a train out of Italy, but Adrian nixed that idea. "Too easy to track," he'd said, adding, "Sending his people to check out the different train stops after the attack in Yerevan might be how Demetrius found us in the first place."

Since I had no intentions of summoning the demon to ask, I'd have to leave it at that. Flying was out for the same reason, not to mention it would mean leaving Brutus behind, and for so many reasons, I wasn't prepared to do that. I thought we'd end up in another remodeled tour bus or an RV big enough to fit four people and a gargoyle, but Adrian had a different plan.

"Careful!" he said to Brutus when night fell and the gargoyle finally came out from beneath the deck. "Remember, do *not* go to the left or the right. Walk straight down the middle."

"We're all gonna die," Costa muttered as he watched the gargoyle attempt to tippy-toe down the center of the boat.

I trusted Brutus, but I could also understand why Costa was nervous. At two tons, if Brutus suddenly lurched to one side of the boat, we stood a good chance of tipping over too far and capsizing. If it weren't a sturdy commercial fishing trawler built for dragging and storing heavy cargos of fish, we probably wouldn't have made it off the dock with Brutus.

But, after driving across the Italian peninsula to the opposite end of the country, Adrian had negotiated our passage with a local trawler owner. Their entire conversation had been in Italian, which meant I didn't understand what was being said. For once, I was glad. Knowing how much Adrian had paid to bribe the trawler owner to give up fishing for the next few days and ferry us around instead would probably keep me up at night.

Still, this was smart. Even if we had been followed by minions—and Adrian had done some pretty impressive driving to prevent that—we were now out in the middle of the Adriatic Sea. Minions and demons would have a hard time finding us here.

The only downside was that the trawler, not surprisingly, reeked of fish. The four of us were breathing out of our mouths to avoid it, but Brutus loved it, proving that even stink was relative depending on the sniffer.

Jasmine came up from below deck next. She'd been upset since hearing that I was going after the spearhead again, but I'd explained why—and more important, that I wasn't planning to use it—so I knew she'd come around. Still, I was relieved to feel her thread her fingers through mine before she rested her chin on my shoulder. She used to do that a lot when we were kids. It had been her way of saying that things were still okay between us after a fight. Feeling it now was like a balm to my frazzled emotions, and I closed my fingers over hers.

"Where are we headed to this time?" she asked.

"Montenegro," I said, repeating what Adrian had told the boat's captain. "The Adriatic is narrow as far as seas go, and Montenegro is on the other side of it. Apparently, there's a church in the Bay of Kotor that Adrian used to hang out at."

That was the reason he'd given me for suggesting that we start our new search there. I had my doubts about his honesty, but we were in very tight quarters with Costa, Jasmine or one of the boat's crew members constantly over our shoulders. I'd wait until we were alone to confront Adrian. Patience wasn't my strong suit, but I'd been forced to practice it a lot lately.

"Gently," Adrian told Brutus when the gargoyle flapped his wings to begin his ascent into the air. Now that it was night, Brutus would want to fish. The boat might reek of them, but there weren't any on it, much to Brutus's disappointment.

The brown-haired crewman whose name escaped me gave Adrian a startled look. "Not afraid your little bird will get lost?" he asked with a heavy Italian accent.

Brutus chuffed and spread his wings to their full length, as if to say, *Who you calling little?* I coughed to hide my laugh as the crewman shook his head, seeing only a squawking, puffed-up seagull instead of a magnificent gargoyle with a wingspan that exceeded the width of the boat.

"This bird won't get lost," Adrian told him, then said, *"Tarate!"* to Brutus.

He took off after one last annoyed look at the crewman, who almost fell over from the sudden, fierce gust of wind from Brutus's wings that the gargoyle had aimed right at him.

"What's that language?" the crewman stuttered, trying to cover up the fact that he'd lost his footing for no apparent reason. I hid my smile. He'd gotten off lucky. He didn't want to know what Brutus could do when he was *really* mad.

Adrian grunted. "Nothing you'd know, trust me."

Then Adrian came over to me, caressing my arm and frowning when I moved away. I pretended not to notice, occupying myself with helping Jasmine control her wildly whipping hair. Mine was already in a ponytail, but she'd forgotten to pin hers back before coming up. Now the wind caused it to attack Jasmine's face as if her locks had been replaced with Medusa's snakes.

"You're not going to win this," I told her, nudging her back toward the opening in the deck. "Come on. I have another scrunchie in my cabin, and there's food in the galley, too."

I walked away, pretending I didn't feel Adrian's sharp gaze on me as I went. Unlike Adrian, I couldn't put on a convincing enough act to hide what I was feeling. And call it the new "darkness" in me, but I didn't mind him stewing over things for a while. After all, I hadn't been able to think much past what I knew he'd been hiding for the past several hours.

That was why I took my time below with Jasmine, first French braiding her hair, then eating some of the rations the boat was stocked with. They were hardly the yummy fare that vacation cruise lines were famed for, but this wasn't a vacation and I wasn't that hungry anyway. I was only eating to keep my lingering queasiness at bay.

"You don't look so great, Ivy," Jasmine said when we came back to my cabin, which was a generous term for the tiny room containing two hammocks and a toilet. We sat on the lower hammock, and Jasmine felt my forehead.

"No fever," she said with relief.

"It's not that," I said. "I'm just nauseous."

Her eyes bugged. "Could you be pregnant?"

"Not possible," I said at once.

She snorted. "We've lived in the same small villa for over a month, and while I don't eavesdrop at night, I'm not deaf. That's how I know it's *entirely* possible."

"That's not what I mean," I said, getting up to shut the door even though with it closed, the tiny quarters made me feel claustrophobic. "Adrian told me that several years ago he had a vasectomy."

Jasmine's brows went up. "Why?"

He hadn't told me the next part. Like too many other things, I'd had to figure it out for myself. "So he stays the last Judian. Otherwise, he'd be passing this awful legacy on to any child he had, and he refuses to do that."

"Wow," Jasmine said softly. "I suppose I get why he did it. But since you're with him, that means no more Davidians, too."

No, there wouldn't be. My hands went to my lower stomach, where I'd never feel life growing. An odd pang of loss hit me. Before I'd found out about my destiny, I'd thought that I'd have kids someday. Now I knew I wouldn't, and despite that feeling of loss, I was glad. I couldn't bear to do what my bio mom had done by abandoning me for my own good. Yet if I had had a child, I might have been forced to do that, too.

"It's not such a bad thing," I said steadily, letting my hands fall away. "If I had children, I'd be passing my legacy on to them, too. Being Davidians would make them prime targets for demons, and I couldn't stand that. So…it's better this way."

Jasmine took my hand, her gaze brimming with sadness. "You don't get to choose much in your life, do you?"

I blinked away the tears that rose unexpectedly. No, not much, and the choices I had made, I was now second-guessing.

"That's life," I said, my voice husky. "We have to try to make the best of it. Besides," I forced my tone to brighten, "we can always change our mind on the choices we do have, right?"

"Right," she said softly, but her eyes were still sad.

I didn't want her worrying about me. She'd had too much worry, stress and pain in her life as it was. "Speaking of choices," I said, still in that fake light tone. "When are you going to admit that you and Costa are a couple?"

Her eyes widened to almost comical degrees. "How did you know?" she asked with a gasp.

Now it was my turn to snort and point out the obvious. "Because you're not the only one who hears things at night."

CHAPTER SIXTEEN

I HADN'T INTENDED to fall asleep in the hammock with Jasmine, but we'd ended up talking for hours, and at some point, we'd put our heads down to be more comfortable. A lot more comfortable, as it turned out.

While we slept, someone had opened the door and left it open, allowing fresh air to come into the stuffy quarters. Having the door open also kept my claustrophobia at bay, and when I looked across the hallway and saw Costa sleeping in one of his room's two hammocks while the other was empty, I knew who'd done it. Adrian.

I got up, taking care not to jostle Jasmine so I didn't wake her. Not that I should have worried. She just rolled into the middle of the hammock with a nasally snore once I'd extricated myself. I smiled at how contented she looked, then my smile faded as I left the room.

Battle time.

Adrian was at the front of the boat. It was still dark out, but a hint of orange showed where the water and the horizon met, so sunrise was on its way. The constant sea spray combined with the wind made me wish I'd grabbed a jacket before coming up, yet I wasn't turning around. Aside from a crew member in the glass-enclosed steering room, we were finally alone.

I went over to stand next to him. Without a word,

he took off his coat and put it around me. It was still warm from his body heat, and his height meant that it fell to my knees.

"Thanks," I said as I put it on. Then I took a deep breath. I wasn't going to open with *We need to talk* or *Isn't there something you want to tell me?* We were way past that.

"You've been lying to me again, Adrian," I said, still staring at that faint orange light on the horizon. "Don't make it worse by denying it. I think I already know most of what it is, but you're either going to tell me the rest of it, or no matter how much I love you, I am going to leave you."

He swung me around to face him, the fading moonlight highlighting the shock on his features. "What?"

I pushed his hands from my shoulders, glaring at him through a sudden surge of tears. "I said, I will leave you if you don't spill right now everything you've been hiding and lying about. As Jasmine noted earlier, I don't have a choice about much, but I can damn well choose not to keep searching for the spearhead with someone who keeps lying to me and undermining my every step. Yes, your bloodline and your upbringing mean that lying's second nature to you, but you still have free will. Whatever you do now, it will be your choice, so don't blame anyone but yourself if you don't like the consequences."

I was breathing hard by the time I was finished, as if I'd been running. In some ways, I had. I'd been running from this moment by dismissing or ignoring all the warnings that had led up to it. Adrian was breathing harder, too, and the silver rings around his eyes were almost glittering in the moonlight.

"You don't get it, Ivy. If I tell you everything, you'll leave me anyway."

"Then I'll do it with the truth you should have told me in the first place," I said, clenching my fists in an attempt to keep my trembling from showing. The thought of leaving him, even temporarily to continue this quest without him, hurt so much that I was shaking, but I wasn't bluffing. I'd had enough of excuses, lies and rationalizations. Now I wanted the truth, all of it. "You owe me that, Adrian."

He muttered a foul curse in Demonish and turned away. I waited several moments, but he didn't speak or turn around.

I took in a shuddering breath, feeling a tightness in my chest that rose to clog my throat. Even now, he still couldn't do it. I'd warned him of what would happen, and I'd meant it.

I spun around on legs that felt like they'd buckle, but they were still strong enough to carry me away from him. "If you have nothing to say, then this is goodbye—"

"I summoned Demetrius." The words sounded like they clawed their way out of his throat. Hearing them made me pause on my way back to the hold. "Right after you decided to go after the spearhead, I summoned him."

I turned around and came back a step. "Why?"

Adrian's expression was tortured. "I knew there'd be demons left over in this world, and they'd all be gunning for you, Demetrius especially. I needed to keep them off your trail, so I told Demetrius we were soul-tied. That gave him a reason to want you alive, since our tie means if you get killed, I might die, too, no matter what Zach said about my demon nature protecting me. I knew Demetrius couldn't stand for that. He might want to torture the hell out of me, but he doesn't want me dead."

It was so close to Demetrius's exact words, it was almost eerie. I hated that they sometimes thought alike. In fact, I hated every one of their similarities, yet I couldn't deny them anymore because they upset me.

My gaze drilled into his as I took another step toward him. "Is that all the two of you talked about?"

A harsh little smile curled his lips. "I also told him that I never wanted you to find the spearhead, let alone use it, and I'd keep you away from the places where it might really be until the countdown ran out."

The air rushed out of me as if I'd been hit. I'd guessed as much, but guessing it and having it confirmed were two different things. Adrian had tethered his soul to mine in order to prove that he'd never betray me again, but he had. Worse, he'd done so for the exact same reason that fate had predicted.

Many people forget that Judas was guilty of three betrayals. His first had been betrayal of trust after he stole funds from the disciples' communal purse. His second was greed when he accepted those thirty pieces of silver and the third was death when he identified Jesus to the guards with that treacherous kiss. Adrian might not have accepted money from Demetrius, but he'd been motivated by the same thing that had done in Judas two millennia ago: greed. For Judas, it had been greed for money. For Adrian, it had been greed for me.

An awful sense of inevitability rose to cover my anger and hurt. Despite everything we'd done, we'd still ended up here.

"And Demetrius was okay with that?" I managed to ask. I had to distract from the crushing weight of fate. If I didn't, it would wreck me, and I was barely holding it together as it was.

His features twisted again. "No. At first, I thought it was because he wanted you to find and use the spearhead, since he knows it'll kill you, and he wants you dead. He hates you, Ivy. If not for the risk to my life, he would have come through that mirror earlier, ripped your heart out and eaten it in front of you, hallowed ground be damned."

I winced. That was a nasty picture, and worse, I didn't think Adrian was exaggerating. For all I knew, he'd seen Demetrius do that exact same thing to someone in the past.

"But after he knew about our tie, he said the reason he wanted you to find the spearhead was so you could keep it safe from other demons. I didn't buy that, but he said you couldn't do anything with it except free some trapped humans anyway, and he didn't consider their potential loss a big deal."

Adrian paused, another bleak smile wreathing his lips. "He didn't tell me about the spearhead's other use, but I didn't ask. Maybe I didn't want to know, but now I know why he was so adamant about you finding it instead of another demon."

"Yet you sabotaged me." My voice was as raw as my emotions. "You took me to places you knew it wouldn't be, and you didn't tell me about the countdown. You were going to let a demon find it and reopen the gateways."

His fists clenched. "I told you—I wasn't sure that's what the weapon would be used for. Besides, if a lesser demon found it, it could kill them. Just like the spear-head would probably kill you as soon as you touched it, it would also kill all but the most powerful demons who dared to attempt wielding it."

The way he said it made me believe him, but it didn't matter. I wasn't about to risk the freedom of count-less humans on the hope that a weak demon found the spearhead instead of a strong one. He was also ignor-ing the obvious: that a weak demon would find it and give it to a stronger one. What better way to curry favor with the new "king" than that?

"I promised Demetrius that I would put you on the right path," Adrian went on, filling the silence that had fallen like a load of bricks. "In return, Demetrius promised to keep the other demons off your trail by directing them away from us."

A breath of humorless laughter escaped me. "But you didn't put me on the right path, so you lied to De-metrius, too."

His gaze never left mine. "Demetrius doesn't know that being around the spearhead will give you an un-controllable compulsion to use it, but I do. I saw it with the staff, and I wasn't risking your life no matter what I promised him. I told you once before, my every ac-tion is driven by my undying love for you, and that, Ivy, is the real truth."

CHAPTER SEVENTEEN

THE SUN WAS coming up, coloring the sky in shades of fire. A dark form rushed by overhead, startling me, until I realized it was Brutus. He hovered above the boat, slowing the beating of his wings by degrees, until he lowered himself onto the deck with only a slight pitch in the boat to show for it.

Adrian said something in Demonish that I recognized as praise for the delicacy Brutus had shown. Then he said, "Wait in the fish freezer, boy," and the gargoyle carefully walked down the stairs of the hold.

"The freezer's off, isn't it?" I asked, although it might not matter. Brutus had spent all but the past several months of his life in a frozen demon realm. He might miss the cold.

"They don't pay to keep it running when there are no fish," Adrian replied, his tone carefully neutral, but his eyes were almost wild when he looked over at me. *Is it over between us?* his gaze seemed to scream.

I wasn't sure. He'd been truthful, but that had been damning in itself. Plus, I felt like there was more he still wasn't telling me.

"This church in Montenegro that we're on our way to," I said, trying to keep my voice from cracking under the strain of holding my emotions inside. "Is it a decoy?

Or is there a real chance that the spearhead might actually be here?"

"Decoy," Adrian said, the single word strained.

I let out a short, hard laugh. "Figures."

Could I get past all the lies he'd told me? It had been so hard to forgive him before, when all he'd done was withhold the truth about my destiny after we first met. Did I even want to put myself through the pain of trying to forgive his much greater lies now? He'd said that tethering his soul to mine would be the proof I needed to show he'd never betray me again, yet he had. He just hadn't done it the way his destiny predicted that he would.

Yet I'd lied in our relationship, too. Sometimes small, like early today. Sometimes big, like the time I'd lured him into a room so I could bash him over the head and get his blood to enter a demon realm without him. Even now, I was holding back what Demetrius had said about the effects of our soul-tethering. If I believed that Adrian's darkness made it impossible for him to redeem himself, what did that say about me, if I now had the same darkness?

But before we got to that... "Is that everything you've been hiding from me? Or is there more?"

The question hung like a sword over our relationship. One more lie, and it would fall, severing the tie between us.

"No," Adrian said, gripping the edge of the ship so hard that the wood creaked beneath his hands. "There's something else. It's about your biological mother."

"My bio mom?" I repeated in surprise.

If I'd thought his expression was anguished before, it was nothing compared to now. "Seven years ago,

Demetrius took me to this world on a hunt. He did that sometimes when he was after another demon or a minion he wanted to teach a lesson to, but when we got to this small village in Guatemala, he told me who we were really there for." His next words were whispered, yet they struck me with the force of a sledgehammer. "A Davidian. The last one, or so Demetrius believed. He'd tracked her there, but the village where she was staying was on holy ground, so he needed me to go into it and get her to come out…"

I turned away, a sob ripping from my throat. *No. No.* I knew that my biological mother was dead, but I had never in a million years thought that Adrian was involved. I could not stand to hear the rest of this. I *couldn't.*

"He told me this was what I'd been training for my whole life." Adrian's voice was hoarse. "That it was my destiny to lure her into his hands. The ugliest parts of me even wanted to, but I'd seen too much of this world by then. I knew Demetrius and the other demons had been lying about humans being the real monsters. Yes, some were, but demons were far worse, and I couldn't help them destroy the last Davidian in order to grow even more powerful. So, I refused."

I looked up, torn between relief, dread and the desperate need to know more. "What happened?"

"I've never seen Demetrius angrier," he said simply. "He beat me unconscious. While I was out, he set most of the grass on fire, then used his shadows like tornadoes to force the fire to spread inside the village. By the time I came to, half the village was burned, the survivors were fleeing and Demetrius had set himself up in the only path they had to escape the flames."

I couldn't imagine the panic from that deadly blaze, let alone having your only way of escape blocked by a demon. It must have been hell on earth.

"Most of the survivors were covered in soot, so he couldn't tell which one was the Davidian," Adrian said, his tone taking on the rough edge of grief. "So he started slaughtering everyone once they left hallowed ground. I tried to stop him, but he sliced me open. I couldn't move, so I could only watch as he kept killing them…until a woman yelled out that she was the one he was looking for."

I sucked in a ragged breath. I couldn't imagine the courage that this had taken. My bio mother would have known what the demon would do to her, and a quick death while attempting to flee with the others would have been far preferable.

"I couldn't see her face very well from the smoke, but she had long dark hair like you do," Adrian said softly. "She stayed at the edge of the hallowed ground and demanded that Demetrius grant everyone safe passage before she came out. He thought that was funny, but she said she'd allow herself to burn to death unless he let everyone else go free. She must have known that he wanted her alive so he could use her to find David's sling."

Good God, she'd had courage! Now a part of me was glad that I'd never met her. What a disappointment I would have been to someone so selflessly brave.

"Demetrius didn't want to risk the fire taking his prize from him, so he let them go. He got as close to the hallowed ground as he could to stare at her while the survivors left, and she didn't back away. Instead, she stared right back at him. But that was a mistake.

Her clothes must have gotten ripped in the stampede when people were running for their lives, because Demetrius suddenly bent down and said, *You have stretch marks on your stomach.* Then he started hopping up and down, screaming, *You have had a child! Where is your child?*"

Adrian looked at me, and in that moment, I caught sorrow, anger and admiration in his expression.

"Your mother's last words were *You'll never find out.* Then she pulled out a gun that she must have been hiding and shot herself in the head."

I couldn't stop my tears, and I didn't even try to. She deserved every one of them. All my life, I'd felt unloved and abandoned by my biological mother. How wrong I had been.

"Demetrius went nuts," I dimly heard Adrian say. "He kicked me into a coma that I didn't come out of for days. When I finally woke up, he told me that he had tortured and killed the remaining villagers, but none of them knew where her child was. They hadn't even known that she'd had a child, so Demetrius said it was now my job to find the child as punishment for my rebellion. But seeing your mother kill herself rather than give up your location was the last straw. I was done being the demons' prophesied savior, so as soon as I could, I walked out of my realm determined to end my life. It was the only way I thought I could be free." Short, harsh sigh. "I overdosed and you know the rest. Zach found me and showed me the truth about Demetrius using his shape-shifting abilities to masquerade as my mother, both to keep me in their world and to cover up the fact that Demetrius had murdered her when I was a child. Ever since that day, I've been fighting demons and my own destiny."

I felt his fingers brush my tears, and I looked up, meeting his dark, tormented gaze.

"Maybe now you can understand why I was so horrified when Zach told me who you were, and why I fought so hard to deny what I felt for you. I hadn't stopped Demetrius from causing either of our mothers' deaths, so I'd failed you before we even met, and my fate predicted that things would only get worse." His voice broke. "A good man would've left you alone, but I didn't because I'm not a good man."

He took my hands, as if he couldn't stop himself from touching me, then dropped them just as quickly. The muscles in his jaw kept twitching as he ground his teeth together.

"I thought if I could defy my destiny, show you how much I loved you and keep you safe, then I'd finally become the man you deserved. But all I ended up doing was proving that I'm not. I'm a betrayer, Ivy. Maybe not in the ways that Demetrius wants me to be, but in ways that hurt you almost as much."

He spun around then, gripping the railing as if it were the only thing holding him upright. I wanted to soothe him, to stop the anguish I could so clearly see, but what was I going to say? That it was okay that he'd repeatedly lied to me?

"When we started this conversation, I thought nothing would be worse than losing you." His words were whispered, yet they vibrated with intensity. "But I was wrong. It's seeing the pain in your eyes from all the ways I've deceived you." He paused to take in a short, sharp breath. "I never want to see that kind of pain again, yet if I stay with you, I will. I love you, which is why I can't promise not to continue sabotaging you in this quest. I can't promise that if you find the spearhead, I won't rip it away, because I would gladly trade every life in this world for yours. I can't be who you need me to be, so I'm the one who has to leave."

Shock had me staring at him as if I'd never seen him before. I barely noticed Jasmine coming up behind me, saying, "What's going on?" in a sleepy voice.

"Get pen and paper and come right back," Adrian told her. His sharp tone caused her to blink in surprise, but she turned around and went back into the hold.

"You're leaving me?" I got out, so stunned I could hardly speak.

He turned around, his jaw set so tight, it looked carved from stone. "You'll have to be careful. Demetrius might not be the only demon that's figured out I'm the map. If the spearhead can do what he says it can, then every demon left in this world will be gunning for it, including Demetrius. It's gotta be why he wants you to keep looking for it. He loves power too much to resist the chance to crown himself king, so he'll use you to find it, then he'll try to steal it from you."

He was speaking as if he was never going to see me again. I grabbed his arm.

"Stop this. You can't really mean to leave. Yes, we have some huge things to sort through, but—"

"You'll be fine," he interrupted. Then that ragged edge in his voice softened. "You'll have Brutus, your sister, Costa, and if you call Zach, I know he'll come, too. You can trust them, but you can't trust me. No matter how hard I try, I'll only hurt you again. Jasmine," he said, raising his voice and looking past me. I hadn't even noticed her coming back. "Write this down."

He rattled off six different names and countries, making her repeat them while I stood there, feeling like I was being pulled beneath the waves that were currently tossing our boat around. Yes, I'd been prepared to leave him if he insisted on telling more lies, but I hadn't dreamed that he'd finally tell me the truth and then leave *me*.

"Why are you doing this?" I demanded, gripping his arms and forcing him to look at me instead of Jasmine. "What is this, payback? Are you trying to punish me for saying I'd leave you?"

"What?" Jasmine gasped, but both of us ignored her.

"Ivy." He uncurled my hands from his arms and then stroked my face. "For once, I'm doing what's best for you instead of what makes me happy. This is as close as I can come to being the man you've always thought I was." He stroked my face again. "The places I had Jasmine write down are where I think the spearhead could be, since they were all my favorite places when I used to escape into this world. Costa has my bank account numbers, so you won't have to worry about money. You'll have all you need—"

"I don't need money," I snarled, hurt and panic forming a toxic mixture inside me. "What I *need* is for you to stop lying so we won't keep having these conversations in the future!"

He closed his eyes. "If I could, I'd rip the darkness out of me and lay it at your feet. But I can't. Let me do right by you this once, before I don't even have the strength to do that. Brutus, come to me!"

I'd thought he had nowhere to go while we were on

this boat, but with the gargoyle, he could go anywhere. "Adrian, wait," I began desperately.

"Brutus!" he yelled again, pushing me back. *"Larastra!"*

Brutus came out of the hold fast enough to send the boat madly rocking. Adrian said another word in Demonish, and Brutus flew over my head. The sudden gust of wind combined with the heaving of the boat knocked me off my feet. My grasping hands slipped from Adrian's arms, and his pain-filled gaze met mine as he walked out of my reach.

"I love you," he said hoarsely. "Never forget that."

Then he grabbed Brutus's low-hanging leg, using it like a pulley to swing himself onto the gargoyle's back. A torrent of Italian from the crewman erupted behind us, but I couldn't tear my eyes from Adrian as I tried to scramble to my feet.

"Don't!" I shouted as Brutus began to beat his mighty wings, lifting Adrian high above the boat. "Adrian, come back!"

My only answer was a mournful whine from Brutus that faded as he and Adrian disappeared from my sight.

CHAPTER EIGHTEEN

I SPENT THE next few days swinging back and forth between denial, anger and depression. This wasn't the first time Adrian and I had been apart, but it was the first time he'd left me. More important, it was the first time I didn't know if I'd see him again, and not because one of us might get killed. Death was always how I'd feared—or more honestly, expected—things to end between us. I certainly hadn't expected this.

It was now our third night in Montenegro. I'd stayed here because this was where we'd originally intended to go, so it would be easy for Adrian to find me. After all, he couldn't have gone far. Brutus had reappeared a mere four hours after he'd left with Adrian. Half that time had to be taken up by Brutus flying back to me, so Adrian was only two hours away. He had to come to his senses soon and come back, right?

When I wasn't in denial about Adrian's absence being permanent, I was alternatively blasting myself for being the one to bring up leaving in the first place, or reigniting my anger by reminding myself that I had every right to tell Adrian that I wasn't going to put up with any more of his lies.

"I mean, no relationship can survive if one person keeps lying to the other, right?" I fumed to Jasmine while I was on the latter part of my emotional roller coaster.

"Right…" Jasmine hedged, but the way she drew the word out and the uncertainty in her tone made me pounce.

"What?"

"It's totally wrong that he lied," Jasmine said quickly. "Look, you know I hated Adrian when we met. I told you that you could never trust him because of what he was, and yeah, he kinda proved that with this, but still…I get why he did it."

My eyes bugged. "You're on his side?"

"I'm on your side," she said hastily, her gaze pleading with me to understand. "Always. But I'd have lied to you, too, if I thought it would keep you alive. How can I get mad at Adrian for doing the same thing I would've done? You were so determined to find that weapon no matter that using it would kill you. Sure, I feel bad about the people trapped in the realms, but I don't want to *definitely* lose you on the chance that you *might* be able to save them. If that makes me a terrible person, then I'll own being a terrible person."

"You're not a terrible person," I said, my heart breaking for another reason. "You've just been through so much—"

"Haven't we all?" she interrupted, wiping a new spill of tears from her eyes. "I've lost everything except you and Costa. You've lost everything except me and Adrian. Adrian lost everything except you and Costa. Is it such a surprise that some of us are willing to do whatever it takes to hang on to what we have left, even if it means becoming people we aren't proud of?"

No, it wasn't a surprise. I could even understand

the desperation that had driven Adrian to make a deal with the person he hated most in order to improve my chances of survival. After all, there wasn't much I wouldn't have done to save him when I thought he was dying right in front of me. The difference was that I would've paid the price and then *told* him about it.

Adrian had kept lying to me. In fact, he would still be lying to me if I hadn't confronted him about it, and that was the crux of it. I could forgive him not telling me about my bio mom's death because he'd felt a misplaced sense of guilt. I could even forgive his knee-jerk reaction of summoning Demetrius and making that bargain when I first decided to go after the spearhead. What was harder to get over was what he'd done every day after that.

"There's a lot about me that I'm not proud of, too," I told Jasmine. "But it's easier to rationalize leaving all those people behind when you aren't the one solely responsible for their possible freedom, or continued imprisonment. Don't get me wrong—I understand why you and Adrian didn't want me going after the spearhead. I'm the one who eventually gave up on it for those same reasons, but that's the point. Adrian didn't respect me enough to let me come to that decision myself. Instead, he made that decision for me."

Jasmine's eyes were still brimming over. "Would talking with you have made any difference? I kept telling you not to go after the spearhead, but you kept doing it, just like you're still doing it now."

That hit me in all the places that felt raw from Adrian leaving me. I blinked, forcing back the new shine in my gaze.

"Demetrius said there's a countdown, and Adrian

confirmed that. If I don't find the spearhead, then a demon will, and countless thousands more people will get enslaved when the realms reopen. We might, too," I added, because like Adrian, her worry for me was stronger than her worry for strangers. "So our only hope is to grab it first, then hide it where the demons won't know to look."

"But if you touch it, you'll die," Jasmine said brokenly.

I took her hand. "Remember how the slingshot had no effect on you because you're not a demon, Archon, Davidian or Judian? The spearhead would have no effect on you, either. Hallowed weapons can't be activated by regular people, so I'll find it, then you and Costa will take it somewhere and hide it where no one can find it again, even me."

Her grip, which had been slack before, tightened. "You're not going to try to use it?"

I squeezed back, blinking harder this time. The words *I promise* hovered on my lips, but somehow, I couldn't say them even though I tried twice. "You're right," I settled on. "You and Adrian are all I have left. Now that he…he—" I still couldn't say *left me*. "Well, now that he's not here, I refuse to lose you, too."

She threw her arms around me and cried in a way that reminded me that she was only nineteen. She looked like a woman, acted like a woman and had lived through more hell than most people would experience even if they lived to be a hundred, but in reality, she still wasn't old enough to legally drink.

Then, surprising myself, I also cried in the kind of no-holds-barred way that was better suited to someone twelve than twenty-one. It was exhausting, embarrassing, and gave me a headache, yet it was also one of the most freeing things I'd done. I *wasn't* prepared to handle everything that was still ahead of me. As for what was behind me, I didn't know if I'd done the right thing, the wrong thing or the stupid thing. Yet in those brief, unrestrained minutes, I allowed myself to simply ache without my usual worry, second-guessing or self-recriminations.

Afterward, I let Jasmine go, trying to push back my battered emotions as easily as I wiped my still-dripping tears.

"We'll be okay," I told her, patting Jaz on the back with a briskness I didn't feel. "We're tough, right? We'll get through this. Then, when all this is over, we can go back to a semi-normal life. We have fake names and fake ID now, so we don't have to worry about the police being after us on top of minions and demons. You could go back to college, make new friends, and maybe I can track down Adrian and see if it's possible to put things back together between us."

He didn't think so, but if the spearhead was out of the picture, then neither of us would have a destiny pulling us in the opposite direction. I'd like to see what our relationship would be like without fate, bloodlines and angels and demons trying to tear us apart.

Jasmine grabbed a nearby tissue box and blew her nose before responding. "You really think that's possible?"

I wasn't sure if she meant finding the spearhead and getting it safely out of everyone else's reach, her going back to college or my finding Adrian and somehow making things work. Either way, my answer was the same.

"I hope so."

CHAPTER NINETEEN

WHEN I WAS LITTLE, I saw a movie called *Planes, Trains and Automobiles*. I now felt like I was starring in one called *Trains, Ferries and Taxis*, because that was what I'd been traveling in for the past two weeks.

I'd waited one more day in Montenegro before leaving. As devastated as I was, I couldn't spend any more time nursing my broken heart. I'd already given any demons that were after the spearhead enough of a head start. So, I'd gotten the bank account information from Costa, nearly fainted at how much money was in them, then made arrangements for the first stop on our spearhead-hunting trip.

Adrian had listed several places where the spearhead might be. The good news was that most of them were on this side of the globe. The bad news was that still left a huge amount of territory to cover. It hadn't been a big deal for Adrian back then. He'd had demon realm vortexes to use for his mode of travel, and those were nearly as quick as teleportation. I, however, didn't have access to either demon realm vortexes or the light realms, which were even better because I could simply *think* my way to wherever I wanted to go in those. No, I had to do this the slow, hard way.

Flying would've shortened things by a lot, but that would mean leaving Brutus behind. At least once over the bumpy, sleep-deprived and seasick two weeks I'd spent traveling, I have to admit that I considered that, but I couldn't. For starters, Brutus was invaluable when it came to his fighting abilities and his capacity to get us away quickly if the fight was unwinnable. More important, however, he was a cherished friend.

Yes, when we'd first met, I'd viewed Brutus as an unwanted protector that Adrian had thrust upon me. After all, aside from his history as a guard gargoyle for a demon realm, he was the size of an elephant and his farts could peel the skin from your nose. He also drooled when he slept, and I feared for stray cats when he flew at night despite repeatedly telling him that he was *not* allowed to eat them. But over the past several months, he'd become much more than a protector or even a pet. If I cried, he'd sit with his head as close to being on my lap as he could manage, and when I'd hold in the pain so I didn't upset the people around me, he'd stare at me, his solemn red gaze seeming to silently promise that he'd fix everything if he could.

Lately, he'd also taken to bringing me back "presents" from his evening flights. When we were in Travemünde, Germany, the departure city for the ferry we were taking, it was a rosebush complete with roots from his tearing it out of the ground. After we'd ferried from Travemünde to Malmö, Sweden, it was a small, fancy marble birdbath that must have previously adorned an upscale backyard. When we had to spend the night in Stockholm because our train didn't arrive until the following day, Brutus brought me back a gold-colored statue of a ten-horn stag. From the damage to the bottom of it, it had been ripped free from some permanent fixture. I only hoped it wasn't a national monument.

He might not be able to speak beyond grunts, chuffs and roars, but clear as a bell, Brutus kept letting me know that he loved me. I loved him, too, weaponized farts and all, and you didn't abandon those you loved just because the road with them was bumpier than the road without them. That was a lesson I intended to teach to Adrian, if I survived all this to see him again.

Our last stop was Jukkasjärvi, a little town in the uppermost northern part of Sweden. Unlike most of the other passengers on the train with us, we weren't here to get a glimpse of the famed aurora borealis, more commonly known as the northern lights. Instead, we were looking for an artifact that had never been associated with this place.

Maybe that's the point, I thought as we got off the train and I got my first good look around at the village bordered by forest on one side and a long, winding river on the other. Who would think to look in a tiny arctic town for an ancient Roman weapon that had last been seen in the heart of the Middle East? Not me, and probably not anyone else, either. This place was so remote, if I wanted to hide something where it would never be found, I'd certainly consider hiding it here.

Brutus chuffed with relief when we collected our bags and he was finally able to leave the luggage car. He'd had a much smaller area to hide in this time, so he was glad to be off the train. He stretched out his wings as if getting the circulation back in them, then beat them until he hovered a few dozen feet from the ground. I didn't know if he was expelling some pent-up energy, or going higher to get a better look at his new surroundings. Either way, it didn't go unnoticed.

"Where did that seagull come from?" the blonde

woman next to me asked, her accent outing her as British.

"He's mine," I said, lowering my voice as if embarrassed. "I take him everywhere with me, so I snuck him in the baggage car when they told me that pets weren't allowed on the train."

The woman gave me a look I was used to, but hey, a seagull was a lot more normal type of pet than what Brutus really was.

"He seems to like it here," she finally said, looking back at Brutus as he made a few wide circles overhead.

He did look happy, and I wondered if it was from more than finally getting to stretch his wings. Jasmine and I were pulling our coats tighter around us because it felt like it was only a couple degrees above freezing, but Brutus appeared to be reveling in the cold. Then again, I suppose he would. He'd been born into a lot colder conditions than this.

If you asked someone to think of a demon realm, they would probably say it contained fire. I don't know how that rumor got started, but the opposite was true. They were frozen because there was no sunlight. If I were looking for a scientific reason for their existence, I'd say they were a mishmash of M-theory and parallel universes. Take a demon powerful enough to manipulate the gravitational field between a spot in this world and the mirror image world next to it, smash the two together to form an overlapping "bubble," and you had a new demon realm complete with whatever buildings, cars and humans had been unlucky enough to be sucked along for the ride. I'd been on that particular ride, and it was like being on a roller coaster set to the speed of "please, someone kill me now."

"Are you here for the Icehotel?" the British woman asked me, dragging my attention back to her.

"Yep, we're spending the night there," I said, trying not to sound as unenthused as I felt about it. Unlike Brutus, I didn't have fond memories of being in perpetual cold.

"So are we! Are you staying in a cold room, or warm?"

I knew what that meant because I'd had to choose between those two options in order to make the reservations. "Cold. We wanted the full experience." This was a lie—dammit, why was I stooping to lying to a total stranger?—but I had my reasons for picking the frozen option.

She elbowed the man next to her. "That's what I said we should do, but this cheap bugger called it rubbish."

The cheap bugger in question rolled his eyes. "She's paying to freeze her arse off while we'll be warm and happy, no offense t'ya, miss."

I didn't take any because I agreed with him. The cost of staying in the ice part of the Icehotel had staggered me, but it was where Adrian would have stayed when he was here. If I was retracing his steps in the hopes that they would lead me to the spearhead, I had to retrace all of them.

"Oh, the bus to the hotel is pulling up," the woman said, glancing up at Brutus once more. "Best call your pet down and hide him in your bag."

I stifled my laugh at the thought of a bag that would be big enough to fit Brutus. "No need. He'll follow by air."

Her brows rose. "You trained him like a hunting falcon?"

That was one way to spin it. "He came to me trained" was what I said.

She gave me another "you're weird" look, but said, "Quite. Well, since we'll be seeing more of you at the hotel, I'm Zoe, and this is my husband, Dylan."

"Iris," I introduced myself, choosing an *I* name so it would be easier to remember. I kept that theme when I waved Costa and Jasmine forward after I'd shaken Zoe's and Dylan's hands. "And this is my sister, Jada, and her boyfriend, Carl."

"Pleasure," Costa said after giving me a startled glance when I called him *her boyfriend.* Hadn't Jasmine told him I knew their secret, as if it wasn't obvious? Men. They weren't nearly as good at hiding things as they thought.

I was surprised when their response to Costa and Jasmine was much stiffer than the friendliness they'd shown me. They shook Costa's hand as if they'd really rather not, and they kept giving Jasmine oddly censuring looks.

"Carl, eh?" Dylan said, looking Costa up and down. "Short for Carlo, I expect?"

What did he mean by that? I wondered, when a deep voice said, "And I'm Zach," right behind me.

I turned around, stunned. Zach stood there, wearing his usual hoodie and jeans, his demeanor as casual as if he'd been traveling with us this entire time. I barely registered the much longer pause Zoe and Dylan had before they accepted the hand that Zach held out to them.

"Is this your boyfriend, then?" Zoe asked me, releasing Zach's hand almost immediately after she grasped it.

"No," I said with all the repellence I felt at the thought. Dating an Archon would be *so* sacrilegious!

"Ah." Zoe's smile turned into a smirk. Then she leaned forward and whispered loud enough for everyone to hear, "I feel the same way about dating another species."

For a second, I panicked. Were she and Dylan minions? Was that how Zoe knew that Zach wasn't human… Oh. Wait. That was not what she meant.

"Are you serious with your racist shit? I've got news for you—I'm half Latina!" I sputtered out even as Costa growled, "You're pulling this with the *wrong* person," with more of his Greek accent than usual.

Zoe and her husband stiffened as if they were the ones who'd just been royally insulted. "That a threat, mate?" Dylan asked, squaring off against Costa.

Costa laughed. "Normally, it would be, but not this time. I can sit back and watch, because if you keep pissing off my friend, he'll get Old Testament wrathful on your ass."

"Doubtful," Zach said in a mild tone. "For one, I do not spill blood unless ordered to. For another, even if it were mine to decide, I would not repay them in full for their sin. My purpose here is to save lives, not to take them."

Dylan looked rattled, as if on some level he sensed that there was more to Zach than he could see. Then he lost that brief moment of intelligence and sneered at Costa and Zach. "I don't need to be threatened by a fucking dago and his n—"

Zach held up his hand and Dylan didn't finish his other appalling slur. Dylan's eyes bulged while his mouth started moving faster and faster, yet no sound came out of it.

"For your trespasses, you will not speak again for three full moons," Zach said, still in that same mild tone. "And if you do not repent of the hate in your heart by that time, your speech loss will become permanent."

"What did you do to him?" Zoe screamed as Dylan's miming became more frantic. Her shrill voice turned several heads among the people who were also waiting for the bus. Zach stared at her, letting a glimpse of his real power out through the tiny, star-like lights that appeared in his eyes.

"Stop speaking," he said, those brilliant lights burning even brighter. "Or you will soon be as silent as he."

She shut up with a gulp, grabbing Dylan and almost dragging him back to the train instead of toward the bus. Guess she'd decided against their going to the Icehotel. I resisted the urge to yell, *And you got off lucky!* after them.

"That was epic," Jasmine breathed.

"So much for not being vengeful," Costa said with a grin.

Zach lifted his shoulder in a half shrug. "If it were vengeance, their bodies would lie slain on the ground. This was merely a lesson."

I gave mad props to Zach for how he'd handled the racist duo, but there was another, more pressing topic I had to discuss.

"Don't take this the wrong way, because what you did to those two was masterful, but you told me goodbye the last time you saw me, and it sounded permanent. Why are you back now?"

CHAPTER TWENTY

THE TINY, BURNING lights in Zach's eyes disappeared, leaving nothing but their normal, walnut-brown color when he said, "Your bus to the hotel is boarding. If you miss it, you'll have to wait an hour for the next one."

"Why are you here?" I continued to prod. I wanted to be happy to see him, but a sick fear had also risen in me. What if he was here because something terrible had happened to Adrian?

"He is fine," Zach said, using his mind-reading skills again. "And I will answer your questions only when I am ready, as you should be well aware by now. Get on the bus, Ivy. You gain nothing from standing out here in the cold."

Now that I knew Adrian was all right, that sick feeling left me. I was still nervous about what Zach's purpose was, but he was right. I did know better now than to keep pestering him. Zach wouldn't tell me what he was up to until he felt like it or was ordered to, period. Even if I threw the biggest fit in the world, all that would happen would be me, Jasmine and Costa freezing our asses off while we waited for the next bus.

"Brutus!" I said instead, and the gargoyle quit circling overhead and landed next to us. "Follow this bus," I told him, pointing at it. He knew what that meant. He'd managed to follow us during all the taxi rides we'd taken between train stops and hotels. To Jasmine and Costa, I said, "You ready?"

Costa hefted two of our heaviest bags, leaving the smaller ones for Jasmine and I. "Yep. Let's do this."

When I turned around to ask Zach if he was coming, too, he had already disappeared.

I DON'T KNOW what I had thought of the Icehotel before I saw it. A tourist trap, of course. An overpriced, hollowed-out ice cube, possibly. I didn't expect it to look like a mythical fairy mound on the outside, with its wide, misshapen silhouette rising up from the ground in uneven heights. Maybe Hobbit house would be more appropriate considering the dry brown grass that covered the low, sloping roof. It had a double door in the middle, and around that, decorative blocks of ice in an upside-down U shape. They weren't melting, and it wasn't from the rapidly dropping temperature as the sun dipped lower on the horizon.

Another neat fact I'd found out while booking our rooms was that the hotel was now opened year-round because it was kept chilled using solar panels. In another couple months, the temperatures would be enough to do the job, but mid-September temperatures still ranged in the forties for the highs.

We checked in through the "warm" side of the hotel, where we were shown the saunas, dressing rooms, showers and relaxation areas we would use during our stay. We were also given our special coats and boots for when we were in the "cold" side of the hotel. Jasmine and Costa were eager to see the ice bar, where even the glasses were made of—you guessed it—ice. I was waiting for Zach to pop up around every corner, and when I wasn't thinking about that, I was activating my hallowed sensor to see if I felt any blips.

So far, nothing, although I doubted that the spearhead was hidden beneath the hotel. It was redone every year as dozens of ice sculptures changed the layout to reflect fresh new themes, we were told by our reservation guide. If the spearhead were here, it was more likely hidden in the surrounding village or the wilderness around it. We'd arranged to go sightseeing and hiking tomorrow, common tourist activities here. With my hallowed sensor picking up strong objects from a half-mile radius, I was hopeful that a sweep in and around the village would be enough to either find it or rule this place out.

When we were finally allowed to check into our custom-designed suites in the cold section of the hotel, I briefly forgot about why I was here. Instead, I looked around at the gorgeous ice sculptures that adorned every hallway and room, and I knew why, out of the thousands of places that Adrian had visited in this world, he'd chosen this among his favorites.

My heart ached as I pictured him returning to this place over and over as he must have to include it on his list. With everything around us made entirely of ice formed into exquisite shapes, this was as close as you could get to a demon realm without actually being in one. Add the upcoming polar winter where there was little to no sunshine from December to mid-January, and this place must have felt like home to Adrian.

They only showed me the beautiful things at first, Adrian had told me when I'd asked how he could have stood to live with demons for as long as he had. And there had been beauty in their world beyond the horrors they'd initially hidden from him. Icy, dreamlike beauty where the impossible was made real, just like this place. Everything in the suite was dazzlingly carved ice, from the chairs, tables, benches and bed, to the multi-room 3-D mural featuring sea creatures such as mermaids and mermen frolicking in the waves of a frozen ocean. Expand this hotel until it was the size of an entire city, add a lot more artistic creativity and bling, and you had a demon realm without the demons, minions or suffering humans.

"Oh, Adrian," I whispered to the empty room.

I should have seen past his hatred of demons long ago to realize that—minus their gleeful cruelty and desire to destroy humanity—he was one of them. He hadn't been fighting only the negative aspects of his Judian heritage and a fate that said he'd be the cause of my death. When he walked out on demons, he'd also disowned large parts of himself. Because he refused to admit that, he hadn't been able to heal from it.

If he accepted who he was without the hatred he normally associated with that, I believed he'd finally be able to overcome the inner hurdles that he now saw as insurmountable. After all, his self-identification and half his genetics might be demon, but that didn't mean he was without choices. Just like he'd chosen to be a different Judian than fate predicted, he could also choose to be a different kind of demon.

"Isn't this amazing?" Jasmine said, interrupting my thoughts as she came into the room. "It's like a little frozen slice of Disneyland!"

I was relieved the Icehotel wasn't giving her flash-backs of the demon realm she'd been a prisoner in for weeks. She'd suffered enough already. "Amazing," I agreed.

"I'm freezing my ass off, of course," she went on cheerfully. "Costa and I are about to hit the bar so we can warm up on the inside with lots of shots. You coming?"

"You guys go ahead. I'm a little tired," I said. She deserved a few hours with Costa without my being a third wheel, or their having to focus on my quest for the spear. Besides, in this country, she was already the legal drinking age, so she might as well take advantage of that. "Think I'll check out how hard the ice bed is," I went on.

She waved at the bed. "Oh, there's a bunch of hides beneath the sleeping bag, so it's not that bad, actually."

I stifled a snort. "You've been in your room for less than twenty minutes, and you already know how the bed feels?"

She shot me a grin that was pure Old Jasmine, before the horrors of the past year had smashed her life to pieces. "Waste not, right?"

Now I didn't bother to contain my snort. "Go have your drinks, but don't forget to eat something, too."

"Yes, Mom," she teased. Then a shadow crossed her face, and just like that, she was back to her new, far-more-burdened self. "God, I miss them," she whispered.

"I do, too," I said softly. "So much that I rarely let myself think about them, even though that's awful."

"It's not awful," she said, taking my hand and gripping it. Then, her voice very intense, she said, "It's survival. I cry every time I think about Mom and Dad. Then I get so furious over their murders, I can barely function from the rage, and I don't have a lot to do, but you do. That's why you need to stay focused however you can. If that means not thinking about them right now, Mom and Dad would be the first to tell you to not think about them."

I blinked hard, refusing to let myself cry, because it felt like crying was all I had been doing lately. "You're right, they would," I said, faking a strength I didn't feel. "So, you go get drunk with Costa, and I'll take a nap like an old person."

She gave me a quick hug. "Join us if you change your mind."

"I will," I said, but I knew I wouldn't.

I waited until I was sure that Jasmine would be at the bar with Costa. Then, instead of taking a nap like I'd said, I left the hotel. It was fully dark out now, but I didn't need to see for what I was about to do. Not yet. I just needed to feel.

I walked until I was outside of the range of lights from the hotel. I could hear the nearby river, but I couldn't see it anymore. It had blended into the darkness that felt like it had swallowed me.

"Brutus," I called out. Then, louder, "Brutus!"

A few minutes later, the gargoyle sailed to a graceful landing not far from me. I walked over to him, scratching him in his favorite spots around his head. Then I climbed onto his back, using the leather harness he always wore to help myself up.

"Let's go for a ride, boy."

CHAPTER TWENTY-ONE

IT TOOK ONLY an hour for my night vision to return. The goggles I'd grabbed helped, keeping the wind from stinging my eyes due to how fast Brutus flew. As expected, he seemed to revel in the cold, undeveloped landscape, dipping low over the forest as if trying to tag the treetops with his clawed toes.

I let him fly wherever he wanted for that first hour, waiting for my senses to kick into a higher gear. Once they did, I directed him in a loose search grid a few miles out in either direction from the hotel. I had to make sure that we kept out of view of the village lights, of course, which made us skip some areas, but those I could explore on foot tomorrow. For now, I wanted to cover a broad search area over parts that couldn't be explored by foot, like the river.

I had Brutus fly over that as low as he could, reassuring myself that if he made a mistake and we crashed, he would fish me out. Sure, I might get hypothermia, but it wouldn't kill me. My body could stand a lot more than most due to the perks of my lineage. In any event, it was worth the risk. If I wanted to hide the spearhead where it would never be found, the bottom of an icy river would be a great place.

I sent my hallowed sensors outward, looking for any telltale blip that might indicate an interesting object.

So far, I'd felt nothing except for an area in the village that the tall steeple outed as a church. Another hour later, and the cold was getting to me even through my thick protective wear. An hour after that, I was pretty sure I was getting frostbite in my fingers. These gloves were made to withstand the interior of the ice hotel, not countless blasts of wind that came from steering a gargoyle at high speeds through the arctic night.

"Let's go back, boy," I said, steering Brutus toward the lights in the distance. This flight had accomplished one thing: it told me that if the spearhead was here, it was warded. Otherwise, I would have felt it, and I'd been within fifteen or twenty miles of the hotel in almost every direction.

If it was warded, it had to be in a box that was buried. After all, no one would leave a big, symbol-covered box out in the open unless they wanted whatever was in it to be found. If it was warded and buried somewhere in the river or the vast wilderness around the village, I wouldn't be able to find it even if I had a map with a big X on it, and if I couldn't find it, then neither could demons.

I was cheered by that thought. Tomorrow, we'd hike around the area plus check out the village, and if we didn't notice a big warded box, we could mark this place off and move on to the next one. That might be interesting. I'd never been to Russia.

Brutus chuffed and dipped in a way that caught my attention. He jerked his head to the left, chuffing again while also slightly altering course. I squinted, trying to see what he saw. At first, all I noticed was the many lights and roofs of the village we were approaching, with the darkness of the river on the opposite side. Everything looked normal. What was agitating Brutus?

Brutus chuffed a third time, this one ending on a growl. A few seconds later, I noticed a lone figure standing in the middle of a field that was bordered on one side by the river. As we got closer, I realized it was a large backyard. It didn't seem strange until I factored in the late hour and the much colder temperatures. It had to be well below freezing by now, and whoever this was really wasn't dressed for a midnight stroll.

The person turned and seemed to stare right at us. I told myself that had to be coincidence. With the black sky as our backdrop, no one should be able to see us. That was why I'd chosen dark colors for my outerwear, and Brutus's blue-gray skin was natural camouflage— Wait. Did that person have long blond hair?

"Ivy!" I faintly heard before the sound was snatched away.

"It's Jasmine," I told Brutus, patting him when he only growled again. I angled him toward her and pulled down on his reins so he'd drop lower. He did, and with every second, I got a clearer look at her. She was wearing a different coat than the one the hotel had supplied us with, and she waved when we got within five hundred yards of her. Yep, she'd spotted us.

Maybe she'd been searching the sky with binoculars. She must have checked on me at some point and seen that I was gone, then figured out what I was doing. I felt bad for worrying her. I don't know why I lied to her about taking a nap in the first place. Damn this new tendency to lie without thinking twice! Was that the darkness from my soul-tethering growing? Or was it me, taking the easy-but-wrong route all on my own? Either way, it had to stop—

Brutus's growl turned into a roar as he pulled his wings to his sides and began to dive right at Jasmine. Good Lord, he would hit her if he didn't veer! I yanked his reins hard to the right, but he ignored me. Jasmine smiled, oblivious to the danger. I hauled on Brutus's reins with all my strength, trying to pull him up, and he only roared louder.

"Brutus, stop!" I screamed. What was the matter with him? He was going to kill her!

I figured it out as soon as I was close enough to see Jasmine's face. It was just as pretty as ever and her eyes were just as blue, but the *look* in them. This wasn't Jasmine.

In the final seconds before we hit, I hid behind Brutus's back and held on for all I was worth.

The impact felt like hitting a brick wall. I was torn free from Brutus and tumbled through the air, limbs flailing, until something hard broke my fall. A fence, I realized dazedly. I'd broken it, too, and every part of me felt as destroyed as it was. It was agony to even breathe, let alone to move, yet I forced myself to scramble through the remains of the wood and wires until I was free.

That was when I got my first look around, and screamed. Brutus was about fifty feet from me, swinging around to put himself between me and what could only be Demetrius. No one else could shape-shift into someone's exact likeness, and Demetrius was well aware of what Jasmine looked like. He'd held her prisoner in Adrian's former realm for weeks. But I wasn't screaming in fear of Demetrius, although I probably should be. I was screaming in horror over what he'd done to Brutus.

His left wing had been torn completely off. It lay, spasmodically jerking, in front of Demetrius as if it were still attempting to take the demon's head off. Dark red blood ran from Brutus's side and he was howling in pain, yet he didn't run. He squared off against Demetrius, lowering his remaining right wing into a chopping formation. Demetrius, still wearing my sister's appearance, smiled at Brutus while a thin trickle of shadows flowed into the shape of a large sword.

"Brutus, no!" I shouted. "Stay away from him!" If Demetrius's shadows could penetrate Brutus's unnaturally thick hide enough to slice off his wing, he could take off his head.

"Listen to Mommy, beast," Demetrius taunted Brutus in his own smooth, accented voice. Hearing it while the demon was still in my sister's form felt like a desecration to Jasmine, but I had bigger concerns, like getting me and Brutus out of here alive.

"Adraten!" I told Brutus, putting all the force I could muster into the command for him to stand down.

Brutus flinched, his wing dropping before he took a reluctant step backward. Demetrius's low chuckle reached me like a poisonous wind.

"Adrian taught the last Davidian the language of demons. How delightfully twisted of him."

"I'm still learning," I said, trying not to panic as blood continued to flow from the hole where Brutus's left wing used to be. I had to get Demetrius to focus on me long enough for Brutus to get away. As for how I'd get away…well, I'd worry about that afterward. "Remind me what *dyaten eskanitta montubule* means. Adrian always said that when he was talking about you."

Demetrius's face darkened and he stalked toward me, his shadow sword dissolving into what looked like a long, thin whip with a knife attached to the end of it. He really didn't like being called *fucking demon trash*. I'd have to remember to use that insult more often on him, if I survived.

I backed away, silently praying that Brutus would do the same now that the demon's attention wasn't on him. From the pain shooting through me, I had busted myself up pretty good hitting that fence. Still, I was able to turn and run, and the Icehotel had a chapel right next to it. It wasn't that far away. If I could reach it before Demetrius could overtake me—

"Take one more step, and I won't stop at killing Adrian's pet," Demetrius spat, his knife-tipped whip moving with blinding speed. A long rip appeared in Brutus's flank, and the gargoyle stumbled, a pained howl coming from him. "I'll kill that bitch you call a sister along with everyone else in the hotel."

I stopped, panicked as Brutus's leg crumpled beneath him. Then my heart ached when he tried to use his remaining wing as a crutch in order to crawl toward me.

"Brutus, stop," I said urgently. "You have to leave!"

Defiance echoed in his answering roar, and he kept crawling. Now I knew what *hell no* sounded like in gargoyle, and my heart broke. Oh God, he'd die like this: brave, bloody and a thousand times more loyal than I deserved. *Please*, I found myself thinking. *Zach, if you're still around, please help us!*

Demetrius regarded Brutus with disdainful amusement. "Foolish beast doesn't know when he's beaten.

Then again, I shouldn't be surprised. He was too stubborn to die like the thousand other experiments we attempted before we successfully bred him, and yet Adrian still believes he was born after hatching from an ancient, previously lost egg." He paused to roll his eyes. "Children, right?"

"What do you want, Demetrius?" I was pretty sure I knew, but I was stalling to give Brutus one last chance to escape. "And drop the disguise. Blond and beautiful doesn't suit you."

He smiled, then Jasmine's face melted as if it were wax under a blowtorch. Black hair seemed to bleed over blond locks and my sister's body contorted, too, though thankfully I couldn't see the details due to his clothes and coat. Moments later, Demetrius stood in his true form of a medium-sized man with shoulder-length black hair, pale skin, average features and a wide mouth. Only the shadows clinging to his outline and his coal-black eyes that seemed to burn with their own inner fire gave him away as nowhere near human.

"You will come with me, or I will lay waste to the hotel your sister is in, then the village after that," he told me.

"How'd you know I was here?" I said, trying to stall so I could think up a way for me and Brutus to get out of this. "Come on, Demetrius, tell me. We both know you love to brag."

"This was one of my son's favorite places when he began sneaking into your world," Demetrius said, glancing around while his lip curled in contempt. "So I sent a realm crashing down on it. Adrian never knew. I evacuated the town first so that none of its sparse population would be swallowed up. That way, I could keep a constant eye on this place." He smiled. Nastily. "Then all I needed was a mirror to travel here once I saw your sister's face at the hotel. You were careful to avoid them, but she wasn't as careful as she should have been. Now, enough chatting. You're wearing out my nonexistent patience."

The house on the other side of the fence I'd wrecked began to shake and crumble. Then it flattened completely as if stomped on by a giant's foot. I stared at it, my mind trying to cope with how it had been a two-story structure a minute ago, yet now the only thing that rose more than a few feet from the ground was all the dust from its sudden demise.

I wasn't aware that I'd spoken, but Demetrius said, "How?" as if repeating me, then laughed. "I can use gravity to smash pieces of this world into their dimensional mirror images to form new realms, and you ask me how I could use that same gravity to force one tiny wooden structure to crumble?" He laughed again, with far more cruelty this time. "The answer is easily. Now, if you don't want me to do the same with this entire village, you will come with me."

CHAPTER TWENTY-TWO

I'D KNOWN THAT Demetrius could make realms. I'd had
the misfortune of being in a place when Demetrius
had used his powers to essentially swallow it up. But
I hadn't known he could use gravity in this world to
smash buildings into smithereens.

It also shook me that I was now in the almost same
predicament my birth mother had been in. I could give
myself up to save this village, or watch Demetrius kill
its inhabitants one by one, starting with my sister. The
only difference was, he'd bargained with my bio mom
because he'd been unable to get to her any other way.
He didn't have that problem with me. I wasn't standing on hallowed ground. So why was he bargaining
with me? Why didn't he just grab me and drag me
back with him?

"You want to use me to find the spearhead," I said,
trying to figure out the answer to my questions. I had
to be missing something important. After all, demons
didn't ask for something that they could take.

Demetrius showed me his teeth the way a shark
showed a seal right before the bloodletting began.
"You're stalling, Davidian. Come with me now, or the
next structure I level will be the ice hotel your sister
is in."

What was I missing? What? "You're saying you'll

let Brutus go free along with everyone else in this town?" I said, trying to eke out a few more seconds, and afraid that it wouldn't be enough. *Where are you, Zach?* I thought desperately. Why had he bothered to come here at all, if he had no intention of putting in an appearance when he was actually needed?

Demetrius inhaled as if he could smell my growing anxiety. Then, as if lifted by invisible strings, a mirror rose up behind him. His entrance into this place, and obviously, the way he intended for both of us to leave.

"They can all live, if you come now without a fight."

What sort of fight was he worrying about me putting up? I had no more hallowed weapons!

Wait. He didn't know that. That had to be why he wanted my compliance instead of trying to force me to come with him. He must've taken my silence as acquiescence, because he took another step toward me. It was weird; the closer he got, the more my body burned. The pain was so intense, I almost doubled over.

I fought not to focus on the pain, but each step he took made it worse. Why? If anything, I should hurt less now, since I no longer had the slingshot or the staff embedded in my skin. Tons of pain had made sense when Obsidiana attacked me at the hotel, because hallowed objects responded to demons like the spiritual version of a terrible allergic reaction. But if I didn't have any hallowed objects anymore, why did my entire body—especially my right side—hurt as if I did?

"Get away from her," a familiar voice suddenly snarled.

I swung around in disbelief. It wasn't Zach, who I'd been hoping would show up. It was Adrian, and I had no idea how he'd gotten here, let alone known I was in trouble.

Like Demetrius, Adrian wasn't dressed for the icy temperatures. He had on only a long-sleeved sweater, jeans and gloves. Brutus whined when he saw him, crawling faster despite the wide, bloody trail he was leaving in his wake.

Adrian glanced at Brutus, his mouth tightening, before the demon claimed his attention again. "Get away from her," Adrian repeated. "Now."

The look Demetrius gave Adrian was half-annoyed parent, half-enraged monster. "If you'd do as you're told for *once* in your life, I would be king, you'd be a prince and we'd both rule the realms. You could even keep this worthless excuse for a Davidian as your plaything. Just don't interfere now, and I'll return her to you once I'm finished with her."

"Liar," Adrian growled. "You'd kill her the second you no longer needed her."

At that, Demetrius laughed. "Probably. I can't remember when I've hated one of these meat bags more."

"You're not taking her anywhere," Adrian said, walking past me without looking at me.

Demetrius took another step forward, his shadow whip writhing around as if hungry to sink into flesh. "And how do you think you'll stop me, my son?"

Adrian pulled something small and white out of his pocket. "With this Archon grenade."

Demetrius jumped back as if stung. He must remember as well as I did what an Archon grenade had done to him. I would've enjoyed his reaction more, except my right hand was throbbing as if something beneath my skin were fighting to be free. At the same time, agony shot from my neck to my toes. It certainly *felt* like the hallowed weapons! A wild hope rose in me. Was that what Zach had really come here for? To give them back to me without my realizing it?

I didn't take my glove off to see if my right hand now had a braided rope around it. Or unzip my jacket to see if I could glimpse a gnarled wooden tattoo running down my body. What if I looked, yet saw only my own normal skin?

"Fine," Demetrius spat. "Keep your little whore for now, but it will cost you. From this night on, I will tell every demon in this world about the spearhead's possible locations. When all of them are chasing after her, a deal with me will be far preferable."

I was horrified for lots of reasons about that, but there was only one he might care about enough not to do it. "If another demon claims the spearhead, they'll round up the others and kill Adrian. You'd risk your own son's life out of spite?"

Demetrius didn't look away from Adrian when he said, "If he won't help me get the spearhead, he deserves what will happen if another demon finds it." Then he raised his hands and stared straight at me. "And I warned you what would happen if you didn't come with me. Say goodbye to your sister, Davidian."

Time seemed to freeze when I heard a mighty crashing sound behind me. My mind replayed the memory of watching the nearby house crumble in mere seconds, replacing it with the ice hotel. As if I were there, I could imagine Jasmine's and Costa's panic as the beautiful, crystal-clear blocks of ice that formed the roof came tumbling onto them. Their pain as the rest of the structure followed suit, crushing them and the dozens of other people in the hotel under the pitiless force of Demetrius's weaponized swat of gravity.

I didn't pause to doubt. Didn't even think about what I was going to do. I just took the entirety of the pain burning its way through my body and shot it toward the hotel. Demetrius flew backward as if he'd been hit by a car. Adrian fell to his knees, and the rumbling beneath my feet abruptly stopped. The crashing sounds stopped, too, replaced with something far softer that I couldn't put a name to.

A dazed moment later, I realized I was on the ground, though I didn't remember falling. I didn't remember taking my right glove off, either, but it was now several feet away from me, its edges blackened as if it had been burned. My jacket smelled like smoke, too, and when I glanced down, I saw that a thin line of fire went from it all the way down to my pants.

I attempted to roll to stop the flames, but my next realization was that I couldn't move. Adrian staggered to his feet, grabbed me up and used his body to smother them, then threw me over his shoulder, yelling, *"Larastra!"* at Brutus.

As Adrian ran us away, I saw Brutus use his remaining good leg and wing to hop after us. His increased exertions sent blood flowing more freely from his wounds, yet I was more afraid of what would happen if he stayed close to Demetrius. The demon was still knocked out for the moment, but any second, he could get up.

The moment we crossed onto the grounds of the chapel that was adjacent to the ice hotel, I felt a little better. Adrian set me down well away from the edge of the hallowed ground, then yanked my still-smoldering jacket and pants off. I helped as much as I could, and as soon as I had them off, I tried to run to the hotel, but I stumbled after only one step. What was wrong with me? My entire body felt drained.

Adrian picked me up again, holding me in his arms instead of slinging me over his shoulder. He turned around to make sure Brutus had cleared Demetrius's immediate reach, although Brutus was nowhere near the hallowed ground we were on. At least Demetrius still hadn't moved. I watched with a mixture of fear and relief as Brutus continued to limp away from the demon's prone form. Then he collapsed about thirty yards from Demetrius. I wanted to go to Brutus, but first, I had to see if Jasmine was alive. I'd done *something* to the hotel—I'd felt that, and whatever it was had been strong enough to knock Demetrius out—but I had no idea if it had saved anyone.

During the short amount of time it took for Adrian to run us there, I looked at my right hand. Tears blurred my vision, but that single glance was enough. The sling was embedded in my skin as if it had never left, the ancient rope darkening from bright gold to brown the farther we got away from Demetrius. I couldn't pull the collar of my turtleneck down enough to see my chest, but I didn't need to. I knew the staff was back, too.

Adrian stopped when he rounded the side of the last building in our way and the Icehotel was finally in view. Or, more accurately, what was left of it. The electricity had shorted out, yet with the lights from the nearby structures and my improved night vision, I could see. Adrian stiffened in disbelief and I gasped.

The ice that had made up the majority of the hotel was now gone. Instead, water poured out, draining into the nearby river as if being sucked in by an invisible wet vac. Without the ice making up the walls, ceilings and other structures, we had a clear view of soaked patrons splashing through knee-deep water as they made their way out of what used to be the stunningly carved Icehotel. The patrons I saw looked understandably confused and alarmed, but so far, no one looked like they'd been seriously hurt or killed.

"You melted the ice."

Adrian sounded awed. I was pretty stunned by what I'd done, too. I hadn't planned to. I'd been overwhelmed with panic at the thought of those heavy blocks of ice crushing everyone to death, so either the staff had somehow decided that instantaneously melting all the ice was the best way to prevent that, or my subconscious had. Either way, I couldn't take the credit.

My momentary daze cleared up when I caught a glimpse of a bedraggled blonde being helped out of the waterlogged mess by a tall guy with dripping black hair, and relief swamped me.

"Jasmine, Costa, over here!" I shouted.

Jasmine heard me and elbowed Costa, pointing at us. They made their way over, and I scoured her appearance for any sign of injury. The long underwear Jasmine wore was soaked, she had a cut on her forehead and she looked like a drowned rat, but she was all right. Costa was just as soaked and both his arms were bleeding from superficial wounds, yet he, too, was okay. I could have cried from joy.

Jasmine stopped when she saw whose arms I was in, then recovered and quickened her pace. "What the hell happened?" she asked when she reached us. "We were sleeping, then a horrible noise woke us and we saw the roof caving in. Right before it hit us, it and everything else turned into water. We almost had to swim our way out before it started draining away!"

"You grab any manna before you got out?" Adrian asked, not answering her question about how this had happened. I didn't, either. There were too many other ears around.

"Here," Costa said, holding up a dripping wet satchel.

Adrian took it, then he handed me off to Costa like I was a football. "I'll be back," he muttered, and ran back toward the direction we'd come from.

"Why was he carrying you? Are you hurt?" Jasmine asked in a worried tone.

"No. Just drained. I'll be fine." Using the staff in such a powerful way had sucked all the energy out of me, but I'd recover. I hoped the same could be said for Brutus. "Costa, think you can carry me about a hundred yards?"

He snorted and started walking briskly in the same direction Adrian had disappeared to. Jasmine kept pace and continued to cast worried looks at me. "Why'd he run off with the manna? Who else is hurt?"

"Brutus," I said, fighting to keep my voice from breaking. "He's...he's really bad."

"What *happened*?" Jasmine demanded. Then she grabbed my right hand, staring at it in shock. "It's back!" she said, immediately followed by, "Oh my God, if it is...then you did it. *You* melted all the ice! Why would you do that?"

"Demetrius ambushed me," I said, not wanting to say how. I didn't want Jasmine feeling any unnecessary guilt over him using her appearance to fool me.

"Take a right here, Costa. Brutus tried to kill him, but Demetrius cut his wing off and crippled his leg. That's why Adrian ran off with the manna—"

"What the fuck?" Costa said, coming to a stop. At first, I thought he was upset for Brutus, which was nice but a surprise. Then I followed his gaze to the demolished house.

"Demetrius did that," I said, hoping against hope it had been empty. "He was in the process of doing the same thing to the ice hotel. That's why I used the staff to melt everything."

"Wow," Jasmine said softly, staring at the flattened remains of what used to be a two-story house. "I didn't know he could do things like that, especially in our world."

"Neither did I," I said with more than a little grimness. "Follow the fence, Costa, until the break. You can't miss it."

"What happened here?" he said when we reached it a couple minutes later.

"I crashed," I replied simply, then my heart felt like it skipped a beat when I caught sight of Brutus.

The gargoyle was lying facedown ahead of us, his remaining wing stretched out as if he'd collapsed while still trying to use it as a crutch to hurry after us. He was so silent and immobile, I couldn't even tell if he was breathing. Adrian was about thirty yards away from him, his back to us, walking slowly while his shoulders heaved as if he were sobbing.

Oh no. No, no, no, no!

"Brutus!" I screamed.

CHAPTER TWENTY-THREE

My shout was a cry of pain mixed with a plea for him to still be alive. Adrian jerked around, revealing that his shoulders were heaving because he was dragging Brutus's very large, very heavy severed wing along with him. Why would he be doing that, if Brutus was already dead?

"Stay down, Brutus!" Adrian said sternly, repeating the command in Demonish. "Costa, don't try to help me," he added when Costa immediately started to put me down. "None of you should even be here. It's too dangerous. Get back to the hallowed ground, where it's safe. I don't see Demetrius anymore, but he could come back."

A wave of relief hit me when I saw Brutus angle his head in my direction. He was still alive. Thank God, he was still alive!

"I have the sling again, so it's more dangerous for you, which is why we're not leaving," I said. "Get some rocks," I told Jasmine, yanking up my sleeve and feeling enormously grateful that the slingshot was back in my arm. I didn't see Demetrius, either, but that didn't make me feel safer. The demon was nothing if not crafty.

Jasmine began rooting around in the nearby field. I squirmed, trying to stretch out my legs to see how they felt. If I needed to use the slingshot, I probably had to be standing. I didn't know if I could do it while being held in Costa's arms.

"Here," Jasmine said, coming back quickly and handing me some small rocks. "I'll keep looking for more."

I kept one in my hand and put the other two in the only pocket available to me now that my jacket and pants were gone—my cleavage. Costa grunted in amusement.

"That's getting the most use out of those."

I ignored the quip. "Take me to Brutus," I said, still trying to wiggle the strength back in my legs. If Demetrius popped up and threatened Brutus or Adrian, I'd be able to use the slingshot to send him back to hell. In the meantime, I'd see what I could do for Brutus's wounds.

As requested, Costa set me down when we reached the gargoyle. I stood for a few seconds to test my legs, then sank to my knees next to Brutus. It wasn't just because my legs were shaking in an ominous way. It was because of the hopeful-yet-pained look Brutus gave me, as if even through his pain, he believed things would be better now that I was here.

I wanted it to be, but I didn't know what to do. "Shh, it'll be okay, boy," I settled on saying in my most soothing voice. Then I scooted until I was half cradling his massive, gorilla-like head in my lap, continuing to croon to him while also keeping a wary eye out for Demetrius.

Brutus whined and tried to lift his head. I didn't want him to move because every twitch seemed to send more blood out of that horrible hole where his left wing had formerly inserted into the bony cradle in his back.

So I bent down to him, kissing his cheek and telling him that he was the best boy ever. When his tongue slimed the side of my face with his version of an answering kiss, I was relieved instead of mildly grossed out like usual. While I continued to praise him, I covered the still-bleeding hole in his back with my hand. Adrian had treated Brutus's leg with manna—that was clear from the newly healed skin where that long, gaping tear had been. But he hadn't treated anything else, and that hole in his back was the worst injury of all. I had an idea why Adrian was waiting to use the manna on that, and I was torn between hope and tears.

Adrian dragged Brutus's severed wing a few more feet before Costa ignored his prior order and came over to help him drag it the rest of the way to Brutus. Then Adrian lined it up next to the hole I was covering with my hand.

"Will that work?" Oh, please, please let it work!

"Hope so," Adrian said shortly, and bent next to Brutus, saying something in Demonish that I loosely translated as "Don't move." Then he grabbed a handful of manna, leaving almost none in the bag. Adrian coated the end of the bone in the severed wing with it, then, with enough force to make me flinch, shoved it back into the bleeding hole in Brutus's back.

The noise Brutus made blasted my eardrums with its volume and squeezed my heart from its agony.

"It's okay. It's okay!" I said, trying to soothe him while he trembled all over yet somehow remained faithful to Adrian's order not to move. I kept repeating those and other useless assurances while we waited to see if the manna would reattach Brutus's wing back to its original functionality, or merely heal up the hole and leave the wing to fall out as soon as Brutus stood up.

After a few minutes, Brutus quit trembling and the pain left his expression. Manna worked quickly, so either he was now healed as good as new, or he was healed yet he'd never fly again. When Adrian had him rise to his knees after letting another few minutes pass in order to be extra cautious, I was the one who was trembling. When Brutus carefully stood up and nothing dropped to the ground, I was holding my breath. When he stretched both wings out to their full span, then flapped them until he rose a few feet in the air, I burst into tears.

I couldn't help it. I'd held it in when I saw that Jasmine and Costa were still alive, but this was the last straw. Joy and relief combined with the emotional crash of surviving yet another life-threatening encounter, and that demolished my resistance. At last, I knew that we were okay, all of us. The guests at the Icehotel seemed to be okay, too, and I had the hallowed weapons back so I could defend us if—when—more demons came calling. The stress seemed to drain out of me with the tears that fell, and though I felt a little embarrassed, I couldn't stop them.

Adrian knelt down next to me, his large hand caressing my face to catch my tears. Our eyes met, and the intensity in his gaze caused a jolt to course through me. I don't know if it was the rare, unshielded emotion in his eyes or our soul-tethering connection flaring, giving me access into him that I shouldn't have. Either way, I suddenly knew that it was taking all of his strength not to pull me back into his arms, and if he lost that fight, he wouldn't be able to let me go again.

I turned my face into his hand and leaned toward him. An almost dangerous gleam appeared in his eyes, and the hand that had gently brushed aside my tears slid down and tightened until he was gripping my hair.

And I wanted—*needed*—him to lose that last vestige of control. I knew the risks, knew exactly who he was and knew that one or both of us might end up with broken hearts. Yet I couldn't do anything except lean in closer and practically dare him to let go of the final barrier that was holding him back.

Do it, my stare urged him as I parted and moistened my lips. His nostrils flared and a low, almost growling sound came from deep in his throat.

"Ivy!" Jasmine shattered the moment by coming over and nudging me. Adrian dropped his hand, got up and quickly backed away. I tried to go after him to force him to confront what he was really running from, but my legs still weren't steady enough to walk and Jasmine wasn't done talking. "Zach's here," she said, pointing behind us.

I turned around, seeing the Archon no more than a few feet behind me. I felt foolish for not noticing him before my sister pointed him out, but he couldn't have been there long. As usual, he was wearing his faded blue hoodie, and he didn't look at all concerned about interrupting my and Adrian's loaded personal moment. Instead, he looked as relaxed as if he'd just come from a long soak in a heavenly hot tub.

"We should leave now," Zach opened with instead of saying hello. "Demetrius fled through the mirror, but what happened to the Icehotel will soon alert others to your presence here."

Of course he knew about what I'd done to the ice

hotel. Had he been here the whole time, concealed from our view, but watching things unfold like our lives were his version of a soap opera? Once again, I found myself torn. Part of me wanted to thank Zach profusely for giving me the hallowed weapons back, while the other part wanted to rail at him for waiting to show up until *after* all the danger had passed.

"Leave?" I settled on saying, choosing to focus on what he'd said instead of what I felt. "How? My passport and ID were back at the hotel, so they've probably floated away by now."

Zach let his gaze slide around the area. I didn't know what he was looking for, but he seemed to find it fast enough. "Not that way. Through a door only I can enable you to cross."

Adrian whistled. "A light realm is nearby, isn't it? And you're offering to pull us into it?"

"A light realm?" Jasmine hopped up and down in delight. "Yes, let's go! It's warm there, and I am *freezing*."

Honestly, it sounded great to me, too. In addition to being sunny and warm, light realms were demon-and-minion-free. They could also act as portals that would instantly transport us wherever we wanted to go, even if that happened to be to the other side of the world. The only reason I wasn't hopping up and down in joy like Jasmine was because I was sure there had to be a catch. There was always a catch with Zach.

"What will this cost us if you do it?" I asked bluntly.

The corners of his lips tilted faintly upward; his version of a broad grin. "Come and see."

Not an answer, but that must be all he was willing to give. I don't know why I expected anything different. We wouldn't refuse his offer and Zach knew it.

We had very limited options with the deluge washing away most of our stuff and more demons expected to show up soon.

"We're taking Brutus," I said. He'd hate the sunlight, but I was not leaving him behind. "That's nonnegotiable."

Zach lifted one shoulder as if he didn't care enough to use both to shrug. "As you wish."

"And we'll need to collect more manna while we're there," I added, trying to capitalize on Zach's rare agreeable mood.

His mouth quirked again. "Of course. And if you ask *very* nicely, I might have a real Archon grenade for you, too."

My gaze swung back and forth between Zach and Adrian as I translated the subtext. "A real one? That wasn't a real Archon grenade you threatened Demetrius with earlier?"

Adrian's snort was immediate. "If it was, I would've blasted him with it. No, I ran out of those months ago. That was a regular communion wafer, but Demetrius didn't know that."

He'd bluffed the most dangerous demon in existence with basically a cracker, all because he hadn't known that I'd gotten my hallowed weapons back. Of course, even if he had known, he still would have done the same thing. Adrian had never hesitated to risk his life when he thought I was in danger. Ever.

It was why, despite everything, I was still willing to risk my heart with him. He might not believe that he could overcome the dark tendencies that were second nature with him, but I did. He'd already beaten his fate. What was a little half-demon heritage compared to that?

"Let us leave," Zach said, holding out his hand. "Adrian, you first."

He looked at me and hesitated. It took me only a moment to realize why. He still intended to stay away from me, or pretend to, anyway. He'd obviously been following me. Unlike Zach, Adrian couldn't appear anywhere in a blink, so the only explanation for his intervention with Demetrius earlier was him following me here. But once in a light realm, Adrian couldn't leave unless Zach pulled him out of it, just like he couldn't enter unless Zach pulled him in. And Adrian must not want the door metaphorically locked behind him.

He opened his mouth, no doubt about to refuse to come with us—and I collapsed like a puppet whose strings were cut.

CHAPTER TWENTY-FOUR

FOR SOMEONE WHO'D never taken acting classes, I'd done a great job of faking a faint. I even let my head bang on the ground hard enough to give me a headache after I dropped in a boneless heap. *Oscar winners, eat your hearts out.*

Adrian rushed to my side like I knew he would. He'd let nothing, even his own deep-seated conviction that I was better off without him, come in the way of trying to protect me when he thought I was in danger. I ignored his gentle shakes and repeated calls of my name, opting for a completely limp pose. I even debated letting my tongue loll out of my mouth, but I didn't because that might be overdoing it.

Of course, Zach could put a stop to this. Even if he'd initially been fooled by my convincing-looking faint, he could hear from my thoughts that I was faking it. Quickly, I sent him a mental directive. *Don't you dare rat me out! Adrian and I need to talk, and this is the only way it'll happen without him running away again.*

I couldn't see his reaction, since my eyes were still closed, but I thought I heard an undercurrent of amusement in his voice when he said, "Lift her up, Adrian. I'll pull both of you in together, then come back for the rest of them. You can collect manna for her once you're there."

Ooh, that sly Archon! None of what he'd said was a lie, but it also was a deliberate misdirection, since he knew nothing was wrong with me. Not that I was complaining about his subtle subterfuge. This one rare time, it benefitted me. Adrian had me hefted in his arms before I could even give Zach a mental thank-you, and then I felt the distinct stomach-flopping, free-falling sensation of crossing from one realm into another.

I didn't have to open my eyes to know when we'd arrived. Light seemed to crash past my closed lids, and the bone-deep cold I'd felt was instantly replaced by the soothing warmth of sunshine on my skin and balmy temperatures. Even though it didn't mesh with my fainting act, I found myself inhaling deeply, trying to see if the air was as sweet as I remembered.

It was even better, like breathing in a combination of fresh spring rain and a flower garden in full bloom. You didn't realize how tainted our air had become until you breathed in something that had never been touched by chemicals, pollutants, car exhaust or everything else that made our world the modern world. I inhaled deeply again, as if trying to clean my lungs with the pristine air, then let myself lie limply on the ground when Adrian set me down.

"I see manna trees," he said, then sounded like he ran off.

"Remember, time passes differently in these realms," Zach called out. "It will seem like hours before I return, yet it will only be minutes as far as Jasmine and Costa are concerned."

Translation: Adrian and I had time to talk without being interrupted. I sat up and opened my eyes just in time to see Zach disappear through a door visible only to him. Adrian looked startled to see me suddenly up-right, then relief crossed his features and he ran back over to me.

"Ivy! Are you hurt? What happened?"

"I tricked you," I said bluntly. "You were about to refuse to come here and we have things to sort out, so I fake fainted."

It was almost funny to watch the shock on his face. Really, he shouldn't be this thrown by my deception. It could more than fairly be said that he had it coming.

"You lied to me," he said, still sounding stunned.

I wasn't going to get into a semantic debate about tricking someone versus lying to them, especially when the intent to deceive was the same. So, I said, "Newsflash—you don't have a monopoly on being dis-honest. Go ahead and get mad at me. I deserve that. But with Zach gone, you're not able to run out on this conversation, and according to him, he'll be a while."

Something like alarm crossed his features and he cast a quick, calculating glance around. I flung my arm out, indicating the beautiful stretch of meadow we were on, the river I could faintly see in the distance and the trees with their bell-shaped blooms that, when crushed up, turned into manna.

"Nowhere to go, Adrian, and I'm fast enough to keep up with you if you run. So quit looking for a means of escape."

"Run? You could barely walk before, or was that an act, too?" he countered.

"Nope, that was real," I said as I tested my legs by standing up and then hopping up and down. Thank-fully, they felt normal now instead of wobbly. "Either I've recovered on my own after the effects of using the staff, or being in this realm did the trick. Either way, yes, I'm capable of chasing you now."

I proved it by walking over and taking two big handfuls of his shirt. His eyes widened, then narrowed as I twisted the material until it resembled handholds.

"Now," I said calmly, "unless you want to run off half-naked, you're not going anywhere until we're done."

His golden-colored brow arched with a hint of his familiar arrogance. "It's a shirt, not a pair of handcuffs. You think I care if it rips?"

"No, but you care about me," I said at once. "You might have left me in a very dramatic fashion, but you've been following me ever since, haven't you?" He looked away, and I pounced. "Come on, Adrian! You didn't *coincidentally* decide to stay in the same tiny arctic village that you told me to check the spearhead for. What, did you use the credit card trail I left behind to figure out which place I was heading to first? Or did you simply follow us the whole way to Sweden?"

"Both," he said, the single word sliding out with obvious reluctance. "I lost you when you took Brutus for a ride, but then I saw you coming back in with him and ran to find you when I heard a crash shortly after that."

That crash could've been me hitting the fence or Demetrius leveling that house. Either way, I was so glad Adrian had decided to investigate it.

"You sound like you hate admitting the truth. Is it really that hard for you to be honest with me?"

"Isn't that the source of most of our problems?" he replied bitterly. "Even at my best, I am still a liar at heart."

I took a tighter grip on his shirt. "That might be

your default setting, yes, and you're also a demon in denial, but—"

"I am *not* a demon," he interrupted, incensed.

If I hadn't been gripping his shirt, I would have thrown up my hands. "See? Denial, but let's look at the facts. You love the dark and cold more than the sun and light. Lying is second nature to you, especially when the truth doesn't give you the results you're looking for. You have tastes that redefine the meaning of 'high end,' and when you want something, you will tear through other realms, this world and even heaven and hell to get it. Sound like any species you're familiar with?"

His jaw was clenched so tightly, I could hear the cartilage start to crack. "Fine. I'm a demon as well as a liar and betrayer, so what else could there be for us to talk about?"

I stared at him as I took a deliberate step closer. "Because unlike other demons or Judians, that's not all there is to you. You're also so brave, you regularly risked your life for strangers when you were working for Zach. You're loyal to a fault to your friends, honest enough to own up to your many flaws, generous to people who could never repay you and understanding even when ignorance would be easier. Most of all—" I took a breath to loosen the new tightness in my chest "—you're selfless enough to leave the person you love most because you think—mistakenly—that she's better off without you, and that's something no normal demon would do."

"You *are* better off without me." His voice was so hoarse, it was almost unrecognizable. "I tried to tell myself otherwise for a while, but once again, I was lying."

"Yeah, you lie when you shouldn't, and yeah, it's mostly because of who and what you are, and yeah, it's caused some huge problems between us." Now I hauled on his shirt to bring him closer. "But again, if you were *only* everything you hated about yourself, you wouldn't have turned your back on your demon family to begin with, let alone rescued Costa and Tomas when you left, or worked with Zach for years rescuing other people, or risked your life for me countless times, and finally, left me when you thought you'd hurt me again. Time and again, you chose to be better than your DNA and your destiny, and that proves you're stronger than the darkness inside you. Yes, it's there and it probably always will be. It's there for me, too, and—"

"How is it there for you?" he interrupted.

I let out an exasperated noise. "*Everybody* has some darkness in them, Adrian! Demetrius says I have some extra now that our souls are tethered together, and he could be right. For starters, I've noticed that I'm lying more, even if there's no reason for it. I'll have to make amends for those lies, and I'll have to fight against my inner darkness harder to stop it and worse things from happening, but I'm not afraid of my darkness no matter the source of it. Know why?"

He gave me a pained look. "Because you're the Davidian. Unlike me, the darkness will never win with you. It can't."

"It can't win with you, either," I said softly. "Not if you accept who you are, all of it."

His snort was harsh. "How will that help?"

"You might be a demon with the extra baggage of Judas's legacy, but you also have all the light you need."

At his doubtful look, I exchanged the crumpled-up

hunks of his shirt for his hands, gripping him while I stared into his tortured sapphire eyes.

"You might not believe that, because I love you, but we also have an objective opinion. See these?" I said, shaking our entwined hands at him. "Two out of the three most hallowed weapons in the world are embedded in my skin, yet unlike when other demons are nearby, they don't react to you. You might have demon blood in your veins, but you are *not* evil. I know that, and these hallowed weapons know it, too. Otherwise, they'd be glowing gold and burning the shit out of me right now."

He stared at our clasped hands. The ancient, braided rope tattoo disappeared beneath his fingers where his hand covered mine, its brown color only a few shades darker than my skin. This was far from the first time that he'd touched the tattoos without them adversely reacting to him, but it was clear from his expression that this was the first time he'd considered the ramifications of that. For the briefest moment, hope lit up his features. Then that hope was buried by doubt.

"Maybe it's nothing more than a loophole. I'm the last Judian and you're the last Davidian, so fate says I'm supposed to get close enough to you to betray you. Hard to do that if these weapons went into alarm mode every time I was near you."

"That's not it," I said, seizing on his brief moment of hope and trying to make it grow. "Not long after we met, I was worried that demons would win this war because there seemed to be a lot more of them than Archons. You told me numbers didn't matter when it came to darkness versus light. Remember why?"

He looked away, muttering, "No," but that was a lie. He did remember, and so did I.

"You said, *One shadow in a brightly lit room goes unnoticed, but shine a ray of light into even the darkest corner, and everything changes*." I gripped his hands tighter. "If you don't trust what I see in you, and you don't trust the hallowed weapons' lack of a negative reaction, then trust the tethering of our souls. It joined us together, right? That makes you part of the Davidian legacy now, too. You might have a lot of darkness, but *you have light*, too. You've had it for a long time. It gave you the strength to turn your back on demons years ago, and it'll give you the strength you don't think you have now. One ray shining into the darkness, Adrian. That's all it takes to make even the deepest shadows scatter, and you have more than one ray. You have so many of them—"

His mouth crushed over mine. At first, I thought he was trying a different method to shut me up. Then I felt the desperation in the way he clutched me to him, and the need seething in his kiss transcended simple lust. It broke the dam inside of me, releasing all my boiling emotions in a rush.

I shoved him back and slapped him with all the pain I'd felt when he left me. Then I was instantly horrified at what I'd done. He only crushed me to him again, his tongue sensually dominating mine. I wanted to tell him I was sorry, that I didn't know what had gotten into me when I hit him, but other, stronger emotions rose, covering my shock and shame. They replaced them with a need that felt almost feral. I ground against Adrian as if trying to make love to him right through our clothing, and when he clutched me tighter, his arms, mouth and body became a cage that I never wanted to escape from.

CHAPTER TWENTY-FIVE

I PUSHED HIS shirt up, needing to feel his skin beneath my hands. Then I needed to feel more of it because that warm, muscled expanse was addictive. Within moments, his back wasn't enough, so I plunged my hands beneath his waistband, reaching for the hard globes of his ass. I could grasp only the tops because the large bulge in the front of his pants combined with the formfitting denim meant there wasn't enough room for my hands.

I made a frustrated noise and he responded with a low, throaty laugh that made things lower in me clench. I knew that laugh. It promised incredible amounts of pleasure.

I wanted him to make good on that promise now. I dragged my hands away from his ass in order to lock them behind his neck. Then I pulled myself up to wrap my legs around his waist. His arms immediately supported me, and our bodies met at exactly the right spot. When he ground against me with that thick, jutting hardness, I barely heard his moan from the sharp cry I made.

His arms tightened until I was plastered to him, then he dropped to his knees. I gloried in the weight and feel of his body as he pressed me against the soft grass, then I made a wordless sound of protest when he pulled away. That stopped when he drew his shirt over his head, throwing it aside to reveal his luscious golden-brown chest. I stared at him, all at once breathless for more reasons than passion.

He was so beautiful, he didn't look real, yet he felt very, very real, especially when I tugged open the front of his pants to free the hardness straining against it. His breath caught when I wrapped my hands around him, and he briefly closed his eyes. Then he almost ripped my top and bra away. I arched beneath the searing warmth of his mouth as he sucked my nipples, and when he pulled my pants off and his fingers found my center, I couldn't stop my moans. I was both desperate for more of his touch and desperate for him to stop so he'd be inside me. When his mouth left my breasts to slide down my stomach, I grabbed his head, shoving myself down until his face was level with mine instead of between my legs.

"Don't. I want you now."

I loved what he could do with his mouth, but I wanted him inside me more. He stared at me, the desire and intensity in his gaze as arousing as a thousand erotic strokes of his tongue. Then, with an arch of his hips that tore a cry from both of us, he thrust inside me, moving deeply and slowly, stoking the fire that already burned within me. Soon, those thrusts became faster.

My nerve endings sizzled, while my mind spun away from everything that wasn't him. There was only his kiss, his taste, the feel of his muscles bunching in his back, the sounds he made and the indescribable ecstasy that each new thrust brought. The first time I came, I was breathless. The second time, I was shaking. The third time, when he finally came with me, I was screaming. I didn't care, either. I'd lost the last of my inhibitions a while ago.

I grabbed him when he tried to pull out of me, wrapping my legs around him to keep him inside. He smiled, clasping me to him when he rolled onto his side. I kept my leg hooked around his hip and my arms around his neck while I waited until my breathing evened out enough to speak.

"You're never leaving me again" were my first words. "I don't care what you think about me being better off."

He sighed, kissing me on the top of my head. "You would be, but even when I left you before, I couldn't go far."

"You shouldn't have gone at all," I said, adding quietly, "And I shouldn't have threatened to leave you, either. I was so hurt by what you'd done, so angry... I wanted to punish you."

"I deserved punishing," he said, his voice equally quiet.

"You did," I agreed. "But not that way."

He was silent for a moment. Then he said, "I didn't only hide what I'd done with Demetrius because I knew it was wrong. I also did it because I knew once I told you, I'd have to let you keep looking for the spearhead. And I didn't want you to."

He rolled onto his back, taking me with him. My hair fell around his face, haloing it in brown swaths as I stared at him.

"Don't kid yourself about me, Ivy," he said softly. "Even now, I'm as greedy for you as Judas ever was for silver."

"I love you," I said, and meant it to my soul. "And

unlike your infamous ancestor, I know you loving me is why you did what you did. But you can't keep taking my choices away from me, Adrian. If I was the type of person who'd let you, you wouldn't love me, because you're too strong willed to let anyone make up *your* mind for you, especially about really important things."

"Even if that were true, in this case, I might make an exception," he said dryly.

I let out a watery chuckle, then got serious again. "I was half-crazed when I thought you were dying in front of me. Right then, I would've agreed to almost anything to save you. And you agreed to terrible things trying to save me. I get why. I do, but no matter what, we have to be better than our instincts to protect each other at any cost."

He stared at me, his gaze turning sad. "You can be that strong. I don't think I can."

"I know you can. Otherwise, you wouldn't have torn your own throat out to take Obsidiana down. Or bluffed Demetrius with a cracker, or had Brutus fly me and Jasmine away so you could face a horde of minions alone, or any of the other countless things you've done. I want both of us to stop lying, but that's changing a behavior. I don't expect either of us to change who we are."

"I should. You shouldn't." His voice roughened. "Tying yourself to my darkness might have given you some bad habits, but it can't touch who you are. You're the girl who should have crumbled when you lost your parents and your sister within two weeks of each other, but you shoved your grief aside to start your own search for Jasmine. Even when you found out you'd have to go through minions, demons, strange realms and an unwanted destiny to get her, you never wavered. Then you tried to help others by repairing the realm walls despite demons dogging your every step. Now you're back to going after a weapon that'll kill you the moment you touch it, yet you're not letting that stop you, either."

I dropped my gaze. "I need to find the spearhead before demons do, but I haven't said that I'm going to use it—"

"Ivy." My name was a sigh. "Yes, you will. You won't be able to stop yourself, and that has nothing to do with you being the last Davidian. It's because you're you. That new darkness might have stalled you, but in the end, it will never stop you."

I looked back at him. His sapphire-and-silver gaze reflected torment, then icy determination, then torment again. Not a muscle on his body moved, but I could practically feel the fierce battle within him.

"But if I'm there," he said softly, "I don't know if I can let you. I want to swear that I'll respect your decision, but I don't trust myself not to try to save you, even if that's not what you want."

I opened my mouth to argue over his surety that I'd use the spearhead if I found it, but no words came out. It reminded me of when I'd been unable to promise Jasmine that I wouldn't use it, either. Was he right? Despite all the good reasons why I shouldn't wield it, deep down, had some part of me always intended to?

I sighed. "I don't know if you're right. So what if neither of us promises the other anything right now? That way, you don't have to worry about lying, and I won't have to feel sorry if I hit you over the head later to stop you from doing something against my wishes."

"If it comes to that, better make sure you hit me hard," he muttered.

"I've done it before," I replied with the same grim humor.

A dubious truce, but an honest one, at least. I rolled off him, finally disengaging the most intimate parts of our bodies. Then I smiled when his arms shot out to keep me close.

"Where do you think you're going?"

"Nature calls," I said, pushing him away.

I donned his shirt because it was the closest piece of clothing in the grass around us. Then I trotted off in search of a bush. There wasn't one nearby, so I settled for going out of eyesight while I tended to my bladder's needs. When I came back up the hill, Adrian was no longer alone.

Zach, Jasmine and Costa were now here. The Archon politely glanced away, but Costa raised an eyebrow as Adrian hastily put on his pants. Jasmine gave me an incredulous look.

"Seriously? You two were alone here for *five minutes*!"

"Your time," I said, buttoning Adrian's shirt as fast as my fingers could fly. "It was, uh, a couple hours on this side."

"Oh." Jasmine's expression went from shocked to mildly censuring. "Better, but still means you're easy."

I snorted. "Get me an Easy Ivy T-shirt, and I promise I'll wear it."

"Speaking of T-shirts, I'm still in soaked jammies," Jasmine said, turning to Zach. "Got anything other than fig leafs for me to wear here?"

"I'll attend to that after I return with Brutus," Zach said, and disappeared.

"With the time difference in this realm, he won't be back for hours," Adrian said, handing Jasmine my discarded shirt. "Here, wear this. Ivy can keep mine."

Jasmine took it, turning her back to discard her soaked top and replace it with my turtleneck. She gave a pointed look at me when she fingered the rip up the side of it. I just shrugged, still too filled with afterglow to be embarrassed.

"Take my pants, too," I offered. "Adrian's shirt is like a dress on me, anyway."

"Thanks," Jasmine said, this time using Costa as her shield when she doffed her sodden pants in exchange for my dry ones.

Adrian came over, handing me something he'd kept out of sight. My underwear and bra, I realized, and gave him a smile of thanks while I darted back down the hill to put them on.

Costa was hanging Jasmine's wet clothes on the branch of a manna tree when I came back. He'd taken his shirt off and hung that, too, but must have resigned himself to staying in the wet long underwear bottoms he still wore.

"You could take those off to dry, too. Promise I won't peek," I teased him.

Costa gave me an arch smile. "Ah, but if you did, then you'd leave Adrian, and I couldn't do that to my best friend."

Adrian laughed and said something in Greek. Grinning, Costa replied in the same language, and Adrian laughed again.

"Not fair," I told them, and Jasmine echoed her agreement.

"Learn Greek if you're curious," Costa said, still grinning.

"Don't worry," Adrian told me, chuckling. "It's mostly lies and wishful thinking on his part, anyway."

Brutus suddenly popped onto the hillside, his broad features expressing alarm at all the sunshine, then relief when he spotted me and Adrian. I ran over to him and reached him right as Zach appeared out of seemingly nowhere, too.

"How'd you do that so fast?" I asked, surprised. "We thought you'd be gone for hours again."

His brow arched. "I deliberately took longer before, and as anticipated, I had reason to delay."

I didn't touch that. There were a lot of things I wanted to talk to an Archon about, but my sex life wasn't one of them.

"Thanks for getting us all here," I said instead. "Brutus, don't worry. We'll find you a tree or something to hide under."

"I can do better than that," Zach said, walking down the hill. "Follow me, and I will take you to a place that has tents he can hide in, as well as food, water and dry pants," he added, with a last glance at Costa.

I exchanged a surprised look with Adrian. We knew light realms had food and water; they had streams as well as fruit and nut trees. But I'd never seen one with tents. Or pants.

"Follow me," Zach said again.

CHAPTER TWENTY-SIX

WE WALKED FOR what felt like an hour. Not that I was certain it was that at all. With light realms, you couldn't really be sure what the actual passage of time was, hence it being hours on our end before Zach returned with Jasmine and Costa, although for them, it had been five minutes.

Demon realms had time anomalies, too. In some of them, what was hours in a realm equated to several days in the real world. Sometimes, it was the opposite. Adrian had spent most of his life in demon realms where time slowed to a crawl. It was how he looked to be in his midtwenties yet was actually around a hundred and forty. Demetrius had wanted to make sure that his son had over a century both to hone his skills and to immerse himself in demon culture, all so Adrian wouldn't hesitate to fulfill his Judian destiny to hand me over to my death.

Some days, it amused me to think about how that plan had backfired on Demetrius.

"Look!" Jasmine said, pointing ahead. "Tents!"

I shielded my eyes and stared in the direction where she pointed. Yep, in the distance, I could see tents. Lots and lots of them. Some were the smaller ones you'd expect to find when camping; some were the size of

modest apartments; and some were as large as football stadium domes.

"What is this place?" Adrian asked before I could.

"A refuge," Zach replied, looking at me when he
spoke. "We told you we would care for the humans
who were rescued from the Bennington realm. This
is where they have been convalescing."

I was speechless as I stared back and forth between
Zach and the tents. The night I'd first used the ancient, hallowed sling, it had been far more powerful
than it was now. In one blinding burst, it had killed *all*
the minions and demons in the realm I'd found it in,
which—once upon a time—had been Adrian's former realm. All that had been left after the sling was
done were ashes and the realm's traumatized human
slaves. After Adrian and I had helped to get them out,
Archons whisked them away, promising to take care
of them. Once I knew they'd be okay, I hadn't really
thought about them. Now, here they were.

A loud horn blast suddenly came from somewhere
inside the tent village. It sounded like a watchman
sounding a medieval alarm, and when the people
stopped what they were doing and all turned in our
direction, I knew that blast was because of us.

"Why are we here, Zach?" The low, almost growling sound in Adrian's voice startled me.

Zach, as usual, appeared unperturbed. "As I said,
this place has dry clothing, shelter for Brutus, food,
water—"

"Bullshit. You did this because of *her*."

Adrian clearly meant me, but I didn't know why.
There was a good possibility that none of these people
would remember me from that day. Even if they did,

they might not recognize me. I think I'd been disguised by Archon glamour back then. Hell, Adrian had a better chance of being recognized than I did. With how slow time passed in the Bennington realm, some of these survivors might be from back when Adrian had been ruler. Since that had been in his demon prince heyday, I didn't imagine he'd be remembered fondly by any who did know him.

"She knew there would be a price for me to bring everyone to safety here," Zach replied, his tone changing from casual to unyielding. "This is it."

I still didn't get it, but Jasmine tugged my arm and said, "Forget whatever they're complaining about. I think I smell food cooking! Come on, I'm starving!"

I gave a worried look at Adrian, but now his features were closed off in a way that I recognized well. He wouldn't be revealing what was really bothering him anytime soon, and that might be for the best. I didn't want him getting into a fight with Zach. The Archon would win.

Besides, whatever it was, I didn't intend for us to be here long enough for it to fester. We'd get a change of clothes, maybe some food, and then be on our way, Zach's baffling price paid. I let Jasmine lead me down the hill and we reached the outskirts of the tent village.

Another horn blast straight out of a battle in a historical movie ripped through the silence. Then people began shouting and rushing toward us. Adrian was at my side in a flash, pushing me behind him while he faced the crowd that was now surrounding me.

"What's going on, Zach?" I asked, only to have my question drowned out by several people excitedly talking at once.

"It's her!" I heard amid the cacophony of voices, and I was confused until one word rose up and became a chant.

"Davidian, Davidian, *Davidian*!"

Looks like I'd been recognized after all.

"Yes, it is she," Zach said, his commanding voice ringing out over everyone else's as he pointed at me. "Your savior."

"No, I'm not," I said at once, but no one paid any attention. Instead, I was overwhelmed by people hugging me even though Adrian tried to hold them back—kisses being pressed to my head, hands and even the edge of my shirt—and most of all, by an avalanche of thanks I didn't deserve.

It didn't take long for me to figure out why Adrian had been upset at Zach. It took even less time for me to wish I hadn't come here. Each smiling face, each jubilant chant of "Davidian!," the way I was repeatedly kissed, all the hands that reached out to touch me…these people were hailing me as their savior, and I wasn't. Yes, I'd wiped out the demons and minions in the realm they'd been trapped in, but I hadn't done it for them.

"Bless you for saving me and my baby," a weeping, dark-haired woman said as she kissed my hand over and over.

"I didn't," I said, shame stinging me. She, her baby and all the rest of them had just been lucky enough to be in the same vicinity when I wiped out that realm to save Adrian. I should have gone back to it even if Adrian hadn't been there. Even closing the realm gateways had directly benefitted me, Adrian, Jasmine and Costa. Had I ever done something just because it was right, and not because it also helped me or the ones I loved?

"All of you, get back!" Adrian shouted, picking me up and shouldering his way through the crowd. "You're crushing her!"

Yes, but not physically. I'd heal from the accidental bruises I'd gotten during some of their attempts to hug and kiss me, but I didn't think I'd heal from what I felt as I looked into the people's joyous, grateful, unknowing faces.

"Let her pass," Zach called out. His command parted the crowd in a way that Adrian's brute force hadn't been able to. "I brought the Davidian for you to see and thank as I promised you," he continued. "But now she must go."

As I promised you...

I met Zach's eyes over the top of the crowd. One glimpse into them, and I knew this moment had been planned since the day I first touched that ancient, hallowed sling. Maybe even since long before that. Zach had known that seeing these people and hearing their undeserved praise would shake me. He'd *wanted* it to.

I was startled by my instant anger. He had no right to try to shame me by bringing me here! I didn't owe them or anyone else anything, least of all my life! They were glad that they were still alive. Well, I was glad that I, Adrian, Jasmine and Costa were still alive. Why did that make them normal while making me the bad guy?

Then, quick as that anger rose, I realized its source. The darkness inside me. Oh, how easy it would be to keep letting it fill me, until I felt nothing except my own angry defensiveness! But that wasn't the right path, even if it was the easy one.

These people mattered. So did the ones still trapped in the realms, and I didn't like who I'd become when I'd let the darkness lie and tell me otherwise. Adrian was right. I'd been kidding myself by believing that I could abandon them. Even if I didn't have a chance at saving them, even if touching that spearhead would do nothing except kill me, I'd at least die knowing that I'd tried. That was a hell of a lot better than living knowing that I hadn't. I'd rather live a short time in victory over the darkness slithering inside me than decades in defeat because it had turned me into someone I wouldn't want to know, let alone be.

Adrian finally got us free from the crowd and almost ran back up the hill. I heard Zach tell them not to follow us, and I heard him also tell someone to find new clothes for Jasmine, Costa and the rest of us.

"You okay, Ivy?" Jasmine called out.

"Fine," I said, and for the first time in a long time, I meant it. "Stay there and get what you need."

Whatever she said was lost to the wind as Adrian ran faster. Soon, we were at the top of the hill and the people below appeared to be more of a large, indistinct mass. Adrian stopped, took one look at my face and began to curse in the filthiest words I recognized in Demonish.

"I fucking hate being right," he finished in English.

"I'm sorry." One of the only things I regretted was how this would hurt him. "But now I know what you meant when you said you'd been wrong to think that losing me would be the worst thing that could happen. I don't want to lose you, either, but there *are* worse things. For you, it was seeing the pain in my eyes after you betrayed me again. For me, it was what I felt when

I looked at these people. What I've been doing is the same as saying I'd rather see them all dead than risk my own life, and that's not who I want to be. I want to be someone I can be proud of."

Adrian's sapphire eyes were brighter than I'd ever seen them. When the sun reflected in their shimmering depths, I realized that brightness came from tears. "You already are someone you can be proud of."

My heart felt like it shredded within me. "I love you," I said fiercely. "But just like you said before, now I know I can't turn away from this. I might have been able to distract myself for a while, or rationalize my actions, but if I'd really made up my mind, if I'd *truly* been okay with my decision not to try to save those still trapped in the demon realms, it wouldn't have hurt so much to see these people, and it did."

"I knew this day would come," he said in an anguished tone. "But I didn't think it would be today. Ivy…just remember that you deserve to live, too."

I let out a short laugh. "I think so, but maybe that's not supposed to be up to me. Maybe I'm only supposed to do what's right and let whether I live or die be up to…someone else."

I didn't say *God*. It felt hypocritical, especially when Zach had said more than once that he'd been given orders not to raise me if I were killed. There was only one source of his "orders," so it didn't seem that Zach's boss was concerned about me surviving. Then again, in the big picture, my death was inevitable sooner or later, so maybe that was why it being "sooner" wasn't a big deal to heaven's head honcho.

It was a big deal to *me*, but I couldn't let that stop me anymore. Of course, I was still hoping for some happy middle ground where I did the right thing and lived, yet I wasn't too optimistic. But since I was going to start doing the right thing even if it was hard…

"I know this is too much for you," I said, fighting not to let my voice betray how hard this was to say. "So I'll understand if you need to leave, Adrian—"

He yanked me to him, cutting off my words from how tightly he pressed me to his chest. First, I felt his kiss on the top of my head, then on my forehead when he leaned down until we were eye to eye, and finally, it was on my lips.

"I love you," he breathed against my mouth. "And I'm not going anywhere, Ivy. Not now, not ever again."

I kissed him back, feeling relief, fear, optimism and dread swirl like a kaleidoscope within me.

I hope I'm not, either, but we'll see.

CHAPTER TWENTY-SEVEN

ADRIAN AND I went back to the place where we'd first arrived in this realm. It was easy enough to find. We just looked for the clothes hanging from a manna tree. Jasmine, Costa and Brutus joined us about an hour later, and I noted with surprise that they'd loaded tents, food sacks and water jugs onto Brutus's back. The gargoyle didn't look like he minded. He probably would have been happier if the fabric from the tents had been draped over his face to block out the sun.

For once, I agreed with him. Normally, I far preferred daylight to darkness, but right now, I longed for the concealing comfort of the dark. Without it, I had to force a smile onto my face as I ate with Costa and Jasmine, not surprised that all the food was vegetarian. The original Eden might have been filled with animals, but the Archon realm equivalents seemed to be animal-free.

After we ate, we pitched our tents: one for me and Adrian, one for Costa and Jasmine and one for Brutus. We gave him the biggest one, and although he wasn't happy with a meal of grilled vegetables instead of raw meat, he was curled up in his tent and asleep within minutes. If I didn't know better, I'd even swear I heard Brutus snoring.

I didn't think either Adrian or I would be able to

sleep, but neither of us wanted to continue to make small talk, so we retired to our tent under the pretext of being tired. I'd have to tell Jasmine what I'd decided very soon, yet I couldn't bring myself to have that conversation now. I told myself delaying it gave Jasmine a chance to relax and enjoy the peace of our surroundings a little longer, but I knew I was only stalling.

I didn't want to break her heart any more than I'd wanted to break Adrian's. It seemed no matter what I did, I was hurting someone. All I could comfort myself with was the knowledge that this way, I was hurting fewer people for the right reasons versus hurting far more of them for the wrong ones.

Even still, as expected, I couldn't sleep, and that was despite Adrian and me making love two more times. My body might be beyond tired, but my mind wouldn't shut off. I didn't want to tell him that or he'd insist on staying up with me, so I pretended to sleep. After a while, his deep, even breathing let me know that he'd drifted off. I stayed there, trying to soak in the contentment of being in his arms, but the knowledge that I'd metaphorically flipped the hourglass on our time together eventually drove me out of the tent.

The river wasn't far. I'd take a quick dip and then try to sleep again. Hey, I'd have to bathe soon anyway. Doing it now meant that I wasn't disturbing anyone.

I took a new change of clothes with me. Someone had loaned us a long green dress that looked handmade, although the fabrics had probably been supplied by the outside world. After my bath, I dried myself with my old clothes, then put on the green dress. It was knee length and sleeveless, which was comfortable with the warm temperatures. I'd made it halfway back up the hill toward where our tents were located when I noticed someone leaning against the trunk of a nearby manna tree.

I walked over to Zach and sat down. He never did anything by accident, so he must have something to say. But after several minutes, nothing happened except him sitting next to me. Finally, I couldn't take the silence any longer.

"Archons aren't supposed to lie, but you told those people I was their savior." I kept my voice quiet so I didn't wake Adrian or the others. "Liar, liar, pants on fire."

"I did not lie." Zach's tone was smooth compared to the edge in mine. "You saved them, so you were their savior."

"We both know I didn't do it *for them*."

He let out the faintest sniff. "They are free and safe when they used to be trapped and in constant peril. Your motivations are your concern, not theirs."

"You're right," I said with a sigh. "And my motivations are the problem, or at least, they were. Everything I did before, I did because it helped me or the people I loved. Now I want to do the right thing because it's the right thing." I paused to give him a lopsided smile. "Sorry it took me my entire life to get to this point."

His head tilted. "You don't owe me an apology, and you're wrong about why I brought you here. You and Adrian believe I did it to shame you into wielding the spearhead if you found it, but I did it to show you that your life *does* matter, even if you don't use the final hallowed weapon. Look at all the people you've saved, and there are many more who are not here. No matter what happens, Ivy, you have achieved much, and I wanted you to know that."

I was so touched by his unexpected kindness that it left me speechless. Zach didn't seem to mind. We sat in silence for several minutes. Again, I found myself wishing it was dark. Then Zach wouldn't be able to see how I kept swiping at my eyes.

"I'm probably going to fail, aren't I?" I finally said. "Even if I give it my best, I'm not nearly up to the challenge. Your side really screwed up by making *me* the last Davidian. Tons of other people could've handled this a lot better than me, and they probably wouldn't have kept saying no first, either."

"Do you know what Moses said when he was first told that he had been chosen to demand his people's freedom from Pharaoh?" Unless I was mistaken, I thought a tinge of amusement colored Zach's tone. "He said that he wasn't a good speaker, so please send someone else."

"I don't remember that," I said in surprise.

Zach grunted. "Nor do most people. They only remember his successes. Jonah refused his call at first, too, and I could tell you millions of other stories like theirs. The truth is that many who are chosen refuse their destinies when they are first called to them. Some, like Moses and Jonah, obey later, but some never do. Therefore you, Ivy, are not the first, nor will you be the last, to say no to your calling at the onset, then change your mind later."

I felt better hearing that. It didn't mean I had any greater chance to succeed, but it helped to know I wasn't the only one who'd said, *Nuh uh!* and run in the opposite direction when confronted with a monumental, destiny-altering choice.

"Is that why you gave me the hallowed weapons back?" I asked. "Because you knew that eventually I'd change my mind?"

The smallest smile touched his mouth. "I didn't give them back to you."

"Uh, yes, you did," I said, tapping the braided rope tattoo on my right hand for emphasis.

"No, I didn't," he said, his smile fading. "Nor did I take them from you in the first place. Since the day you wielded them, the hallowed weapons have not once left your flesh."

I stared at him. "That's not possible." Then I said it again. "That's not possible. For weeks, they were *gone*!"

"From sight only," he replied, his voice deepening. "Your guilt over forsaking your destiny was so strong, it compelled the images of the weapons to fade. But they were never gone. That is why, when Demetrius was near you, you felt them again."

"But when I saw him before in the bathroom, I didn't feel anything," I said, still swinging between denial and shock.

"He had not crossed over into your realm," Zach replied. "He was only a reflection in a mirror. Those weapons do not activate by the reflection of a demon. Only one's presence."

I didn't ask how he knew the details of my bathroom encounter with Demetrius. Zach seemed to know everything. I don't know why I bothered to ever think otherwise.

"The weapons never left me?" This wasn't me arguing with him; it was me trying to accept the truth.

"No, Ivy." Zach's voice was soft. "Even when all your senses were telling you that they had, you were not alone. You have *never* been alone."

I had to turn away because I didn't want him to see the tears that sprang to my eyes. He wasn't only talking about the presence of the weapons, and we both knew it.

"Why didn't you tell me this before?" I said, trying to get ahold of myself. I didn't know why I was crying at the drop of a hat lately. Yes, things had been very stressful, eventful and emotional recently, but *come on.* I was starting to resemble a leaky faucet.

"Because you wouldn't have believed me, so you still wouldn't have seen them."

I looked back at him. "That doesn't make a lot of sense."

He gave an oblique shrug. "Some things you need to believe before you can see them."

"O me of little faith, huh?" I said with a small, self-deprecating laugh.

Zach didn't say anything. He didn't have to. His expression all but screamed *Exactly.*

Yeah, well, having faith was hard. I believed in a lot of things, mostly because I had no choice due to my firsthand experience. But faith wasn't just overcoming the hurdle of believing—it was the far more difficult act of *trusting*, and I still wasn't there yet.

I didn't want to get into that with Zach, however. He might be practically all-knowing, but some things—especially this—I'd have to figure out for myself. Instead, I said, "So, am I going to see you again after we leave here?"

"Yes."

I waited, but he didn't elaborate or say anything else. As the silence continued, it was obvious that he wasn't going to. From the faint tilting of his lips, it seemed to amuse him that I was frustrated about that, too.

"Great," I finally said, my voice edged with false flippancy. "I can't wait to be surprised when it happens."

Then Zach did something so unexpected, so shocking, I could only stare at him in complete disbelief.

He laughed.

CHAPTER TWENTY-EIGHT

WE GOT UP the next morning, or whatever time of the day it was. Hard to tell when it was always bright and sunny, let alone when time passed differently here. In any case, Adrian no longer had dark circles under his eyes. After my talk with Zach, I had finally slept, too, so he wasn't the only one who felt better.

When Jasmine came out of her tent, it took only one look for me to know that she hadn't had a restful night. Her eyes were red rimmed, and her movements were stiff and jerky from anger. Costa gave me a guarded look when he came out of the tent after her, and I noticed that he gave her a wide berth.

"Did you two have a fight?" I asked without beating around the bush.

"I don't want to talk about it," Jasmine said shortly.

"Yes," Costa replied, matching my bluntness with his own. "She knows what you're intending to do, and she's furious both with you for doing it and me for supporting your decision."

My mouth sagged open. "What?" I hadn't told her yet. I'd intended to today, but it looked like that wasn't needed anymore.

"I got up to pee in the middle of the night and overheard you and Zach talking," Jasmine said with an accusing look.

I closed my eyes. Zach would have known that she was listening. No human could sneak up on an Archon. He'd known, and he hadn't bothered to warn me. He'd just shockingly laughed at my retort and then disappeared.

"I'm so sorry you found out that way," I said, opening my eyes. "I was going to talk to you—"

"You promised," she interrupted me, anguish in her tone. "You *promised* you were only going to find the spearhead and hide it, not find it and use it!"

"No, I didn't promise." Even then, I must have known that I was only running from my destiny, but I couldn't hide. "Besides, things have changed—"

"Yeah, your guilt trip over seeing those people," she interrupted. "What about feeling guilty over what you're doing to me? Or to Adrian? I know *he* can't be supporting this!"

"I'm supporting Ivy," Adrian said very quietly. "This is her decision, not mine."

"Jasmine," I began.

She gestured at me almost violently. "Don't. I don't want to hear you explain why you chose strangers over your own family."

"I didn't," I said, frustration mixing in with my sorrow. "I chose right over wrong."

Tears started to stream down her face. "Fine. You throw your life away on a weapon you know is too powerful for you, but don't expect me to watch. I'll stay here, with the people you care about more than you care about me."

I took in a deep breath, trying to absorb the emotional blow while also reminding myself that this wasn't the real Jasmine talking. It was her anger and her fear speaking.

"That's fine," I managed to say calmly. "You have every right to decide where you want to be, and I'm glad you'll be safe. I love you, Jasmine." My voice wavered when I said her name, but then I forced myself to continue in a strong, steady tone. "I'll always love you. Remember that."

"Yeah." Her voice broke like a wineglass dropped from a high ledge. "I'll put that in my memory banks next to the rest of my dead family members."

Couldn't she see that I didn't want to hurt her, Adrian or anyone else? If I had a choice, I would never have been born with this destiny. But I didn't have a choice about that. All I had was trying not to screw up even more than I already had.

Adrian came closer, drawing me into his arms. "That's enough, Jasmine. Maybe you should take a walk, before you say anything else to Ivy that you'll regret."

She sniffed hard, her tears still flowing. "Doesn't matter," she muttered as she started striding down the hill. "All I have left are regrets now."

I didn't speak as I watched her go. I'd told her I loved her and I was sorry. The rest was all noise to her. Maybe even that was, too. Right now, nothing that came out of my mouth would make her feel better, except the one thing I couldn't say.

"You're doing the right thing," Costa told me quietly.

The sound that came out of me was too strangled to be a laugh. "You're literally the only person aside from Zach who thinks so."

Costa came closer. "Not true. Adrian knows it, too,

deep down beneath his fear of losing you. More importantly, you know it's true. That's why you're strong
enough to do it."

I looked down the hill where my sister was walking
away as fast as her legs could carry her. Her blond hair
whipped around her shoulders from her rapid pace, and
her shoulders were shaking from tears.

"I don't feel strong," I whispered as Jasmine disappeared from my sight. I might never see her again,
and that knowledge felt like a weight on my chest that
wouldn't lift.

"Fifty-two years."

That turned my attention back to Costa even as I
felt Adrian stiffen behind me. "What?"

"That's how long I was trapped in the Bennington realm, measuring by the time that passed in the
real world." Costa's lips thinned, and something dark
flashed over his expression. "I don't want to know how
long it was over there. It's awful to have no control over
a single part of your life, right down to whether you
live or die. It's even worse when there are actual monsters around you. I saw some people I used to know
from the realm in the village down there," he added, almost offhandedly. "Since they were in the same realm
I'd been in, I wasn't surprised to run into them. I was
only surprised by how few of them were left. All the
rest are dead."

A tremor went through Adrian, yet his grip on me
remained secure and comforting. "That's on me."

"Some of it," Costa acknowledged, his deep brown
gaze unflinching. "It's also on Demetrius, since he took
over after you left. Turned that place into the same shit
hole as the other demon realms, to hear them describe

it. Our prison was cushy by comparison under you, and you took me and Tomas when you left, so as I've said before, you and I are good. But the rest of them... you still owe them, Adrian. I know you've been paying on that debt since you walked away from the demon prince life, but you've gotta ante up some more before this is all over."

Was he trying to make me feel better, or make Adrian feel worse? My expression must've said what I was thinking, because Costa addressed it head-on.

"You're at the center of this decision, Ivy, but it's not only about you. Adrian has a part to play, too. Years ago, he rescued me and Tomas, and after what we'd been through, we deserved the chance to make new lives for ourselves. All those people still trapped deserve that chance, too, and you might be the one destined to give it to them, but you can't do it alone. You need Adrian's help, and him giving it is payment on the debt he still owes—not to me, but to a lot of other people." His voice became deeper and more resonant. "And I'm going to stand by your sides to help you to do it. I want those people to get their shot at a second chance. After all, it's the best thing I can do with the second chance that I was given."

I blinked hard, wondering if I was going to spend every day of what might be the very short remainder of my life trying not to break into tears.

"Thank you, Costa." My voice husky from my continued attempts to stem the waterworks. "But if you want to help me help those people, don't go with us. Stay with Jasmine." He opened his mouth to argue, and I held up a hand and said, "*Please.* If things don't go well with me, she'll need you. Like she said, she has no one else left."

He still looked like he wanted to argue, but Adrian said, "You're right, Costa. This isn't just Ivy's fight. It's mine, too, and like you said, for many more reasons than just me wanting to keep her safe. You've already fought against demons and minions many times. You have no debt to pay off, but I do, so let me take this, bro. You take care of Jasmine. She needs someone as strong as you to help her get through this."

Costa still looked like he wanted to argue, but finally, with an audible click of his jaw, he shut his mouth and nodded. *I'll stay*, that nod said. *I don't like it, but I'll do it*.

"Thank you," I said fervently. "I can't tell you how relieved it makes me to know that Jaz won't go through this alone. If it's not too much, I have one more favor to ask."

Costa looked surprised. "What is it?"

"Brutus," I said, turning to look at the tent the gargoyle was hiding in. "I know he's not your favorite person, but he also has no one aside from me and Adrian. If something… If something happens to both of us, will you take care of him?"

I couldn't bear to think of Adrian possibly dying, but Brutus was my friend. That meant I had to deal with the fact that neither Adrian nor I might make it out of this. If the worst happened, I wanted Brutus taken care of, and I couldn't ask Zach. Brutus would rather die than live out his days in a perpetually sunny realm with only vegetables to eat.

Costa cast a look at Brutus's tent, too, his expression showing his reluctance. Then a deep sigh came out of him.

"I'll do it, but I can't promise to cuddle him or let him lick my face like you do."

A breath of laughter escaped me even as I fought back more tears. "Deal, but you'll be surprised how fast he grows on you."

"I hope I never find out," Costa said dryly.

I laughed again even though these topics made me feel like I was being devoured from the inside out. Still, the least I could do was refuse to wallow in the sadness.

"One more thing before we go, Costa," Adrian said.

Costa raised a brow. "What is it?"

Adrian let go of me and went over to Costa. Then he put his arms around him and hugged him. Hard.

"When I walked out of that realm with you and Tomas, I had no friends, no family, a raging drug addiction, a past filled with unforgivable sins and a future filled with an even worse destiny. You told me to take all that and use it to fight instead of allowing it to destroy me. Before anyone else thought so, especially me, you believed that I could be more than what I was. Thank you, Costa. Thank you from the bottom of my heart for being the first person to believe in me."

Costa hugged him back. Though his long, thick black hair hid most of his face, I caught sight of a new, shiny trail on his cheek that had nothing to do with a trick of the sunlight.

"Anytime, bro," Costa said in a choked voice.

This time, I didn't even try to hold back my tears.

CHAPTER TWENTY-NINE

ZACH HAD SAID that I'd see him again, and he was right. Not long after Adrian's emotional goodbye to Costa, the Archon appeared to ask Adrian and me if we were ready to leave. I cast a long, pained look in the direction that Jasmine had disappeared to, but said yes.

"I'll get Brutus," Adrian said, and went into the gargoyle's tent. Moments later, both of them came out, and Brutus gave a wary look at the bright sunlight around him.

"We don't have passports or money," I reminded Zach.

"Here," Zach said, producing slips of paper out of thin air with the ease of a magician pulling coins from behind a child's ear. "You can use these two for passports and the rest for currency. Adrian has accounts he can access for more."

I looked at the blank slips of paper. This wasn't the first time Zach had given me the equivalent of sticky notes to use as formal identification and/or money. Normal Archon glamour was only good for a specific illusion, like making Brutus appear to be a seagull to everyone except me, Adrian and other Archons. *This* type of glamour was next level. It not only fooled the human and demon eye—it also fooled computer scanners, too.

"What part of these are the passports?" Since I could see through Archon glamour, it all looked the same to me.

Zach pulled out two strips from the others. "Passports."

I turned to Adrian. "This dress doesn't have pockets."

He took the two "passport" strips and put them in his right pants pocket. In the left, he put the money strips. "What names are on the passports?"

"Whatever names you tell them to be," Zach replied.

Well, that was convenient.

Zach held out his hands. Adrian and I shared a weighted look. Once we took Zach's hands, there was no turning back.

I placed my hand in the Archon's open palm. Adrian did, too, and held on to Brutus with his other hand. With that, Zach pulled all of us through the gateway and that familiar stomach-flopping, free-falling sensation hit me.

The realm-traversing ride ended with me throwing up on the banks of whatever river we'd been deposited on. A city was in front of us, and across the river, it looked like another one was behind us. Thankfully, we appeared to be on the edge of the town in front of us, so we didn't have an audience for either our impromptu arrival or my hurling. Brutus sprinted off in search of shade, and for a few wrenching moments, I was too sick to be embarrassed by how I was puking like a teenager after a bout of binge drinking. Then I mentally scolded myself.

Way to start off the new quest, Ivy! Demons of the world, beware—the last Davidian is back, and she's got vomit!

"What a rookie reaction to a realm trip, right?" I said out loud, brushing aside Adrian's concerned hovering. "Don't worry. I'm fine. Did I get any puke on my dress? Dammit, I did!"

"We'll need to get new clothes anyway. It's much cooler here." Then Adrian's eyes narrowed as he looked around. "But this doesn't look like Moscow. Where are we?"

"Trier, Germany," Zach replied.

"Germany?" I repeated. "That wasn't on the list of places you gave me, Adrian." If it had been, I would've picked going here before going to the arctic end of Sweden. Hell, we'd had to travel through Germany in order to *get* to Sweden!

"Why are we here?" Adrian asked. "This didn't make the list of favorite places."

"It should have," Zach said mildly.

I gave Adrian an exasperated look. "Were you sending me to the wrong places on purpose again?"

"No," Adrian said emphatically. "I swear, I didn't even think of this place as a possibility because I only came here once. I'd been to those other places many, many times."

"Quantity isn't everything," Zach said, still in that mild tone. "The place you visited here left an impact on you."

I arched a brow at Adrian. "Oh? How so?"

He shifted uncomfortably. "The one time I came here, I got ragingly high and tried to set fire to the Aula Palatina."

"What?" I said even as Zach asked, "And how many other times in your life did you attempt arson?"

"None," Adrian replied, his tone defensive now.

"I mostly stuck to hurting myself when I visited this world."

"You see?" Zach said with satisfaction. "Impact."

"Or a temporary case of 'like father, like son,'" I noted. "Demetrius burned down one of your former favorite places, remember? You probably got the arson idea from him..."

My voice trailed off as an idea began to form. Zach looked at me, his mouth doing that not-quite-a-smile thing. "Exactly."

I glanced up at the sun's midlevel position in the sky, then down at my vomit-spattered dress. "We need to hurry. We have to get Brutus, get some new clothes and then get to whatever place you tried to torch, Adrian. Something very important is there."

WE ARRIVED AT the Aula Palatina, or Basilica of Constantine, with two hours of sunlight left. That should be enough to feel around for something hallowed, hopefully find it and get to somewhere safe before nightfall. If worse came to worst and it took longer, Emperor Constantine's former palace entrance hall was now a church, so we'd be on hallowed ground. I'd rather wait out the darkness hiding on the property than take our chances looking for a hotel. Zach—of course—had disappeared on us while we'd been waiting for a taxi.

"I will see you again," he'd said right before vanishing.

With him, that could mean five minutes or five weeks. Either way, we couldn't count on him to pull us into the safety of a light realm if we finished after dark. We had to assume that we were on our own, and with Demetrius declaring open season on us to all the other demons in this world, I was paranoid about being caught on non-hallowed ground once night fell.

At least this place hadn't been known as one of Adrian's "favorites." That was how Demetrius had found us last time, so without that, we might be okay. Just in case, I'd bought my new outfit without trying it on, since dressing rooms had full-length mirrors, and I'd made sure not to look into any of the mirrors in the main area of the store.

I'd also made sure to pick pants and a long, loose sweater instead of another dress. Not only was I warmer, it allowed me to stuff rocks into my pockets for the sling, and the longer, generous cut of the sweater hid the bulges. Adrian had changed, too. Gone were the homespun white top and drawstring pants he'd gotten from the light realm's inhabitants. Now he wore a dark blue silk shirt and a black jacket over black tailored pants.

No, we hadn't been able to afford all that from the strips of paper Zach had given us. Our first stop had been the nearest international bank. The Archonglamoured "passport" Adrian used for identification had worked as well as predicted. Since it was also good for any name Adrian selected, he'd picked one of his many bank account aliases to take out enough traveling money.

Now we looked like regular tourists instead of slightly suspicious hippies. If not for the "seagull" that followed every taxi we took by flying over it, we'd seem downright normal.

We got out at the Aula Palatina, which was in a populated area with several shops, offices and restaurants. Adrian had given me a brief history on the way

over, so I knew it used to be part of Emperor Constantine's palace. The former entrance hall didn't look very
palatial today. It was a tall, rather plain-looking red-
brick structure shaped like a long, covered stadium.
The basilica's only outward decoration that I could
see were two sets of cathedral windows. Still, it was
enough of a tourist draw that we were far from the
only people there.

"No!" I told Brutus when I caught him giving hungry, lingering looks to a dog that two other tourists
were walking nearby. At least, I hoped Brutus was
looking at the dog.

Brutus chuffed as if to say, *Hey, I was only reading
the menu, not ordering!* But he stopped eye-munching
the group, and I gave him a couple pats in praise.

In all of our rushing, we hadn't stopped to get him
any raw meat, so no surprise that he was hungry. I was
ravenous, too, but neither of us could add an early dinner to our schedule. We'd eat after we'd checked the
entrance hall, which hopefully wouldn't take long.

When Adrian and I went inside, leaving Brutus to
guard the exterior, I *really* didn't think it would take
long. The interior was almost as sparse as the exterior,
with only rows of wooden chairs, some overhead lights
and a small altar interrupting the vast open space. No
paintings, no shrines, no carved figurines, no statues,
no frills at all, which meant no apparent place for a
two-thousand-year-old hallowed weapon to be hidden.

"Feel anything?" Adrian asked in a low voice.

"Not yet." And from the sparseness of the interior, I
had no idea where to begin looking for hallowed-blocking
wards. If not for my suspicion for why Adrian's "like
father, like son" sole brush with arson was at the same

place Zach had specifically brought us to, I might have walked out.

But Adrian had inexplicably tried to burn this place down, just like Demetrius had burned down a former hiding place of the staff of Moses. Demons had natural aversions to hallowed objects, which was why they couldn't touch them without lots of pain. Maybe Adrian's demon side had subconsciously reacted to the spearhead by attempting to destroy it, just like Demetrius had almost destroyed Moses's staff without knowing it.

It was possible, and since Zach had brought us here, there had to be *something* of value to find. I gave my whole body a shake, as if that would work free whatever kinks must be blocking my hallowed sensors.

"Let's start with the altar," I told Adrian.

It was only a wooden podium with some ferns on either side, but no need to ignore the most obvious hiding place. With the podium's height, it could fit a two-foot-long, ancient iron shank inside it. In this spartan, relic-free environment, no one would probably give it a second glance even if they did see it. They might confuse it with a construction tool.

We wandered over to the podium casually, as if it weren't our intended target. The church wasn't full, since it was a Thursday evening instead of a Sunday morning, but it wasn't empty, either. I managed to walk behind the podium and check out the interior—empty except for a Bible and loose papers that looked like sermon notes—before we were stopped.

"Can I help you?" asked a woman with salt-and-pepper streaks in her black hair. Her accent was German, no surprise, and she had lovely dark brown skin and deep black eyes. A light splattering of wrinkles cut deeper around the corners of her eyes and the sides of her mouth. Smile lines, I realized, and took that as a good sign.

"Sorry," I said, trying to think up a reason that wouldn't result in her calling security. "I, uh, thought I heard a kitten mewling back there."

From her expression, she wasn't buying it, but she smiled and said, "What a relief that you were wrong. I would hate to have one jump out and startle me during my next sermon."

"You're the pastor?"

"Yes," she said. "For a few weeks now."

Damn. I'd been hoping she'd been there for a while and might—dare I be so optimistic?—know the location of the relic we were after. Hey, it had happened once before.

"Ivy," I said, taking a risk by whisking up my sleeve before I extended my right hand. The sling tattoo was now on prominent display. Between that and my real first name, if she was in on any of the supernatural secrets that had brought us here, she'd have no doubt as to who—and what—I really was.

She gave the tattoo only the barest, uninterested glance before she shook my hand. "Pastor Helena. Pleased to meet you."

My hopes sank. I couldn't feel anything powerful dinging my hallowed radar, and the pastor seemed not to recognize my name or my very famous tattoo. Still, something had to be relevant to our quest here. Maybe I just had to be more direct.

"My husband tells me this hall was built in the fourth century by Emperor Constantine." I looked around as if admiring what I saw. "If these walls could talk, right? Bet they've seen a lot of amazing people and relics come and go. Didn't I hear a rumor that the Spear of Longinus was once housed here?"

That was pretty direct, but Pastor Helena only shook her head. "*Nein*, I've never heard of that."

I gave it one final try in case she was feigning ignorance because she thought I was a nosy tourist. "I'm the last Davidian," I said bluntly. "And I'm here for the spearhead."

She frowned as she gave me the look that countless doctors and therapists had given me when I told them that I could see icy, dark, duplicate images of places. The look that said, *Oh, you're batshit crazy, huh?*

"*Fraulein,*" she said carefully. "I think—"

A loud, cracking noise sounded above us, as if a thousand branches had snapped all at once. I looked up to see something large and dark dropping down right on top of us.

And at the same time, every hallowed sensor in my body went berserk.

CHAPTER THIRTY

HAVING MY BODY light up with countless sensors on instantaneous overload caused me to involuntarily freeze despite the danger. Adrian shoved me and Pastor Helena out of the way mere moments before those dark-colored objects smashed to the floor right where we'd been standing. We landed in a tumble of limbs in front of the first row of congregant chairs.

Most of my senses were still stuck on supernatural red alert, so for a second, I thought the wooden pieces around us were from the pew chairs breaking under the force Adrian had used to get us out of the way. Then I realized the colors were wrong. The chairs were made of light-colored wood, yet the pieces that littered the space around us were dark, and the ones that hadn't smashed were shaped in perfect squares.

Adrian looked up at the same time that I did. The ceiling was made of a series of similar boxlike dark wood squares. It was the most decorative part of the entrant hall, and now it had a large hole above where the altar podium used to be.

A flurry of German sounded as about half of the church's occupants ran to see if we were okay, and the other half ran for the exits. Pastor Helena got to her feet, giving a shocked look at the pile of smashed ceiling planks where the three of us had been standing.

"Danke," she said in a shaky voice to Adrian before switching to English. "Thank you. We might have been very hurt if not for your quick actions. Now, however, you must leave."

Pastor Helena raised her voice, presumably repeating the directive to the tourists and congregants who'd stayed behind. After she finished, the rest of them began to head toward the door. I stayed on the floor, staring up at the ceiling. Something super hallowed was up there, and every cell in my body was reacting to it. If I could have climbed the walls to get to it, I would have. But at the moment, I was having a hard time moving. Much like what happened when I first came in contact with the staff, my body was momentarily overloaded and useless.

"Please," Pastor Helena said to Adrian and me. "You must leave. There is obviously some structural insufficiency in the ceiling, and it still might not be safe—"

"Ivy," Adrian said, ignoring her. "I can see something up in the hole where those pieces fell out."

"I don't need to see it." My voice sounded hoarse, as if I'd been screaming. "I can *feel* it."

"Please, go," Pastor Helena said again.

"Brutus!" Adrian yelled in reply. *"Larastra!"*

The gargoyle barreled through the front doors, knocking down anyone unfortunate enough to be in his way. I heard shocked yelps as people tried to figure out what had suddenly knocked them on their asses. All they could see was a squawking seagull running into the entrant hall, which didn't track with the wide swath that had been cut through their midst.

Adrian barked out commands in Demonish while pointing up at the hole in the ceiling. Brutus flapped his great wings, knocking down another person in the process, and soared upward to reach the hundred-foot-tall ceiling. Once there, he flipped upside down, his wings beating faster to hover him beneath the hole while he rummaged inside it.

More pieces of the ceiling began to fall. They were smaller this time, but Adrian still picked me up, getting me out of the way. Pastor Helena ran to the far side of the hall, pulling out her cell phone and shouting at it in German. Moments later, several uniformed guards came into the hall.

They ushered the remaining people out, and when they reached us, Adrian let them hustle us toward the doors, too. We were now the last ones inside aside from Pastor Helena, who seemed to be staying. Right as the guards pushed us through the doors, Brutus let out a roar, and I saw him fly away from the ceiling with something long and thin clutched in his talons.

Adrian sprinted us to the side, shouting, "Hit the deck!" to the guards, who were still blocking the doors.

They glanced around in confusion but didn't move or duck as warned. Then they were thrown forward from the force of a two-ton gargoyle flying right into them. Brutus didn't have his wings in his infamous head-chop formation, nor had he been trying to hurt them, which was the only reason they survived. But from their groans and their pitiable impacts, they'd be taking some sick days after this.

Brutus kept going after he cleared the doorway. Once outside, he flew higher, until he was well over the roofs of the nearby buildings. The farther away he went, the better I felt as my hallowed sensors powered down, allowing my body to function normally. I didn't need Adrian to keep carrying me anymore and told him that, but he didn't stop. Instead, he picked up his pace, until everything we passed turned into a blur.

After a few minutes, we were clear of the metropolitan area and into what looked like the warehouse district. Then we passed that, too, and ended up back on the soft banks of the winding river. Brutus was about fifty yards away, hiding from the sun under a tree, the object he'd taken from the ancient hall's ceiling in the grass by his feet.

Adrian finally set me down, but he kept a tight grip on my hand. "Easy," he warned me. "Give yourself a minute."

Now that I was back in the proximity of the mystery object, he was right: I was back to feeling like every nerve ending had been set on fire and then rubbed raw. I could stand under my own power, though, so the initial effects of being blasted by a supernatural shockwave seemed to have worn off. Now all I had was what felt like a case of full-body hives…and an almost overwhelming urge to grab the unknown object at Brutus's feet.

"I can feel it pulling me toward it. Once I let go of your hand, I won't be able to stop myself from grabbing it."

A ragged sigh came out of Adrian, and his sapphire eyes filled with pain. "I know."

Part of me didn't want to move. I wasn't ready to say goodbye to him yet. I needed more time, just a little more! But for once, I didn't need my willpower to slap down the selfish parts of me that would choose Adrian over the world. The object's lure was too strong. It pulled me to it with a relentlessness that only grew the more I hesitated, until soon, I felt like it would rip me apart if I didn't go to it.

Yet if I told Adrian to take me away, he would. In a heartbeat. The urge to grab the relic would pass as soon as I was out of its range, and Brutus could fly it to safety. We could have the extra time I so desperately wanted, if I told Adrian it was okay to do what I knew he wanted to.

"It won't get any easier if we wait," I finally said, starting to tug my hand free of Adrian's tight grip. "I'll never be ready to say goodbye to you. Not today, tomorrow or even a hundred years from now. So let's not try to say goodbye. Instead, I want to say that I love you, Adrian. More than I ever knew it was possible to love anyone. Being with you has been the best thing to ever happen to me. Never doubt that."

His gaze grew wild, yet he let me pull my hand free. "I love you, Ivy. You made every moment of the hell I experienced worth it because it brought me to you. You're the only part of my life I don't regret, and I will love you from now until the moment I see you again."

I stared at him, unable to look away even as I began to back away. My feet were moving me toward Brutus and the object he guarded, but my whole heart felt like it was straining toward Adrian. I couldn't do this! I couldn't! But I couldn't abandon those people. I was the only chance they had.

"We will see each other again one day." My voice was ragged from my throat closing off. "I know we will."

He set his jaw and his hands closed into fists. I kept backing away, feeling my heart break with every step. This was the right thing to do; I *knew* that. Yet it didn't lessen the pain, and when Adrian's gaze began to brighten from unshed tears, I missed a step and stumbled.

He started forward to grab me, then stopped, fists clenching again until his bones strained whitely against his skin. I steadied myself, holding out my hand in silent plea for him to stay where he was. No matter what I knew to be right, if he touched me again, I didn't trust what I'd do.

To give myself strength, I looked away from Adrian and at the object at Brutus's feet. It paid off. That single look felt like a shot of adrenaline to my body. The power in the object tightened its hold on me, moving me toward it with greater speed. Right then, I knew I couldn't turn back and go to Adrian even if I wanted to. It had me now.

The sky, which had been a hazy blue before, was filling with dark clouds. They grew thicker and higher, until they choked off the rays from the sun. Their darkness matched my pain at the knowledge that I would probably never see Adrian again, until I was sure that I was the cause of the abrupt change in weather. My emotional wounds had activated the staff enough to make it rain inside a hotel hallway; it made sense that the heartbreak I was feeling now had manifested into the roiling, pitch-colored clouds that now covered the sky.

"I'll always love you," I said, but I didn't dare turn around. I couldn't bear to see if his face mirrored the agony I was feeling. Thunder boomed and lightning flashed across the sky, causing Brutus to growl. He might like the new darkness, but he obviously wasn't fond of the coming storm.

I wasn't, either. It signaled the end of my relation-ship and probably my life. I took a deep breath, and another round of thunder boomed across the sky.

"This is the right thing to do," I whispered, and though I still knew it to be a fact, it *felt* less true.

Then, before I abandoned everything just to feel Adrian's arms around me one more time, I reached down and grabbed the long, thin object at Brutus's feet.

CHAPTER THIRTY-ONE

THIS ISN'T IRON.

That was my first thought when I touched the object, immediately followed by an internal screech as power shot up my arm. It rocked me back on my heels, but it didn't drive me to my knees like the staff had. Nor did that feeling of power grow like it had when I first wielded the slingshot. Instead, it seemed to settle inside my bones with a low, uncomfortable hum that reminded me of the aftereffects of an electrical shock.

This wasn't the spearhead. It was way too long, not to mention that if it was, I'd be comatose at best and dead at worst. Not picking the object up and cocking my head as I examined it while I wondered what it was. If I didn't know better, I'd say it was a long stick, but that made no sense. The only famous stick I was aware of was the staff that was still embedded in my skin... Wait. That's right. *Embedded.*

"Adrian," I called out, and felt the rush of air from how fast he ran to me. "This isn't the spearhead, but I think it's the pilum that the spearhead used to be embedded in."

A first-century Roman javelin was no more than a long wooden stick with a nasty iron shank fastened at the end of it. A simple weapon, but deadly enough to impale someone right through their armor, let alone through vulnerable flesh.

This part of the weapon shouldn't still exist. Zach had told me that the spearhead was all that was left of the weapon, yet here it was. Had he actually been *lying* to me?

Adrian looked at the wooden shaft but wisely made no move to touch it. If holding it felt like getting repeated electric shocks to me, it might really injure Adrian.

"The base of the holy lance," he said with a surprising amount of awe in his tone. Then he let out a harsh laugh. "No wonder Zach sent us here. Most hallowed objects are reduced to mere fragments because of the passage of time. Those pieces might be powerful in and of themselves, but they're nothing like what they could be if the objects were reassembled again."

I stared at him in understanding. "Now we have half of the lance, so if we find the spearhead and put it back together—"

"Boom," Adrian said succinctly.

As charged as this was, the shaft was the equivalent of an accessory. But putting it back together with the spearhead would turn it into the equivalent of a supernatural bomb, and we all knew what happened to anyone in the direct path of a bomb.

Boom, indeed.

I set my chin and refused to feel sorry for myself. I'd done too much of that already. Yes, dying young sucked. Yes, losing Adrian would suck even worse, but if nothing else, the combined power of the shaft and the spearhead rejoined meant that I had a real chance to save those people. Reassembling it should blast that lethal power out through me and into every demon realm. I'd die, but I'd die knowing that I was delivering a knockout punch to every demon in existence.

They might get back up eventually, since—as Zach reminded me—the final fight was between Archons and demons, not humans and demons. But unlike what I'd been afraid of before, my death wouldn't be in vain. Instead, with the ultra-amped, reassembled final hallowed weapon, it should allow countless humans to escape a fate worse than death.

Hey, if I was going to die, I might as well go out with the biggest bang possible. Maybe I'd tell Zach to have my headstone read "Suck on THAT, demons!"

"Okay, one piece down, the other half to go," I said, carefully setting the lance back down. "The spearhead's got to be at one of the five remaining places on your list…"

My voice trailed off as I stared at the tattoo on my right hand, then looked at the sky. I wasn't in an emotional frenzy anymore, so the sky shouldn't be as eerily black with clouds as it still was. And my tattoos shouldn't be activating, but the one in my hand was turning a lighter shade of brown and starting to throb, as was the other tattoo in my body.

I cast a new, horrified look at the sky. It hadn't been the staff altering the weather because of the pain I'd felt at leaving Adrian. I hadn't caused any of this. And if I hadn't, then I could think of only one creature that would have the ability—let alone the desire—to darken a sunny afternoon into midnight-like darkness.

Demons.

I wasn't the only one who'd figured it out. "Ivy." Adrian's voice thrummed with intensity. "Get on

Brutus's back and have him fly you back to hallowed ground. Now."

"What about you?" I protested.

He shoved me toward Brutus. "I'll hold them off until you're safe."

"I'm *not* leaving without you," I began, but stopped as something in the sky caught my eye.

At first, I didn't understand what I was seeing. Then ice felt like it blasted through my veins as memory pieced together the impossible image and gave it context.

"Too late," I whispered. "None of us can fly out of here."

Adrian spun around. I knew the instant he spotted the thing, and he figured out far quicker than I had what it was.

"Blinky," he hissed.

Such an innocuous-sounding nickname. Mocking, in fact, considering that Adrian had called his former demon captive that due to the dozens of sets of eyes covering him. Blinky had them because he had once been a seraph, one of the highest levels of Archons. In addition to his freaky sets of eyes that covered his entire upper body, he also had three separate sets of wings. Blinky was now using all of those wings to fly toward us with the speed of a proverbial bat out of hell.

"No one holds a grudge like a demon," Adrian muttered.

"Especially one you tortured and imprisoned for years," I added, yanking at my tattoo. I kept yanking until the sling was all the way out of my arm, then I notched it with one of the rocks I'd stuffed into my pockets. As soon as it was armed, I began to spin the sling.

"Back away from me, Adrian. One clean hit—"

"He's not alone," Adrian interrupted.

I squinted, but I couldn't see anything except the darkness around Blinky. It radiated from him as if he were a black hole that sucked in all the light around him. Still, I took Adrian at his word and got more rocks at the ready.

He stripped off his shirt and used it to pick up the wooden lance. Even with the layers of material between him and the hallowed object, he still winced as if it hurt him to touch it. Then he stuffed it between the leather belts of Brutus's harness while saying something in Demonish to the gargoyle.

"No matter what, we can't let them get this," he told me, switching to English. "If it's a choice between me or it, you save it, Ivy. Otherwise, we're all dead anyway."

I wasn't sure I agreed, but we had to live through this in order to fight about it later. Blinky was only about a hundred yards away now. Close enough for me to see his brown hair, his pale skin and, worst of all, his eyes. One look into them, and revulsion hit me like a splash.

I didn't know how his eyes seemed to pour evil onto everything they looked upon, but they did. Then he smiled, and gooseflesh rippled across my skin with the speed of the lightning flash that finally showed me what Adrian had already seen: half a dozen demons flying behind Blinky. Three were covered in eyes and had those extra sets of wings, letting me know that they were seraphs, too. Wherever they flew, the darkness around them thickened until it felt like it had tangible form.

"Go for Blinky and the other seraphs first. They're the most dangerous," Adrian said, pulling out two long knives from a weapons satchel that Brutus also had attached to his harness. He couldn't kill the demons with those, but he could slow them down, and then I could finish them.

But I couldn't risk a strike with the sling until they were close, and letting seven demons get that close was almost suicidal. Still, we had no choice. I spun the sling faster.

Two of the seraphs broke formation and disappeared into the clouds that kept all sunlight at bay and thus allowed them to come out before nightfall. Adrian said something in Demonish to Brutus, who turned his back to us and thrust his wings out in chop formation. Now our backs were guarded.

Adrian took point to the left several feet away, giving me ample room for my sling. I kept spinning it faster, my gaze darting around as I waited for one of the demons to get close enough to attack. Strangely, I wasn't afraid. Maybe it was because I hadn't come this far only to get killed by *demons*. If anything was going to kill me, it was going to be that damn spearhead!

With a speed I didn't believe possible, two of the seraphs suddenly torpedoed into Adrian with such force that it left a hole where he'd been standing. The hole was so deep that I couldn't see him anymore, but I saw the madly flapping wings and hideous numerous eyes of the seraphs. I was in the process of hurling a stone at them when agony exploded in my body. The last thing I remember was seeing dirt explode all around me while a third grinning, eye-covered seraph filled the rest of my vision.

CHAPTER THIRTY-TWO

THE PAIN WAS so ferocious, it must have briefly knocked me unconscious. That was all I could figure when I looked up and the hideous seraph was gone. Instead, all I saw was dirt. It covered me so much that I had to blink several times to see anything else. Then that ominous black sky met my vision. I was in the hole that had been made when the seraph used the force of his attack to plow a deep furrow into the ground. If I didn't have a supernatural lineage that made me far tougher than the average human, I would be dead twice over.

Apparently, the seraph thought I had been killed. I caught a glimpse of him dancing around the perimeter of my hole, his wings reminding me of three sets of eye-dotted elephant ears.

"Dead!" the seraph howled in glee. "Dead, dead, dead!"

Not yet, although I'd never felt worse, and that was saying something. My head rang, and my spine and ribs felt like they had been replaced with razors that shredded me with every breath, yet I was still alive. That was the good news.

The bad news was that Adrian didn't know I was alive, and if I called out to tell him, the demon would finish me off. I had to take him out first, yet right now, I didn't know if I could move.

"No!" Adrian roared, followed by an answering bellow of rage from Brutus. Then all I heard were the awful sounds of a fierce battle that I couldn't see.

I'm coming! I silently swore to them, biting my lip to keep from screaming as I tried to sit up. Blood gurgled from my mouth, my breathing cut off and I collapsed almost instantly. After I managed to take a few searing breaths, I realized my ribs were *definitely* broken, and from the fresh agony shooting through my left arm, it probably was, too. This was very, very bad. How could I save myself if I couldn't even sit up?

Then I saw the sling, slithering toward me through the dirt like a golden snake. It gave me the courage to force myself to ignore the pain and try to sit up again. That crushing feeling returned and I hemorrhaged more blood out of my mouth. One of my lungs must be punctured or collapsed, but there was manna in the satchel Adrian had strapped onto Brutus. If I could take the seraph out, I had a chance to get it and heal myself.

But first, I had to kill the seraph, and I couldn't spin the sling to release one of those lethal stones without sitting up. It wouldn't work if I just lashed him with the sling. Yes, that would hurt him, but I needed the seraph dead. Not wounded.

The seraph was still dancing around what he thought was my grave. His back was to me, but he had eyes all over that, too. Right now, they were looking away, but when I tried moving again, they suddenly shifted in my direction. I stilled, hoping the dirt I was having a hard time seeing through concealed me enough to hide the fact that I was still alive.

"Davidian is dead, dead, dead," he chanted in a sing-song voice. "Dead, dead, dead!"

My relief that he still hadn't spotted the error of his assumption lasted only a second. Then the sound Adrian made tore through me with the same impact as the seraph's crater-making blow. It wasn't merely of rage, pain or grief. It was something so far beyond the three, it chilled me as if I were in the belly of a blast freezer. It also caused the seraph to look away from me with all his dozens of eyes, which then widened in what could only be called fear.

I didn't know what had freaked out one of the most powerful creatures in existence, but this was my chance. I grabbed the sling, feeling a familiar jolt as soon as I touched it. My agony was already so intense, it didn't even hurt like it usually did. Instead, it filled me with a welcoming surge of energy. I drew upon that while digging one of the rocks from my pockets. Then, with a breath that I held instead of exhaled, I forced myself into a sitting position.

Pain stabbed through every inch of my torso. My chest felt like it was being crushed. I fought to quell the crippling aspects of my anguish and the instinctive panic that came with not being able to breathe. If I did this right, it wouldn't take long. I notched the sling and spun it as best I could while in a deep ditch with a broken arm, broken ribs, lots of internal bleeding and nonfunctioning lungs. The sling flopped around awkwardly, not having enough circulation or torque to hurl the stone. It was enough to get the seraph's attention, though. All those eyes on his back shifted my way, widened in surprise and then narrowed with murderous purpose.

"You're dead!" he shouted as he spun around.

Not yet! I thought back defiantly, and found the

strength to spin the sling fast enough to hurl the stone at him.

I'd always wondered if the supernatural power that had made the sling unbeatable when I first wielded it meant it also couldn't miss its target. When my badly flung stone still hit the seraph between his many sets of eyes, I got my answer. The sling didn't need me to be skilled at wielding it, apparently. It only needed me to have strength enough to try, and then it could take things from there.

The seraph exploded into embers that shone brightly for a moment before fading into ashes. Seeing it reminded me of a fireworks display burning out, but I didn't pause to savor the image. I slumped down long enough to get in some desperate breaths of air and got more stones out of my pockets, too. I was notching one into the sling when a roar filled the air.

"Ivvvvvyyyyy!"

That couldn't be Adrian. It sounded inhuman, as if the thunder that had been booming in the stormy black sky had been given a voice. Yet who else would scream my name? Brutus couldn't talk, and the demons always called me Davidian.

The ground shook, then a form was hurled over the top of my ditch. It happened so fast, I couldn't see who or what it was. Then more dirt began blasting me from every direction and the ground shook even harder.

I sat up and tried to spin the sling as fast as I could. Then I lowered it and let out a wordless cry as Brutus appeared above the ditch. Dark demon blood spattered him as if he'd been showering in it, and I saw deep tears in his wings, body and arms, too. Unbelievably, his gorilla-like face looked happy, and he gave me a joyous lick before hauling me out of the ditch.

The movement drove what little breath I had out of my lungs. It also caused such new agony that my vision started to darken and an ominous ringing filled my head. I tried to reach the satchel attached to Brutus's harness before I passed out. If that happened before I got the manna, I might not wake up.

By the time I grasped the satchel, my vision was completely black and that ringing had deafened me to everything else. My mind was starting to go, too, but with the last amount of mental clarity I had, I felt around inside the satchel. Knives cut into me, telling me Adrian had left some weapons behind, but I ignored that and kept blindly searching for the cellophane bag of manna. When I thought I had it, I grabbed a handful of its contents, stuffed it into my mouth and swallowed.

If this was the bag filled with Adrian's blessed communion wafers instead of manna, I was a dead woman.

Fireballs erupted inside my chest. I cried out and got in the first full breath of air I'd had since the seraph plowed me deep into the earth. My vision also cleared with the suddenness of a light switch being flipped on, and the ringing stopped, too. I had gambled on eating the manna because all my injuries were internal instead of external, and that gamble had paid off. Even my broken arm stopped throbbing, and when I took in another deep breath, the pain in my lungs and ribs was gone, too.

Then new sounds filled my ears with the same volume and intensity as that threatening, you're-about-to-pass-out ringing. They were shrieks, and they were coming from up ahead.

I turned as much as I could manage while still being clutched to Brutus's chest by one of the gargoyle's massive arms. He used the other as a club to pummel any demon who got close to us, but there weren't that many of them anymore. Once I found the source of the shrieks, the reason why was clear. I stared, unable to believe what I was seeing.

Adrian stood about twenty yards away. Like Brutus, he was covered in demon blood, his blood and multiple injuries, but that was not what had me staring while my mind froze with shock. It wasn't even the seraph on his knees in front of Adrian, his wings being ripped off while his many eyes were being strafed with countless thin, dark knives that went all the way through.

It was the shadows surrounding Adrian. At first, I'd thought they were part of a dark fog, or maybe even a case of the demonically formed clouds descending until they covered the ground around him. But when I saw those shadows form into knifelike shapes that kept tearing into the seraph until nothing remained of him except a pile of smoldering ashes, I knew what they were. And I totally understood why the seraph I'd killed had looked terrified.

He hadn't been afraid of me. He'd been afraid of Adrian, and he'd had damned good reason to be.

"You have Demetrius's shadows."

My voice was raw from more than my recent brush with death. Adrian's head snapped up, and I gasped. Even his eyes seemed to have a dark haze over them, as if the shadows weren't just emanating from behind him like a living, malevolent cloak, but were inside him, too.

Then he looked up, and I followed his gaze to see

Blinky hovering about fifty yards above him. The demon looked back and forth between me and Adrian, his expression reflecting equal parts rage and frustration.

"You still live," he said to me with naked hatred.

I squirmed until Brutus put me down. I wanted plenty of room to hurl a stone at him, if he came any closer.

"I would stop looking at her if I were you."

Adrian's voice was light, yet it vibrated with all the unexpected power that caused me to stare at him in continued disbelief. I knew his half-demon side had gifted Adrian with unusual strength, speed and agility, making him by far the deadliest Judian to ever walk the earth. But I had never thought he'd inherited the ability to manifest Demetrius's deadly, infamous shadows. I hadn't even known such a thing was possible.

Neither had Blinky, from the way he regarded Adrian with a wariness he'd never before displayed. He also made sure to keep well out of reach of those dark, lethal swaths that could form into whatever weapon Adrian wanted.

"Why do you continue to fight us?" Blinky asked, his demeanor suddenly changing from hateful to conciliatory. "Never has it been more clear what side you belong with, Adrian."

"I belong with her," Adrian said, his shadows starting to flare and swirl. "And you nearly killed her."

"It wasn't me," Blinky began.

"Yes, you!" Adrian roared while his shadows struck out like soaring knives. Blinky flinched even though he was out of reach, then he stopped trying to win Adrian over and looked at me.

"Don't you wonder how I found you, Davidian?"

Actually, yes, now that he mentioned it. I hadn't had time to ponder that before, what with getting my insides pureed by the pile-driving seraph, but it was a good question.

"How did you?"

"Remember when Adrian repeatedly lashed me with the cloths that had covered Moses's staff?" he asked in a silky tone.

Adrian smiled. "Good times."

I wouldn't have said that. I was still trying to forget what happened to an eye-covered demon when you keep flinging a highly hallowed object onto him. Gross, gross, gross.

"The damage left scars," Blinky said, briefly extending all six of his wings before flapping them to stay aloft again. That glimpse revealed hardened, burned-looking patches all over him, and I mean *all* over.

"Nasty," Adrian said with obvious pleasure. "Remember why I did that to you? Because you were tormenting Ivy. Guess how much I'm going to hurt you now that you tried to kill her?"

"But if you kill me, then you'll never know how we were able to find the Davidian," Blinky all but purred.

What was Blinky up to? Yes, I wanted to know how he had found me, but why would he tell us? It wouldn't cause Adrian to show him mercy; he couldn't have been blunter about his desire to kill Blinky. The demon wasn't trying to kill us at the moment, either. He couldn't risk getting closer. My slingshot and now Adrian's shadows were lethal to demons, as one very dead seraph could attest. Yet Blinky wasn't running away so he could regroup and attack with reinforcements later. That would have made the most sense, and Blinky wasn't dumb, yet here he was, gabbing away like we were all girlfriends at a slumber party…

"He's stalling," I said, looking around in quick, jerky glances that still allowed me to keep one eye on Blinky. "Other demons must already be on the way."

"Look who isn't as stupid as I've always believed her to be," a hated and familiar voice drawled from the river.

I spun around, already hurling a stone. It sailed true, yet Demetrius was out of its range. It splashed into the water several feet in front of him, and he glanced at the ripples it made with contempt.

"Once again, you fail, Davidian."

Then he looked at Adrian and his expression changed, mirroring the same shock I'd felt when I first saw those shadows haloing him with tangible, deadly darkness. Finally, a slow smile spread across Demetrius's features.

"I have never been more proud of you."

The compliment didn't sway Adrian. His new shadows flared. "Come closer and tell me that."

Demetrius responded to the death threat with his smile sliding into a smirk. "No, thank you, my son. Tell me, how long have you been concealing that magnificent power?"

"Didn't know I had it until today," Adrian replied, his voice becoming tight. "The shadows burst out of me when one of the seraphs said he'd killed Ivy."

"Ivy." Demetrius spat my name out as if it tasted foul. "She ruins everything, including this father-son moment. When will you give up on the little Davidian? She is doomed."

Adrian's shadows grew and began to swirl faster,

until they resembled a group of tightly clustered tornadoes behind him. It reminded me so much of Demetrius when he'd been at full power that it was stunning. Adrian no longer looked half-demon. He looked one-hundred-percent demon, and the sight of it shook me.

"I'll never give up on her," he growled to Demetrius, that dark haze over his eyes changing until the silver rings around his irises flashed. "Never."

And screw how scary he looked! He was still Adrian. That meant he was mine lock, stock and now shadow-loaded barrel.

Demetrius sighed again. "My strong, foolish son, even with your glorious manifestation of my powers, you have no chance to save her. You are completely outnumbered."

I looked behind us toward the outskirts of the city, but no one was there. No one else was in the sky except Blinky, and Demetrius was all alone in the river... Aw, *shit*. No, he wasn't.

At least two dozen more heads broke the water to line up behind Demetrius. Some were human looking, but Demetrius wouldn't have brought regular humans as backup. If I had any doubts that he'd brought a demon horde with him, the misshappen and horned heads among them cleared that up.

"As I was saying," Demetrius continued. "You are completely outnumbered, and the Davidian is doomed."

"No," said an unexpected voice behind us. "She is not."

CHAPTER THIRTY-THREE

I WHIRLED, THE TENSION of the situation causing me to hurl a stone even though I'd recognized his voice. Thankfully, the rock bounced harmlessly off Zach's chest, proving that hallowed weapons can't harm Archons. Zach looked at the stone, then at me, and a single dark brow arched.

"You could have simply said hello."

I also could have hugged him. Demetrius had stopped his advance from the river as soon as he saw Zach. Getting his ass kicked by the Archon once before had been an experience that Demetrius clearly didn't want to repeat, and seeing it made me so happy that I got cocky.

"What's that about me being doomed?" I taunted Demetrius.

If Demetrius was rethinking his attack, Blinky wasn't. "You hesitate because of one Archon?" he asked him with open scorn.

"He is no normal Archon," Demetrius replied darkly.

"I am a seraph," Blinky hissed, more to Zach this time now. "No Archons were greater in power, and I have even more power now. Who are you to think that you can stand against me?"

Zach pulled off his faded blue hoodie, which made

me blink because I had never seen him do that before. I barely had time to notice the plain T-shirt he wore underneath it before that was thrown aside, too. Then he reached behind him, and when I saw the skin around his face bunch up while light burst from the back of his head, I knew what was coming next and flung my arm over my eyes while squeezing them shut.

Not even that blocked out the explosion of light as Zach discarded the human suit he wore and revealed his true form. I didn't look because I'd seen him like this once before. From the few glimpses I'd caught, Zach's true form looked like someone had stitched together lightning bolts and blindingly bright solar flares to form a winged, vaguely humanoid shape that, like the sun, was impossible to look at for more than a few seconds.

I heard shouts in Demonish, then splashes, and guessed that at least some of the demons in the river were beating a retreat.

"Michael," I thought I heard Blinky say, but his voice was drowned out by all the other shouts in Demonish. Then I heard him again, far more clearly this time, and that same name was echoed by other voices, as well. *"Michael. It's Michael!"*

"Michael." Hatred dripped from Demetrius's voice. "I should have known when you muted my shadows in the desert. Only an archangel has that power, yet I couldn't believe you'd lower yourself to masquerade as a mere errand boy to mortals."

"I do what I am commanded," Zach replied, still in that mild tone. "If you had, you would never have fallen so low."

"Michael," Adrian said, shock in his voice. I risked a

glance in his direction, although I still used my arm as a shield. It was hard to see Adrian through the dazzling bursts of light that continued to erupt from Zach, but from the glimpses I caught, he had backed away, too.

"You're not only a secret archangel, are you?" Adrian continued, his tone turning accusing. "The archangel Michael is also supposed to be the general of heaven's armies, right?"

"Yes," Zach—*Michael*—said. "And that is why none here can defeat me."

That seemed to be the overall opinion, judging from the tiny glimpses I caught between squints. Adrian wasn't the only one who'd backed up at this revelation. All the other demons had, too, and I didn't even see Brutus anymore. All that light bursting out of Zach must have looked like his worst nightmare.

But maybe it wasn't just Zach's newly disclosed, archangel-plus-general status that kept them back. It might also be the light shooting from him in a wide enough circle to encompass me, too. Light hurt demons, and Zach had *all* the watts going off.

"Leave the Davidian and get Adrian instead," Demetrius suddenly said. "Wherever he goes, she will follow."

"Stop them!" I told Zach when Blinky and the rest of them began to converge on Adrian, who was well out of reach of Zach's light show. His shadows weren't out anymore, either. They'd gone from resembling a cluster of terrifying tornadoes to no more than a dark outline around him. Zach's explosion of light had muted Demetrius's shadows once before, too. Adrian had nothing left to fight with except his fists, and against over two dozen demons, that wouldn't be enough.

"Zach, hurry!" I said. "You need to get Adrian under your light, too!"

But Zach made no move to include Adrian in the bursts of light that were keeping the other demons away from me. He also didn't walk toward him so that Adrian would be safe within the dazzling glow around him. Worse, from their triumphant bellows, the demons realized that. Zach was leaving Adrian on his own to fight them. Again.

Well, I wasn't about to stand back and watch Adrian get beaten and abducted by demons. I started to run toward Adrian, my sling out and spinning, when an unbreakable grip on my arm hauled me back. I struggled against Zach with everything I had, but I soon found out that it was useless. I'd have a better chance at ripping my own arm off than at breaking an archangel's grip.

"I was not sent here for him." The calmness in Zach's tone lit my every fuse as he confirmed his refusal to help. "I was only sent to ensure your safety."

"*Now* your boss wants me alive?" I asked bitterly. That would've been great under other circumstances, but not if it meant leaving Adrian behind to get kidnapped.

"At the moment," he replied with infuriating casualness.

"You can't do this, Demetrius!" I shouted, switching tactics and trying to appeal to the demon's love for Adrian. "They won't stop at trying to kidnap him. They'll kill him!"

"Then I'll raise him," Demetrius shot back coldly. "This isn't like before, when I expended too much of my power spilling a realm into your world. I can bring him back easily now."

I'd forgotten that a select number of powerful demons could raise the dead the same way Archons could. If memory served, Demetrius had even told Adrian he'd already done that after Adrian's former drug addiction caused him to overdose. But that only increased the danger Adrian was in. They'd tear into him without concern for consequences.

Zach might be able to watch this happen, but I couldn't. The demons had manipulated the weather enough to form a sun-blocking barrier. I could use the staff to tear it down and flood this area with light. We had an hour left before night fell. It should be enough.

The first horde of demons jumped Adrian. I dropped the sling, pulled my sweater off, grabbed the staff tattoo with both hands and then yanked on it as hard as I could.

The staff came out of me with a burst of pain that brought me to my knees. I didn't care, so I didn't pause before holding the staff over my head and pointing it at the sky. Then I let all that lovely, agonizing energy pour through me as I screamed out one word.

"Clear!"

Power blasted through the staff before boomeranging back into me. An even more intense pain knocked me all the way over and also left me blind and dazed. A new, echoing sound reverberated everywhere, and I wasn't sure if it was a sonic boom from the staff's explosion of energy, or something else, but it was loud enough to deafen me. Then another surge of power knocked me completely out.

CHAPTER THIRTY-FOUR

I COULDN'T HAVE been out long, which was a vast improvement over the last time I used the staff and it put me into a coma. When I opened my eyes, a blindingly bright sun was above me and there wasn't a single cloud left in the sky. The sight of it made me smile even though I was still in a great deal of pain. Then I smelled the nasty odor of burned meat and looked around to see where it was coming from.

Bad idea.

Both my hands and arms had split open, and the blackened flesh around them was still smoking. I hadn't imagined the power of the staff overloading my body like an electrical surge shooting through insufficient wiring. My hands and arms looked like I'd been trying to bitch slap a lightning bolt. Any other day, I would have been horrified at the sight, but at the moment, I was too tired. Using the staff had taken too much out of me. All I could muster up was a weary thought of *I really hope we have enough manna left to heal this.*

"Ivy!"

Adrian appeared above me, his face even more blood-spattered than it had been before, but seeing him let me know that I wasn't too tired to feel relief.

"Are the demons...gone?" I managed to rasp.

"Yes, but don't try to talk," he said, his head whipping around. "Zach! Zach! *Michael!* Ivy's hurt! Where are you?"

"Retrieving your beast," a calm voice said from farther away. "Not only does he have the manna you need, he also has the lance that cannot be allowed to fall into the wrong hands."

"Be right back," Adrian told me, and disappeared.

I closed my eyes. I might be too exhausted to get worked up over the state of my hands and arms, but I had no desire to keep looking at them. And I'd thought Blinky's burns were the grossest thing I'd seen. Karma was quick to get me this time.

Moments later, Adrian returned. Then I bit my lips to keep from screaming as he spread manna over the large, burned rents in my left arm. To my credit, I managed to stay silent through his treatment of that one, but when he started on my right arm, the damage must have been worse or I was all out of willpower. Either way, a shriek escaped me that I couldn't stuff back.

"You could heal her instantly," Adrian growled, and I opened my eyes. His shadows had all but disappeared earlier, but now that Zach had put his human suit back on, they were flickering down Adrian's back like a living, growing cape.

Zach—I'd never learn to call him Michael—gave the shadows a look that, on anyone else, I'd translate as *You think you're threatening me? Bitch, please!* "These few extra moments won't matter in her overall healing."

Easy for someone to say whose arm wasn't currently resembling a hot dog left too long on the grill. But it was useless to point that out, not to mention ungrateful. Zach had saved both of us today by showing up.

If I berated him about not doing more to save Adrian, he'd probably remind me that he hadn't needed to. I'd had all the necessary power myself. Granted, if it had occurred to me to blast the clouds away sooner, we wouldn't have needed Zach's intervention at all, but better late than never as far as that inspiration went.

"Thank you," I whispered, and I wasn't only saying it to Adrian, who'd finished smearing manna on my arm. I was also saying it to Zach.

"You shouldn't stop at thanking me," Zach said, a gentle reprimand in his tone. "I was sent here, remember?"

I closed my eyes. My complicated feelings over how Zach seesawed between helping us and refusing to help us didn't begin to touch the tangle of emotions I felt when I thought of his boss. Yet Zach was right. I was quick with my complaints, yet I had rarely thanked the Great Being when Zach's actions helped us.

I kept my eyes closed, but in my mind, I directed them upward. *Thank you*, I thought, surprised when that simple acknowledgment released a slew of emotions I'd been trying not to feel. *You've saved us a lot through Zach, and through other people, too. I really am grateful, but to be honest, I'm also mad at you. You didn't save my parents, or my birth mother, or my bio dad, or Tomas, or all the other people who were much better and more deserving than me. And why did you let me fall in love with Adrian, only to take me away from him so soon? I know you're not cruel, but why do you let so many terrible things happen? There's so much pain in the world. Do you not care? And if you do care, why don't you do something about it?*

My tears increased with every question, until they

drenched my cheeks. At the same time, I was inwardly cringing. So much for displaying some long-overdue gratitude! I hadn't intended to turn my thanks into an indictment, yet I had, and if there was one thing I knew, it was that the supernatural was real and pissing it off had consequences. If a lightning bolt suddenly struck me, I wouldn't have been surprised.

"You're not going to be struck by a lightning bolt."

That's right. Zach could hear everything. I opened my eyes, expecting him to be glaring at me, since he was pretty defensive over his boss. That was why it surprised me to find that his dark gaze was kind.

"He doesn't strike people down for being honest about their questions, doubts and pain," Zach continued. "He already knows everything you're feeling, so there's no secret to be kept by refusing to bring your struggles to Him."

I glanced at the sky, embarrassed that moments ago, I had half expected to see a lightning bolt at the ready, or a cloud formation in the shape of an upraised fist.

"Good to know," I said softly. "But I'm not going to get any answers, am I?"

"Not the way you want." Zach's gaze was steady. "As I told you before, sometimes you have to believe before you can see, and some things can never be seen this side of eternity."

Cop-out, I thought. He might as well have said that cliché "mysterious ways" line, too.

Zach's mouth curled. "I still can, if you like."

"Save it," I said, gripping Adrian's hand now that mine had finally healed enough to do so. "We need to get this stick and ourselves back on hallowed ground before the sun sets. Hey, speaking of the stick, you said before that the spearhead was all that was left of the weapon. What's up with that?"

Zach gave me a sardonic look. "Archons do not know everything. When I told you that the spearhead was all that remained, I believed it. I only found out when I was ordered to direct you to this place that the shaft of the weapon still remained."

I snorted. "Guess it's nice to know that humans aren't the only ones kept in the dark. Well, as I was saying, we need to get ourselves and this stick back to hallowed ground right away, unless you can pull us into a light realm?" I added hopefully.

That slight curl wiped from Zach's mouth, leaving it in a thin, straight line. "I cannot."

I blew out a sigh. "Orders, huh?"

Zach nodded, and I reminded myself that he'd already helped us plenty. He'd probably end up helping us again later, too, so—

"I will not help you again," Zach stated. "It has been ordered." Then, incredibly, something like sadness flickered across Zach's features. "And without my help, both of you will likely meet the same fate."

My breath expelled from me as if I'd been punched. The finality of his words couldn't be clearer. He wasn't just saying that we were on our own from now on. He was saying *both* of us were going to die.

Adrian's hand tightened on mine. When I looked at him, the grimness in his features told me that he'd come to the same conclusion. But he smiled when he met my eyes, and when he spoke, his tone was light.

"It's fine. I never wanted to outlive you anyway, and now I know I won't have to. Hell, I'm relieved."

"Adrian, I..." My voice cracked under the weight of everything I wanted to say.

He squeezed my hand again, then let it go to stroke my face. "Don't. It's taken me too long, but I finally believe that you, Costa and Zach are right. This fight is too important for us to sit out." His mouth twisted. "Besides, long before I met you, I swore I'd do anything to even the score between me and demons. You're giving me the chance to do that. Don't feel guilty, Ivy. I've waited a long time to make them pay."

How could he tell me not to feel guilty? By being with me, he was heading right to his own death. He didn't want me to feel bad about that? How could I *not* feel bad about that?

"Don't cry," he whispered, leaning forward until his forehead touched mine. "Maybe being tied to the Davidian-heritage light has finally started making a difference in me. Otherwise, I'd be screaming at you not to do this, or scheming to stop you, but instead, I want us to finish this. Together."

I threw my arms around him and kissed him. Words failed, so I tried to tell him with my body and my lips that I was in awe of his bravery, that I was so sorry we had so little time left together and that I would love him forever because the rest of my life wasn't nearly enough to cover it.

He kissed me back with the same intensity. Soon, I forgot that we had an Archon audience. Didn't care that we were still covered in our blood, demon blood and demon ash. Didn't mind that his shadows were wrapping around me in a dark embrace to draw me closer, or that we had less than an hour left until the sun was down. There was only the two of us. Nothing else mattered.

Far too soon, Adrian drew away, smiling again as he brushed the tears from my cheeks. "Don't think about tomorrow or the next day," he whispered. "However many hours, days or weeks we have left, we're going to make them count. I promise you."

Then he turned to Zach, who hadn't left, to my surprise. He'd already said his version of goodbye, and he'd never been big on watching me and Adrian make out, so I expected him to be gone. Yet there he was.

"You can't take us into a light realm, but do me a favor," Adrian said in a steady tone. "Take Brutus. Give him to Costa, and tell Costa to split what's in my bank accounts with Jasmine. There's enough to take care of both of them for the rest of their lives, plus keep Brutus in plenty of high-end raw meat."

Another sob clawed its way up my throat, but this time, I held it there. I couldn't keep breaking down no matter if it felt as if my heart were being repeatedly ripped out. Adrian was going through everything that I was, yet he was holding it together. I had to hold it together, too.

"Please," I said to Zach, and also echoed the plea silently in the direction of where his orders came from.

Moments later, to my relief, Zach nodded. "I will do it."

Thank you, I thought with a glance upward. Then, even though it hadn't been Zach's call, I said it to him, too.

"Thank you. Just give us a minute to say goodbye to him."

"Brutus," Adrian called out, and the gargoyle reluctantly came out from under the nearby tree that had been shading him.

I drew in a deep breath. *Don't cry*, I told myself sternly. *It'll only upset Brutus, and he's already not going to like this.*

Yet when he came out, giving first a wary look at the sun and then a baleful one at me for forcing him to be out in it, I felt new tears roll down my cheeks. To cover them, I smiled at Brutus and gestured for him to bend down so I could hug him.

He did at once. He might be unhappy about the sun, but he'd never turn down a good cuddle. My arms couldn't make it around his big body, of course, but now my tear-streaked face was hidden in his chest as I gave his wings, his ears and the back of his head a good scratch.

"Who's the best boy?" I told him, fighting to keep my voice from breaking. "You are. You're the smartest, best, most handsome gargoyle in the world, yes you are—yes you are!"

He began to wiggle with joy. I continued to pet, scratch and praise him, knowing the time until dark was drawing nearer, yet also knowing that this would be my last chance.

"I am going to miss you so much, but I know Costa will take great care of you."

My heart squeezed when a whine came out of him. He'd understood that, and when Adrian said something else to him in Demonish, Brutus's whine turned into a wail.

"It's okay," I said quickly while Adrian continued to talk to him in Demonish. He put his arms around

Brutus and his face against the gargoyle's while he spoke to him in soothing tones.

I didn't understand the words, but I knew when Brutus accepted what Adrian was telling him. His head dropped onto Adrian's shoulder, and his great body heaved out what could only be called a dry sob.

I had to look away so I didn't dissolve into tears. Adrian had been given Brutus right after the gargoyle was born. He told me once that Brutus used to be so small, he could carry him around as if he were a baby, and that later, Brutus had broken everything in his house while he was first learning to fly. If leaving him was hurting me this much and I'd known him only less than a year, I couldn't imagine what it was doing to Brutus and to Adrian, who'd been together for decades.

"You'll be fine," Adrian finished in English, chucking Brutus under his chin. "Costa doesn't realize it, but you'll have him wrapped around your talons in no time flat. Jasmine, too, I'll bet."

"Adrian," Zach said quietly.

He glanced up at the sky, which was turning a softer shade of indigo as the sun dipped lower. "I know." He sighed.

I gave Brutus a kiss on the side of his face and didn't pull away when he slimed both my cheeks with a lick. "Love you, Brutus," I said, then forced myself to walk away without a backward glance. If I looked back, I'd lose the last shred of control that I had, and there was no time left for that.

I felt a hand on my shoulder while still hearing Adrian say his final goodbyes, so I knew it wasn't his.

"Thank you," I said to Zach. "I know you'll say you only did what you were ordered to, but you still saved us, helped us, revealed things to us and, every once in a while, just talked to us, too. That means a lot to me, and I'm sorry I didn't say that enough before now."

His hand stayed on my shoulder. "You've often questioned why you were chosen to be the last of the Davidians. I, too, have wondered that same thing many times."

Thanks a lot, I thought with an internal sniff.

Then Zach's voice deepened. "Know this, Ivy Jenkins—I don't wonder it any longer."

A choked sound escaped me. "Thanks," I said with awed sincerity. "That's probably the best compliment I'll ever get."

His hand left my shoulder. "As I told you before, I do not indulge in idle compliments. I only state what I know to be true. Farewell, Ivy."

"Goodbye, Zach—"

I turned around, but he was already gone. So was Brutus. From the stunned look on Adrian's face, they'd both disappeared without any warning. All that was left was Brutus's harness, the satchel that had been attached to it and the stick that used to form the base of a two-thousand-year-old Roman weapon that had been used in the most famous execution in history.

Adrian looked around as if making sure that Brutus and Zach were really gone. Then a short, mirthless laugh left him.

"I don't know why I'm surprised. Zach had never been big on saying goodbye."

I forced out a false laugh. "Archons, right?"

I wasn't about to tell Adrian that Zach had said an unexpectedly thorough and kind goodbye to me. Adrian didn't deserve to feel left out any more than he already did. I didn't know why, either. Adrian was sacrificing just as much as I was, if not more. Why couldn't Zach have told him that before he left?

He'd been blunt about the fact that he wasn't coming back, so of course, I wouldn't get an answer. Instead, I went to Adrian and linked my hand with his. He squeezed back at once, then let go to pick up the satchel and sling it around his neck.

"Don't forget to grab the pilum," he said, not touching it.

As if I would. I took it, noticing then that the slingshot and the staff had resumed their normal position as tattoos on my body at some point. I hadn't noticed them returning, but I'd had a lot to claim my attention. I pulled my sweater back on and checked to make sure that I still had rocks in my pockets, then nodded to Adrian that I was ready.

We had two and a half out of the three hallowed weapons we needed to finish this. Now, on to finding the rest of the third one, although we couldn't start our search until morning. I looked at the deepening indigo sky and shivered. It would be dark soon, and the demons would be back. Guaranteed.

"Where to now?" I asked Adrian.

He glanced at the sky as if judging exactly how many minutes of sunlight we had left. "I know just the place."

CHAPTER THIRTY-FIVE

WE DIDN'T GO back to the Aula Palatina. After part of the ceiling had fallen out and three of the guards had been flattened by a gargoyle disguised as a seagull, it would invite too much chaos to return. To avoid dealing with hiding inside a church, mosque or synagogue and risk being caught and kicked out, Adrian had chosen a cemetery as our hallowed ground for the night. We got there with ten minutes to spare before sundown, and it was large enough that I wasn't concerned about being spotted by the living. As for the dead, they didn't care that we were there, and right now, I appreciated the peace and quiet.

"How did you know about this place?" I asked as Adrian and I walked through what looked like the military burial section. I couldn't be sure because I couldn't read the German signs or inscriptions, but the headstones were all the same size and shape, plus they were laid out with grid-like precision.

He glanced at me. "I went here after I set fire to the Aula Palatina. I didn't want to go back to my realm, religious houses felt too foreign and I couldn't stay where I was."

I sighed. "I can only imagine how hard it must have been for you. It must have felt like everything you loved and believed in had shattered when you saw this world.

No wonder you flipped out and tried to burn that place down. Aside from your demon side subconsciously reacting to the pilum being there, it must have also felt cathartic to try to destroy something that conflicted with what you were taught."

"Some days," he said pensively. "But not that one. I came here in the 1940s." He led me to another section of the cemetery. This one had a brick-and-stone monument showing a man bent down on one knee, his upper body slumped forward as if in weary, helpless agony. The inscription on the base was in German again, so I couldn't read it.

"It's to mark the victims of Nazi tyranny." Adrian's tone held a grim note of remembrance. "You can bet Demetrius took me to see this world during the Holocaust. That indescribable cruelty, all those merciless slaughters…back then, it was easy to keep believing that demons were far better than humans."

I said nothing. During that period of time, it had been more true than not. It didn't excuse what demons were or everything they'd done before or afterward, but forgetting the depths of depravity that humanity could sink to only meant that we were more likely to sink to those depths again.

I gave a longer look at the statue of the broken, kneeling man that represented millions of oppressed, imprisoned and slaughtered Jews. With my Davidian lineage, if my biological mother's side of the family had been in Germany during that time, they might have been slaughtered, too. Instead, due to my Latina makeup, at some point, they must have migrated to Mexico or South America. They had survived, so I had survived, yet far too many had not.

I squared my shoulders as I continued to stare at the statue. I now had a chance to fight for others who were without hope because they were being oppressed and slaughtered. I might not be able to save all the ones trapped in the demon realms, but if I could save some, half or—dare I be so optimistic?—most, it would be more than worth it.

It was ironic; now that I'd reconciled myself to dying in this fight, I wasn't afraid of it or angry about it anymore. Instead, I only wanted to make sure that my death struck the blow to demons that I hoped it would.

But first, we had to find that spearhead and put the weapon back together. Only then would I have my best chance to blast a humans-only doorway into all the demon realms. Yet we still had five places left on our list to search, and the demons had managed to find us at the last two almost as soon as we arrived. For all I knew, they'd been tracking me this whole time, just like Adrian had been secretly tracking me when I went to Sweden. Blinky had even taunted us over how the demons now had a foolproof way to find us. They were probably letting us do all the hard work of finding it, then planned to rip it away and transform it into a weapon of unimaginable evil.

I couldn't let that happen. No more pauses for last kisses, goodbyes or regrets. As much as I loved Adrian, if we found that spearhead, I had to grab it and slam it onto the pilum as soon as I laid eyes on it. That was my best chance to make sure the demons couldn't use it for themselves. That statue represented the millions who'd died without having a chance to save the ones they loved, or strike a crushing blow against their enemies. I had those chances. They were slim, yes, but slim was still something, and I didn't intend to waste them.

Speaking of making the most of every remaining chance… "Is there anywhere a little more private in this cemetery that we can go to?"

Adrian gave me a startled look, as if that was the last question he'd expected from me. Yeah, our surroundings hardly lent themselves to romance, but we couldn't leave the cemetery, since it was after dark, and I wasn't about to waste one of our last remaining nights together.

To lighten the mood, I winked and said, "Don't look so shocked. They do call me Easy Ivy, remember?"

He laughed, and hearing it was like a balm on my soul. "No one's ever called you that except you."

"Then come here, and I'll give you a reason to call me it, too," I said in my most seductive voice.

His sapphire eyes glinted, but then he looked at the shadows cascading around him like a dark waterfall, and his expression clouded. "Ivy…I can't seem to make these go away."

"I don't care," I said, enunciating each word. "They're part of you, so that makes them beautiful to me."

A harsh sound escaped him. "I wish that were true, but they're his. Even now, I feel like they mean he's here, too."

I set the pilum down and came toward him. With every step, I slowly drew off my sweater, until I was clad only in my bra and pants when I stood before him.

"Demetrius is not here, and you might have inherited those shadows from him, but they are *not* his.

They're yours, and you proved that today by using them against him and other demons."

His gaze raked over me, but he made no move to touch me, and that wasn't like him.

I stared at him. "What's really bothering you?"

"I think I'm turning more demon than human," he whispered. "Earlier, I wanted to get close to you to protect you, but I couldn't because of these shadows. They burned and then exploded as soon as Zach's light touched them, and when that happened…I felt like I might explode, too."

I took in a deep breath but didn't drop my gaze. "I don't care if your demon side is outgrowing your humanity, Adrian. You could sprout horns next, and I still wouldn't care. None of that changes who *you* are." Then I shrugged even though I had never felt less flippant. "To me, it means that we can now fight demon with demon, and I say let's give them hell, pun intended."

He let out a strangled laugh, yet some of the stiffness left his frame. "How can you still believe in me so much?"

"Easy," I said, putting my arms around him and bringing my body flush against his. "You keep proving you're worth it."

He kissed me then, his mouth hot, hard and hungry. I kissed him back with equal need and closed my eyes, giving myself up to sensations and emotions that didn't hurt, for a change. At some point, he picked me up and carried me over to a tree-shaded grotto, where he used his clothes as a makeshift pallet. There, he made love to me with all the wildness of his demon side, followed by holding me with all the tenderness of his humanity as we lay panting in each other's arms.

"You see?" I said when his shadows continued to curl around me as if, like his hands, they couldn't stop caressing me. "*Definitely* more than one use for these."

His laughter was low, sensual and oh so enticing. "Now I don't mind them. You make everything better, Ivy."

That wasn't true, but to say I wasn't in an argumentative mood was to put it mildly. I was, however, in desperate need of a shower, I realized as I glanced down at myself. In addition to all the dirt and grime I'd already had on me, all the blood and ashes on Adrian had somehow transferred to me, too.

"Do I remember passing a fountain in this place?" I asked.

His brow rose. "A little one, why?"

"I need to wash some of this dirt, ash and blood off me, and a little fountain is better than nothing."

His mouth quirked. "Right now? What if I intend to get you dirty again very soon?"

"We need to get the pilum anyway," I said, poking him. "Wash now, play more later."

"Play more now," he murmured, grabbing me and flipping me over until he was on top of me. I mock struggled, but that was only so I could keep rubbing against him.

"Want to make sure I'm really, really dirty before my bird bath?" I teased.

His mouth lowered until he breathed his response into me. "Oh, Ivy. You have no idea."

We didn't make it to the fountain until the moon was very high in the sky. I stopped by the memorial statue to grab the pilum first, wanting it close even though no demon could cross onto this ground to take it. Even minions, should they guess where we were, would have less than a needle-in-a-haystack chance of finding it in this large, multi-acre cemetery. I'd left the pilum in a pile of autumn leaves, where it looked to be just another branch shed by one of the many trees in the area.

After I retrieved it, I made sure it didn't graze Adrian as we walked to the fountain. Once there, I set it down and used my hands to cup enough water to wash the many stains from my body. I did a decent enough job, but my clothes were another story. They'd need soap to get all the blood, ash and dirt out, and we didn't have any. Even still, I debated washing my sweater to lessen the worst of the stains against whether it would be dry by morning. What would be worse: walking around in a red-and-black-splattered top that might draw unwanted attention, or shivering in a partially clean wet one?

"We'll need to get new clothes tomorrow," I remarked, deciding against washing the sweater. I'd probably need it for warmth tonight. The temperatures had dropped a lot, and while Adrian and I could snuggle, a covering would still be nice.

He shrugged. "No problem. I still have cash in my pants."

I sat on the edge of the fountain, watching the ripples in the water diminish now that I wasn't grabbing handfuls of it.

"Good, but we'll need more for a plane ticket, and I hope you still have those slips of paper Zach gave us for ID."

He rummaged in his pocket for a moment. "Yep, still do."

Now we could fly to where we needed to go, since

Brutus was no longer with us. I stifled the instant pang of grief that came with knowing I'd never see him again. *No more regrets*, I reminded myself firmly. There was only moving forward.

The water stilled, revealing my reflection when I glanced down. My hair was a tangled mess, no surprise, and I'd apparently missed a large spot of dirt on my cheek. I wet my hand again and cleaned that off, waiting until the water stilled once more to see if I'd gotten all of it. Eh, most of it. Either way, I'd have to remember how well the water displayed my reflection. Normally, I used shiny metal surfaces as faux mirrors, but they were hazy, and more than once, I'd ended up with very erratically drawn eyeliner or lipstick. The water actually worked much better. Hope that didn't mean it was dangerous like mirrors were…

"Mirrors," I said aloud, an idea bursting into my mind.

Adrian frowned, not getting it. "There are no mirrors here, Ivy. You're safe. Even if there were, we're on hallowed ground—"

I gave him an impatient wave. "That's not what I mean. I'm saying that we should *use* them."

Now he really looked confused. "How?"

"What if you're right?" I said slowly. "What if your demon side *is* growing, or at least, getting much more powerful. Your shadows are proof of that, and maybe it also means you have other demon abilities lurking beneath the surface."

He regarded me warily. "What do you mean?"

At my steady stare, he finally got it. "Oh," he said simply. "I don't know if that will work. I've never tried it."

"You've never tried it because you didn't know until a few months ago that you were half-demon," I pointed out. "Since then, you've manifested new and ever increasing abilities, so if you think about it, there's no reason you shouldn't be able to travel through mirrors like demons do. And according to what you told me before, Demetrius could've yanked me into that bathroom mirror, so that means you should be able to pull me through with you, too."

Adrian said nothing for several minutes. I didn't break the silence. We were both mulling what this could mean.

"They wouldn't expect that," he said at last. "And if they are somehow able to track us, this might be the break we need to travel faster than they can catch up to."

I stood up, giving the reflective image of the water a last flick while thinking, *Thanks for the inspiration.*

CHAPTER THIRTY-SIX

DESTINY OR NO, and dirty and disheveled or no, as soon as dawn broke, I insisted that we get some food before we did anything else. We found a street vendor, and I wolfed down two plates of sides plus whatever greasy meat he'd been grilling in the back. No surprise, from how fast I ate plus the greasiness of the food, I was sick to my stomach soon afterward.

"I should've stuck to one meal, not fried, and eaten it slower," I told Adrian after I emerged from the thankfully close public bathroom. "That food came up as fast as it went down."

He gave me a worried look. "You still look pretty pale. Sure you want to try doing any of this today?"

"No time like the present." I'd stalled way too long as it was. "But I'd kill for some toast to help with the new acid in my stomach. Oh, and some, ah, fruit."

I stammered over that last word because I'd almost said watermelon, which was ridiculous. I didn't even like watermelon, and late September in Germany was hardly watermelon season, so I had no idea why it popped into my mind. And yet thoughts of that bright pink fruit suddenly consumed me, prompting my taste buds to nearly scream *Gimme!*

Well, too bad. Craving toast to soothe an upset stomach was one thing; inexplicable urges for *watermelon* could shove it.

"No watermelon," I said out loud, as if my sudden, senseless cravings needed both an internal and verbal rebuke.

Adrian's expression grew even more concerned. "Are you sure you're okay, Ivy?"

"Fine," I said in a firm tone. "Now, let's see if that fried-food peddler has any plain toast, and then let's get some new clothes so we don't scream *Demon attack survivors!* to any minions who might be in this city looking for us."

Adrian gave me another I'm-not-buying-that-you're-fine look, but he didn't argue as we went back to the street vendor. He didn't have toast, but he had hoagie buns, and I ate two of them far slower than I wanted to. Wow, I'd gone from ravenous to puking to ravenous again. Maybe my body was trying to stall even if my willpower had no intention of doing that.

Then we went in search of new clothes. We didn't go back to the same clothing store we'd been to yesterday. We might have been spotted there. The demons probably thought we'd left Trier, but still, no need to show up at the same places we'd been to yesterday if they were tracking us and knew we were here. Instead, we went to a clothing store that was so small and cramped, most of its walls were covered with merchandise instead of mirrors. Perfect.

I had covered the mirror as soon as I entered the dressing room to change into my new outfit, which was essentially an unstained version of my old one, since I went with a sweater and jeans again. After I was done, Adrian squeezed into the tiny dressing room and changed, too. Then he stuck his head over the top of the door but didn't open it.

"Stay here. I'm going to try this without you first."

"Oh, no, you're not," I snapped.

He gave a pointed look at the pilum, which most people seemed to regard as nothing more than a walking stick. "I have no idea what will happen when, or if, I go through the mirrors. We can't risk bringing that into it if we end up coming face-to-face with a bunch of demons. We also can't risk leaving it behind if that doesn't happen and this *does* work. We need a trial run first, Ivy, and I'm the only one who can do that."

My teeth ground together from how much I wanted to argue, but he was right. We couldn't risk the pilum until we knew what would happen inside the mirrors. Yes, we knew they worked as portals, but *how* was still up in the air. I hated to leave Adrian to find out on his own, but he wasn't defenseless. He had his shadows, which thankfully, no one here seemed to notice. Demetrius's shadows had been like that, too. Maybe they came with a natural version of demon glamour that made them invisible to regular humans. Either way, this was what it meant to put the mission above my own wants, so reluctantly, I nodded.

"Fine. I'll wait for you here."

"Wait by the exit," he told me. "I don't want you anywhere near this mirror if someone other than me comes out of it."

Once again, I didn't argue. "Be careful" was all I said.

He flashed me a smile that was far too impish for someone about to embark on a dangerous expedition with unknown outcomes and consequences. "Careful? Never. Ready? Yes."

Then his head disappeared from the top of the door, and I walked over to the front of the shop.

"He's trying on more outfits," I told the clerk, who had proved to speak enough English to understand that. Then, because I had no idea how long this would take and I didn't want him nosing around the dressing room, I added, "He's so indecisive. Best to leave him alone to figure out which one he likes."

"Ah, of course, *fraulein*."

The clerk busied himself at his register. It probably helped that we'd already paid for what we were wearing. Otherwise, he might have been less laid-back as the minutes started to tick by and Adrian still didn't emerge from the dressing room. When it was nearing the twenty-minute mark, he left his register and began to wander toward the back.

"Can you help me with this dress?" I blurted out, holding up the first garment close to me. "I…I'm not sure if this looks good with my coloring. What do you think?"

That stopped him, and I spent the next ten minutes acting as if I were in dire need of reassurances that yellow didn't make my skin look sallow. I bought that dress and another one, then lingered at the register in apparent indecisiveness over whether I wanted to add a pair of hoop earrings to my tally, or go with the plain stud ones.

"You pick which. I check on your husband now," the clerk told me in an exasperated tone.

I could understand why he was fed up, but he didn't know what being stressed out was. Each minute seemed to grab a new nerve ending of mine and pull on it. Now all of them felt like they were at the snapping point. It was no wonder I felt nauseous again, and I tried to use that to my advantage.

"I don't feel well," I said, putting a hand on my stomach for emphasis. "I think I'm going to be sick. Do you have a trash can or bucket? I don't want to get vomit on your nice clothes."

He was back by his counter in a flash. Moments later, a trash can was shoved in front of me. I was surprised when I made good on what had started out as a false, empty threat by using it. Ugh. Worry for Adrian plus that greasy mystery meat from earlier must have really done a number on me.

"Thank you," I said, accepting the tissue he handed me next. I wiped my mouth with it and tried to ignore the smell emanating from the trash can. It was so disgusting, I felt like I was going to hurl again.

That also didn't turn out to be an empty threat, and my hands were slightly shaking after I finished my second round of puking and wiped my face with another tissue.

"Sorry," I said in an uneven voice.

The clerk gave me a look that was still partly annoyed yet also laced with sympathy now. "Don't worry about it. Is this your first *kind*, *fraulein*?"

"Kind what?" I asked, not really caring about the answer. All my attention was on the fact that Adrian had been gone too long for things to be okay. Or did time pass differently in the mirrors, like it did in the realms?

"Child," he said, enunciating the word carefully.

That got my attention. "I'm not pregnant!"

His brows rose and he gave a meaningful glance at

the puke-filled trash can in front of me. "Are you certain, *fraulein*?"

"I think I would know," I said in a huffy tone, but then a question roared into my mind that shattered the confidence behind my borderline-snippy reply.

How long *had* it been since I'd had my last period? Not since Adrian and I had gotten back together, but that had only been for a few days. I thought back to the long train, boat and car trips from Montenegro to the Icehotel in Sweden. Nope, although Jasmine had gotten hers then, because she'd borrowed some of my tampons during the train ride when she couldn't get to a store.

Okay, so I must have gotten it right before that when we were staying at that villa in Vatican City, except…

Oh, shit. I didn't remember getting it there, either.

But I *couldn't* be pregnant! Adrian had had a vasectomy! It must be all the stress that caused me to skip one—okay, maybe two—periods. That had to be it, because weren't vasectomies a hundred percent effective against pregnancy?

Wait. Was anything a *hundred* percent effective?

In response to my inner query, I threw up again.

Moments later, the shop door flung open and Adrian came in. My first reaction was relief, then I was back to sheer, panicked denial. To hide the evidence of what might be morning sickness, I kicked the trash can beneath the space under the clerk's desk. Only once it was safely out of sight did I wonder why Adrian had come in through the front of the store instead of the mirror in the back. And why was he soaking wet, to the point that he dripped water all over the floor when he went straight to the back of the store?

I heard the distinct sound of glass shattering seconds

later, which had to be Adrian breaking the mirror in the dressing room. The clerk began sputtering out protests in German, but those stopped when Adrian threw a stack of bills on the counter that would more than cover the damage.

"Sorry," he muttered to the clerk. "But believe me, I did you a favor." Then he took my arm. "We have to hurry. They might not be far behind me."

In spite of the danger he implied, part of me was glad that Adrian hadn't seemed to notice how I'd been bent over a trash can when he entered the store. I grabbed the pilum and our satchel, then threw a hurried "Sorry, and thanks!" over my shoulder to the clerk, and left.

CHAPTER THIRTY-SEVEN

"USE YOUR POWER to find the nearest hallowed ground, Ivy," Adrian said as soon as we were outside.

I wanted to ask why he'd taken so long inside the mirror, why he was sure that "they" wouldn't be far behind and why he looked like he'd gone swimming in his clothes at some point, but I did none of those things. Instead, I stopped in the street, set the pilum down and sent my hallowed radar outward.

At first, no surprise, it kept being drawn to the pilum at my feet. After a few minutes, I was able to bypass that and zero in on the intangible thrum that denoted hallowed ground ahead.

"Follow me," I said, picking up the pilum. But as soon as I touched it again, the ultra-hallowed item jammed my radar toward the other place. I dropped it with a frustrated sigh.

"You'll have to carry it for this to work, Adrian."

He drew his soaked shirt off and used it as a make-shift glove to pick up the pilum. I tried to ignore his wince when he touched it and closed my eyes, sending my senses outward again. I found the other hallowed signature quicker this time and began to walk toward it even before opening my eyes again.

"This way."

It turned out to be a brand-new mosque, from what

seemed to be the equivalent of a grand-opening sign at the front of it. When we approached the entrance, we were greeted by a smiling older man, although his smile slipped when he looked at Adrian.

I doubted it was because of the shadows that the store clerk hadn't noticed. It was probably because Adrian was a large, bare-chested guy walking up to him brandishing a big stick. I'd stare at Adrian with mild alarm if I were him, too.

"Please help us," I said to the older man, hoping he understood English. "My husband chased a thief into the river to get my bag back, but they fought and... well, look at him."

Ugh, I inwardly groaned. I had to get better at making up believable excuses. Then again, the river was nearby, robberies happened everywhere and how else was I supposed to explain how I was clothed and bone-dry while Adrian was half-naked and soaking wet? I didn't even mention the stick. Hopefully, it would be chalked up to a weird American souvenir thing.

"Of course," the older man replied in very good English. "How terrible for you. Please, come inside. We have clean prayer clothes that he can change into."

We were escorted inside, and I breathed a sigh of relief when I felt the safety of hallowed ground envelop us. I was surprised when we were politely asked to remove our shoes, but I didn't argue, and we were given paper slippers so at least we weren't in bare feet. The greeter, who introduced himself as Hasan, again expressed his sympathies over our fake robbery attempt. Then he said something in Arabic to two younger men. Within moments, they came back with a long high-necked white garment that looked kinda like a dress, and with white pants.

"I'll be back as soon as I change," Adrian told me, setting the pilum by the bench that I'd been hustled over to. Then he cast a deliberate look at the door. "Stay on your guard."

With that, he went with the two younger men, presumably to a bathroom. I tried not to worry about the mirrors it contained.

"You have no need for concern," Hasan said quietly.

I gave him a startled look. Had he somehow known that I was concerned over the mirrors? Maybe he'd recognized who we really were and pieced it together? It wouldn't be the first time that we'd been recognized by strangers.

"What do you mean?" I asked in a careful tone.

He gave me a sad smile. "You have no need to stay on your guard while you are here. Islam is a religion of peace. We strongly renounce all despicable acts of terror in its name."

He thought Adrian had warned me because they were Muslim? Hell, I was worried about our possibly being a danger to *them*, not the other way around.

"That's not what he meant," I said, wanting to explain, but not able to say much. "He meant, um, for me to keep an eye out in case the thief had followed us."

Hasan drew himself up to his full height. "No one here would allow any harm to come to you."

"That's very kind," I said sincerely. "But it shouldn't be necessary. We won't be staying long." At least, not that I knew.

Hasan gestured to someone I couldn't see. "Bring

some water for our guest, please. Shall I also call the authorities while you wait?"

"No," I said a little too quickly, then smiled to cover it up. "We'll file a report later. I just want to get back to our hotel. I'm not feeling very well."

That last part wasn't a lie, at least. My stomach was no longer repeatedly clenching in preparation to heave its contents, but it was letting out warning rumbles. I tried not to think about the potential underlying cause and accepted the glass of water that someone new offered to me. I was halfway through finishing it when Adrian reappeared.

The white outer garment did hang as long as a dress would, but it had slits in the sides that accommodated Adrian's long strides. His hair was still wet, though. From the looks of it, Adrian hadn't even taken the time to towel it dry, although curiously, he did have a towel wadded up in his hand. I wondered why until I saw him pick up the pilum with it.

Yeah, that would work better than using his former shirt, which was currently leaving a puddle on the floor.

"Thank you for the clothes and the assistance," Adrian said, giving Hasan a small bow. "We have one more request. Is there somewhere private where my wife and I can talk? I want to make sure she's okay after her encounter with the thief."

"Of course," Hasan said, gesturing for us to follow him.

We did, and I played the part of shaken robbery victim by keeping my head down and my shoulders hunched. It probably helped that I *was* shaken over a question that kept booming through my mind despite my best efforts not to think about it.

Was I pregnant?

I hoped with everything I had that I wasn't. I wouldn't live long enough to give birth, and the thought of taking my unborn child with me when I died was too horrible to contemplate. *I can't be pregnant. It's just the stress that's causing the nausea and missed periods...and the excessive crying, strange cravings, increased appetite and recent weight gain.*

It was sounding less and less plausible the more I tallied up my symptoms, but I wanted to believe it more than anything.

Hasan led us to an office that had family pictures on the desk and various plaques on the wall. The desk was neat enough to look organized, yet it had enough mild disarray to inspire comfort. I didn't trust people who had impeccable work spaces.

"Please," Hasan said, gesturing to the two chairs across from his desk. "I will return in a few minutes to check on you."

He shut the door behind him, surprising me that it hadn't taken more than Adrian's single request for him to leave us alone in here. What if we were crazed Islamaphobes with cans of gasoline in our satchel because we were intent on arson? What if we were hackers intending to upload a virus onto his computer?

"We don't have much time," Adrian said, unwrapping the towel around the pilum. A small, plastic object fell out. When Adrian flipped it over and it reflected my wide-eyed expression back at me, I realized it was a mirror.

Adrian gave me a quick grin. "Took me a few attempts to figure out how to navigate these things, but I think I've got it now. We'll need to stay frosty, though. I was spotted before, so I had to shake my tail by jumping into a mirrored portal that led into an ocean. Did I ever tell you demons hate salt water?"

"An ocean?" I repeated.

"Yep," he said, holding his hands over the mirror fragment. "Lots of mirrors have made their way into oceans, rivers and ponds over the years, and each one is a portal waiting to happen. It's how Demetrius and the demons with him must've transported themselves into the river yesterday."

I hadn't gotten around to wondering about that. A lot had happened between then and now, like how I was wondering what Adrian thought he was doing with that mirror.

"Wrap the satchel around you, hold the pilum tight and take my hand," Adrian said, holding his out.

I stared at him. "You're kidding, right? We couldn't even fit the satchel through that thing!"

"Sometimes, size really *doesn't* matter," Adrian said, flashing me a quick grin. Then it faded as he added, "It might be small, but it's unbroken, so it can still work as a portal. Remember how Demetrius came through your old locket necklace?"

I did, but I thought he'd been able to do that because he was a shape-shifter who also happened to kinda be made up of shadows. From Adrian's expression, I'd thought wrong.

I didn't know how this was going to work, but I put the satchel's strap diagonally around me, then tucked the pilum between that and my body while grasping it tight. Finally, I took Adrian's hand.

"How does this—"

I never got the rest of the sentence out. The mirror seemed to stretch to an impossible size, and then it swallowed me.

CHAPTER THIRTY-EIGHT

I MUST HAVE closed my eyes in fear, because when I opened them, everything had changed. The small, comfy office was gone. So was the mosque, the streets around it and, in fact, the entire city of Trier.

In its place was an endless, 3-D corridor filled with what looked like countless television screens. Each one showed different people, places and things, right down to various animals, birds and fish. If it were possible to have the satellite feed of every television on earth simultaneously streamed to the same place, it would look like this.

"They're all mirrors."

Adrian's voice held an odd echo. His shadows were even more prominently on display now, swirling around him like dark swaths of silk even below his feet. How did they do that?

I looked down and wished I hadn't. There was no ground beneath me. It was only blackness interrupted by countless mirrors showing whatever was in front of them at the moment. I clutched Adrian's arm, trying to stifle my instant surge of panic. Now I knew what cartoon characters felt like when they looked down and discovered that they'd run off the edge of a cliff. I even had to fight the urge to start flailing my arms and legs the way they usually did right before they fell.

"Why is there no ground?" My voice was a squeak.

"I don't know," Adrian said, closing his eyes. "There just isn't, but I need you to trust me and stay quiet for a moment. We're alone in here now, but we won't be for long."

That wasn't helping me control my fear! Yet I clamped my mouth shut and didn't ask any of the other thousand questions I had. Adrian was obviously trying to concentrate enough to do something, and if that something got us out of this groundless, endless oblivion, I was all for it.

We were suddenly jerked forward with the momentum of a roller coaster gearing up to do a double loop. I might have screamed, but I couldn't be sure. Noise now surrounded us, indistinct yet roaring. Then light exploded in the darkness and we hit something. Hard.

Adrian rolled until I was on top of him and his back took the brunt of our impact. I looked around, squinting at the halogen lights above us that, after the former darkness, seemed like long, thin slices of the sun.

"You okay?" he asked, helping me to my feet and then immediately smashing the mirror on the wall.

"Yes," I said, then proved that to be a lie when I threw up. Good thing we'd tumbled into a bathroom. I made it to the sink just in time.

"That might be worse than traveling through Archon and demon gateways," I croaked.

Adrian was giving me a very concerned look. "This is the second time today you've gotten sick. You might have gotten food poisoning from that street vendor this morning."

"Wouldn't that be wonderful?" I said fervently, and got a strange look in response.

Right, Adrian had no idea about my pregnancy concerns. He'd been gone for three weeks during the time frame that I should have gotten my period, so he probably didn't realize that I was almost two months late. And he didn't know I'd gotten sick multiple times today, too.

I should tell him all these things. I really, really should. But as I stared at him, I realized that I couldn't. Saying it would make it real, and I wasn't ready to face that possibility myself, let alone dump it onto Adrian. Besides, it *might* be food poisoning. The thought cheered me.

"I'm fine," I repeated, and didn't hurl after saying it this time. To prove it, I rinsed my mouth out and splashed water onto my face, dried it with a paper towel that felt rougher than sandpaper and then stared at him expectantly.

"Now where?"

Adrian took my hand.

"Now we see if you feel anything hallowed."

The bathroom door opened and a group of women came inside. They stopped short when they saw us and the broken mirror behind us, then started speaking in a language that wasn't German.

"Where are we?" I whispered, following Adrian as he shouldered past them with a muttered reply in the same language.

"Moscow. One of the places on my list."

We left the bathroom and went down a long hallway with red carpet and numerous doors. When I saw tall cardboard display posters featuring famous actors and actresses every few feet, I realized where we were.

"One of your former favorite places is a movie theater?"

"No," Adrian said with a snort, leading me to the nearest exit. Once we went outside, he pointed at a building with dazzling splashes of color that stood out in stark relief against the drab gray sky. "That's where I want you to search."

I recognized Saint Basil's Cathedral at once, and not just because I was a history major. Many people would know it from the famed, brightly colored domes in the shape of Hershey's Kisses chocolates. At least, that was what they'd reminded me of when I first saw pictures of them as a child. Even now, the cathedral's exterior struck me as so fantastically whimsical, it seemed better suited to be located in Whoville from *How the Grinch Stole Christmas* than reality.

"Good choice," I told Adrian.

He grunted. "I denied it to myself at first, but now I think the extravagant architecture reminded me of home."

What an endorsement. Come to Saint Basil's—it's just like visiting a palace in a demon realm! There was something no tourist group would use as an advertisement anytime soon.

"Well, let's see if it's got something even more impressive inside it."

"IT DIDN'T," I TOLD Adrian an hour later. He'd stayed on the outskirts of the cathedral because when I walked up holding the pilum, I was flatly denied entry. I'd tried to say that it was a necessary balance support, like a cane, but that lie hadn't gone over. The entrance staff had simply told me to rent a wheelchair. Despite Adrian arguing with them in Russian and even attempting to bribe them, they hadn't budged. In the end, we decided to have him wait outside with it while I searched.

He gave a short nod. "Four more to go, then. Do you want to stop for the day? You're still looking a little pale."

"No," I said instantly. "Let's keep going."

I couldn't stop yet. If I did and we found hallowed ground to wait out the rest of the day and night in, I'd have nothing to distract me from what I suspected to be true, and all the ramifications of that. More mirror hopping was far preferable.

Adrian glanced at the sky, where the sun was shining hazily through the clouds. "It's a little after one o'clock here, so the sun should be coming up in Ohio. We'll go to the ancient Serpent Mound that's there next. That should give us plenty of hours of sunlight in case we're still being tracked."

"Sunlight didn't stop the demons from attacking us before," I pointed out.

He gave me a jaded look. "Yeah, and using that kind of power is draining. It probably took both Demetrius and Blinky to pull that off. They'll be able to do it again, but it might take them a day or so to recharge enough before they can try."

Even more reason why we had to keep searching the places on Adrian's list right away, I told myself. See? It wasn't only me trying to hold on to my paralyzing state of denial.

"But we need to find a more private place to make the next jump," he said, nudging me.

Yeah, the heart of Red Square was hardly clandestine. I let Adrian lead me past the other impressive buildings while trying to ignore the tantalizing aromas that came from the restaurants and cafés interspersed between all the famous landmarks. If I ate now, I'd probably puke again. Wasn't it called morning sickness for a reason?

If I had that, I corrected myself at once. If.

Adrian bought a small makeup mirror from one of the shops, then picked a narrow alley with a smelly Dumpster for our portal jump. Like before, it didn't take long for him to do whatever prep work was necessary to make the small mirror navigable, and for that, I was thankful. If I had to smell that garbage container one more minute, I was going to spray it with puke.

This time, when it seemed like the mirror swallowed us, I was less panicked to find myself suspended in the strange floating waiting room, which was how I thought of the bottomless expanse containing countless live-action mirror feeds against a backdrop of pure darkness. But my relative calm didn't last.

"Davidian," a familiar voice hissed, sounding oddly echoing and disembodied. Then every alarm bell in my body went off as I saw a dark form streak by the screens, heading right toward us.

Demetrius.

"Fuck," Adrian muttered, and dived us through the nearest mirror.

We landed with the same painful thud as last time, and Adrian immediately leapt up and smashed the mirror we'd come through with a roundhouse kick. Glass rained down on both of us, yet Adrian didn't pause to brush any of it off. Instead, he began jumping up and down on the larger shards.

I got why he was doing that, and I set the pilum

down to start stomping on them, too. Demetrius shouldn't be able to get through these pieces, since breaking a mirror somehow negated its use as a portal, but Demetrius had surprised us before. No point in taking any chances now.

The pilum, oddly, spun around for a second, then seemed to hop toward the wall, the floor no doubt vibrating from the impact of Adrian and me both jumping up and down on the mirror pieces. Good thing I was wearing sneakers instead of sandals or heels. Even still, it didn't take long before red drops splattered the broken pieces. Whether it was my blood or Adrian's, I wasn't sure, but we had manna in the satchel, so I didn't stop. Whichever one of us had gotten cut, we'd heal ourselves once we made sure that Demetrius wouldn't be following us through to here.

"I think we're good," Adrian said, then cursed when he got his first good look around. "Damn. This is someone's home."

It was, and an expensive one, too, from the looks of the sumptuous furnishings, artwork and other high-end items. We were in a bedroom, and we'd broken the large, lovely mahogany dresser we'd landed on after we came through the mirror that it had been positioned behind.

"It probably has a bathroom mirror, too," I said, gesturing at the partially open door that I was betting led to an en suite master bath. Adrian went inside, and moments later, I heard the sound of more glass breaking. Guess I'd been right.

He came out, and both of us froze when we heard mutterings in a different language downstairs, followed by the unmistakable sound of a shotgun being cocked.

Someone was at home in this fancy house, and that someone was armed.

"This way," Adrian whispered, and strode over to the bedroom window. It had a sweeping view of a large lake in the distance, but what really claimed my attention after I hurried over was the drop below. It had to be three stories.

"We don't have a choice," Adrian whispered grimly.

I grabbed the pilum, surprised when it felt resistant, as if it had suddenly become sentient and didn't like the idea of jumping out a three-story window, either. I didn't have time to wonder about that, so I wrestled it between my body and the satchel straps, then put my arms around Adrian's neck. He hissed when the hallowed object came into contact with him from our tight proximity, but he clamped his lips shut and tightened one arm around me. With his free hand, he opened the window. It was a slide-up, thankfully, and large enough that we both fit through. Right as I heard the sound of running footsteps coming up the stairs, Adrian jumped.

CHAPTER THIRTY-NINE

WE HIT THE ground with even more force than the mirror landing. Adrian rolled to lessen the painful impact, and I was shocked and grateful that the pilum didn't snap under the combined weight of our bodies rolling over on it. Then he pulled me up and we ran, spurred on by the boom of a shotgun blast and the explosion of grass right next to us.

It didn't take long for the angry shouts of the shotgun-toting homeowner to fade. Not with how fast we were running. We headed toward the lake, away from the lines of very expensive-looking houses and condominiums that we passed. I was so focused on getting away, I'd stopped wondering about the odd thing the pilum had done before. But when Adrian grabbed my hand and tried to pull me away from the exposed lake's banks, the pilum suddenly yanked itself back toward the water. Since it was still between my body and the satchel strap around my neck, it ended up yanking me, too.

"What's wrong?" Adrian said when he felt my resistance.

"I don't know," I said, stunned by what was happening with the pilum. "Stop for a second."

He did after giving a wary look behind us, but we weren't being chased, and we hadn't seemed to attract anyone else's attention, either. It was a sunny afternoon here, wherever "here" was, and lots of people were out walking, riding bikes and generally seeming to mind their own business.

Testing a theory, I took the pilum out from between the satchel straps around me—and nearly had it tear from my hands with its sudden lurch once it was free. I grabbed it just in time, then tightened my grip as it kept pulling me in the direction of the water. I followed its pull until I was up to my knees in the lake, yet still, that pull didn't decrease.

"What are you doing?" Adrian sounded impatient as he waded in and took my arm.

I pulled my arm free because it felt like I would need both hands to keep holding onto the pilum. "Something's up," I said, which was a huge understatement. "The pilum's suddenly acting like a missile seeking its target. I can feel it trying to pull itself farther into the lake, but my hallowed sensors aren't picking up on anything that would be drawing it."

Adrian looked at it, and his expression turned grim. "You might not sense anything, but it's one half of the most hallowed weapon in existence. Its power is much greater than yours."

That was what I'd been thinking, and I was torn between excitement and a near-overwhelming urge to let the pilum go so that it could slip out of my hands, my life and my destiny. If we were right, if something was drawing the pilum to it…well, it was obvious what that something had to be. The spearhead.

If so, then *today* I would die trying to wield the re-assembled hallowed weapon. I'd thought I was done being scared by that, yet a sliver of fear wormed its way into me regardless. It was quickly followed by a wave

of grief that I tried to push back as I stared at Adrian.
If I was dying today, I wanted to make sure I had his
face memorized so I could take its image with me.

But despite my own fears, grief, certain death and
the daunting odds against my being able to wield the
spearhead long enough to save all the people trapped
in the demon realms, I'd come too far to give up now.

"Then we need to follow it to find out where it's
leading us to," I said in a steady voice.

Adrian looked away, muttering a string of words
so softly, I wasn't sure if they were prayers or curses.
"We don't even know where we are yet, Ivy," he finished with.

He was stalling. I understood the knee-jerk, emotional reasons behind it, but I couldn't let that stop us.

"Wherever we are, we're here for a reason."

I didn't risk letting go of the pilum with both hands
for fear that it would pull from my grip and disappear
into the lake, so I leaned against Adrian in order to
touch him.

"You picked the closest mirror to jump through
when Demetrius came at us. That mirror led us to a
place that has the pilum suddenly acting like a compass
and a tractor beam combined. It can't be coincidence,
Adrian. You know that."

He inhaled sharply through his nose. "I know. I also
know that I hate it."

I let out a choppy breath. "I do, too, because of
what it means for us, but we have to stop looking at it
through such a narrow lens. This could be liberation
day for thousands of people who've suffered for too
long. That means it could also be Demon Payback Day,
and it's been too damn long for that, too."

Adrian looked at me, a range of emotions skipping across his features. Longing, love, anger, frustration, admiration, pain…they kept repeating like a recording stuck on a loop. I took in another deep breath, trying to smile despite feeling all those same things. *No turning back now. No matter what.*

"This day was always going to come, Adrian. Now that it's here, let's not allow it to break us. Instead, let's show it what we're made of."

A harsh laugh escaped him. "You don't want me to show you or anything else what I'm made of, Ivy. Especially now."

"Yes," I said softly, holding his gaze. "I do. I know you, Adrian. All of you—light and dark, good and evil, human and demon, heroic and selfish, savior and betrayer. You're amazing. You are, and you'll beat the worst of what you're feeling now. I know you will, because there is *nothing* you can't do."

He let out another ragged laugh. "I guess we'll find out. Until then, we need to rent a boat. Whatever the pilum is leading us to, we sure as hell can't swim our way there."

It turned out that we were in Bahir Dar, Ethiopia, which wasn't on Adrian's list of favorite places at all. In fact, he said he'd hated Ethiopia from the first time he'd realm-gateway hopped into this country decades ago. Apparently, he'd never been back since. It sounded all too similar to what had happened with the Aula Palatina. Granted, it could have been because Ethiopia had had a horrible famine back then, which wouldn't have made it anyone's favorite place. However, I thought there was more to it than that.

The pilum in the Aula Palatina had subconsciously set Adrian off enough to attempt burning the whole building down. Now *something* here had caused Adrian to never come back despite his easy access to every place in the world through the demon realm gateways. Like I'd told him before, I doubted that anything happening was coincidence.

Yes, Adrian had been subconsciously drawn to the places where the slingshot and the staff had been, so much that he'd made his homes in both of them. That was why Zach had referred to Adrian as "the map." But this final hallowed weapon was showing us how different it was. With it, both parts appeared to repel Adrian on some level. It was as if it were saying, *All bets are off with me.*

At least it wasn't hard to charter a boat from the local Maritime Transport Authority to take us in the direction the pilum was pulling itself toward. As it turned out, boat trips on Ethiopia's Lake Tana were very popular due to the lake's scenic beauty, its various islands and, more significantly, its historical churches and monasteries.

Yeah, no coincidence with that, either.

After paying the fare, Adrian helped me onto the boat, since I was still holding the stick with two hands. If Gelila, our charter boat captain, thought it was unusual that I was clutching a long stick as if it were a lifeline, she didn't comment on it.

"Is the boat to your liking?" she asked us.

"It's great," I said. And it was. Adrian and I sat in the open section in the back that had two benches and an attached cooler that doubled as a third bench once the lid was closed. The rest of the boat was covered, offering protection against the intense sunlight or the rain, if the day turned stormy.

"Please help yourself to refreshments in the cooler," Gelila said, swinging the boat around to head out into the horizon of the lake. "People can dehydrate quickly out here."

I requested a chilled water bottle from the cooler, which Adrian handed me. Then I ended up clenching the pilum between my knees and keeping one hand on it while I used the other one to drink. Adrian chose a beer, and it looked so much better than my plain water that I almost asked for a sip. Then I stopped myself with a stern rebuke.

Are you crazy? You can't have alcohol. You're pregnant!

A rush of emotions immediately followed my unexpected inner scolding. I'd been denying my condition all day, busying myself by coming up with reasons for why my symptoms had to be something—anything!—else, yet I knew the truth. Admitting those two small words to myself had only confirmed it.

You're pregnant.

Such a simple sentence for something so life-altering. I tried them out again in my mind, and this time, I felt a swell of nearly overwhelming wonder.

You're pregnant. Would it be a boy or a girl? Would it have Adrian's dazzling, sapphire-colored eyes, or my chocolate-mint hazel ones? His blond hair, or my dark brown? His features? Mine? A combination of both? Or something wonderfully, beautifully individual?

Just as quickly, anguish gripped me, so pitiless and intense, I had to bend over and let my hair fall around my face so Adrian didn't notice my instant spurt of tears. I would never know any of these things about my baby. I would never feel it grow, be awakened by its kicks or experience the unsurpassed joy of holding it in my arms.

I was all out of time in my life, and that meant my unborn child was, too. One way or another, I wouldn't make it. Even if I gave up on every single one of the thousands of people trapped in the realms, it still wouldn't be enough. Demetrius was too close on our tails. Blinky had confirmed they had some way to track us. They'd keep coming, and if not them, then all the others like them. We could keep running, but we'd get caught eventually. My baby was as doomed as I was.

The thought made me ache in a way that nothing had before it, and that was saying something considering the carousel of pain I'd been on this past year. I forced back the sob building in my throat and tried to steady my breathing that had become ragged with grief. I couldn't let Adrian see me this way. He'd insist I tell him what was wrong.

Yet how could I tell Adrian that I was pregnant? It would only hurt him on what would already be the worst—if not the last—day of his life. Doing that would make me a monster. Or was it more monstrous to keep something this momentous to myself? No, I decided. I might not be able to do anything to ease the pain I was feeling, but I could spare Adrian from feeling that same pain, too. I wouldn't wish this agony on anyone, let alone the person I loved most.

"Which of the islands are you wanting to visit, then?"

Gelila's accent sounded faintly British. I continued to take in deep breaths while I tried to concentrate on that and not the agony clawing at my heart. Fortunately for me, I'd had lots of practice at pushing back unbearable pain. Within a few minutes, I was breathing normally, and I'd surreptitiously splashed a couple handfuls of the icy bottled water onto my face to lessen the redness from my tears.

When I picked my head up, Adrian was staring out at the water, obviously lost in his own thoughts. Gelila had to ask her question again to get his attention. When he looked up, I busied myself with studying her so I didn't do something reckless when I stared into his eyes, like blurt out the truth.

Gelila looked to be in her early fifties, with wide shoulders, lovely deep brown skin, shoulder-length black hair and a cheery smile that couldn't be more opposite from what I was feeling.

"We're not sure which island we want to visit yet," Adrian said distractedly, then added, "We'll tell you when one of them interests us after we see what sights the lake has to offer."

She nodded. "Lots of sights on Lake Tana. It's the source of the famed Blue Nile, you know. Bit late in the day to see the hippos, but you'll catch sight of more than a few crocs before we're done, I expect."

Hippopotamuses *and* crocodiles? I shuddered. To think that I had waded into this lake earlier! It would have been just my luck to get eaten by the local wildlife before the spearhead could kill me. I could just imagine demons and minions laughing their evil asses off at that.

As if it could sense that I'd been thinking about the spearhead, the pilum felt like it began to thrum with slowly building energy. Of course, that could also be the vibration from the boat's motor, but I didn't think so. It was leading us to its other half, and once I found it, well, I had to try to look on the bright side of my death. If I was able to hold on to the reassembled spearhead long enough, it would blast that humans-only escape route into every demon realm in existence. I might not be able to save my life or my baby's life, but I could save so many other lives. I might not have much left, but one way or another, I'd make sure that I—and they—had that.

"Beautiful day for a boat ride," Gelila commented.

"Uh-huh," I replied with as much politeness as I could muster.

"I love being a captain," Gelila said, continuing to make small talk. "It's what I always wanted to do. That's why, when I finally got my own ship, I named it *Eddel*."

"*Eddel?* What's that mean?" Adrian asked, his tone telling me that he wasn't really interested in the answer.

Her smile grew. "It means destiny."

I stared at her, my grip tightening on the pilum. "We're on a boat named *Destiny* right now? You've got to be kidding me."

Gelila's smile slipped. "No. Why?"

I managed to say, "No reason," in a far more casual tone, yet I felt anything but casual as I met Adrian's darkened stare.

If either of us had had any doubts that today was the last day of my life, those doubts were now gone. Sometimes, Zach's boss wasn't vague at all. I guess writing Time's Up, Ivy! in the sky using the clouds would've been too flashy.

Despite feeling as if I'd throw up again, then burst

into tears, then throw up once more, I smiled. "It's okay," I said to Adrian in a soft voice. "We've still got this."

And amazingly, most of me even believed that. I'd heard once that the grace to face death was only given to the dying. Well, someone must be giving me something, because I knew I didn't have the strength to handle this on my own. Not after finding out that I was pregnant. Yet here I was, not falling to pieces.

Thank you, I sent upward, even more surprised that I could say it instead of just think a silent, endless scream. But as it turned out, I had even more to say. *Please. Whatever happens...please don't let me fail all the people who are counting on me.*

Adrian looked away even as his hand closed over mine, and by proximity, the pilum, too. A spasm went through him, yet he didn't let go despite the pain. I knew how he felt. I'd brave whatever pain came my way in order to touch him, too, although mine came from my heart feeling like it was being shredded one layer at a time. Still, I closed my eyes, trying to soak in the feel of his touch one last time.

"Settle in, lovelies," Gelila said in her cheerful voice. "We'll reach the first of the islands before you know it."

CHAPTER FORTY

Two hours later, I saw a small landmass on the horizon. Then Gelila said, "We're approaching the island of Tana Kirkos."

With that, the pilum began to emanate so much power that holding it burned my hands. I wasn't the only one affected. Adrian pulled away from me with a gasp, and his shadows retracted as if they'd been burned, too.

"You feel that?" he asked roughly.

I clenched my jaw. "Towel?" I managed. If I tried to say more, I might scream from the blistering pain, yet I couldn't let go. The pilum would shoot away from me if I did.

He leapt up. "Gelila, I need a towel, quickly!"

"In the cabin," she said, slowing the boat and giving us a concerned look. "Did you hurt yourself?"

Adrian ran into the covered section of the boat, and I tried not to think about how the flesh felt like it was being scorched from my hands.

"What's on that island?" I gritted out, trying to distract her from questions I couldn't answer, and myself from the pain.

"An ancient monastery with ties going back to the fourth century. It was even rumored that the Ark of the Covenant was once kept there for nearly eight hundred years."

"You don't say." It hurt so much, I had to let it go! But I couldn't let it go! Dammit, where was that towel?

Adrian ran back and gave me a beach towel. He tried to hold the pilum in order to let me peel my hands from it, but as soon as he touched it, he was knocked backward with such force that he nearly fell overboard.

"It's not in the mood for a threesome," I gasped out, using my knees to grip the pilum, then almost screaming at the fresh pain. Still, I managed to wrap the towel around it in several layers, since thankfully, beach towels were oversize. When I was done, I gritted my teeth and grabbed it with my blistered hands.

The towel made touching it tolerable, but the damage had been done. Every move I made tore at the burned and bubbled-up skin on my hands.

"I need manna," I said, but Adrian was already moving.

Gelila stopped the boat completely. "What has happened?" she demanded as she came over to where I was. Then she stared in shock at my hands and knees. "You've been burned!"

"Move," Adrian said, pushing her aside none too gently as he retrieved the plastic bag of manna from our satchel.

He grabbed a handful, then rubbed it on my scorched knees. I closed my eyes and breathed through the pain, which thankfully didn't last long. When I opened them, Adrian had his clean hand hovering by the towel-wrapped pilum, while the manna-clumped one was extended to me.

"Let go, Ivy, one hand at a time. Don't worry. If the pilum starts to get away from you, I'll grab it."

I didn't want him to, even with the towel covering it. His shadows already looked as if they were cringing behind his back. His mere proximity to the pilum since its new power surge had to be hurting him. That was why I pulled my left hand away first. My right one was stronger, and I gripped the pilum with no regard to what that did to my burned skin.

The pilum tugged hard toward the island. I tightened my grip even more and wedged the bottom of it between my feet for extra anchoring. Once again, I was beyond glad that I'd gone with the less pretty, thick sneakers. All that foam and rubber was an extra barrier against the pilum.

Adrian spread the manna onto my left hand. Gelila let out a gasp as those scorched, blistered welts began to lighten at once, and then they disappeared entirely.

"What. The bloody. Hell?" she said, staring in disbelief.

"Long story, no time," I replied, grabbing the towel-wrapped part of the pilum with my left hand and wincing as I pulled away my right one and saw that it left some scorched skin stuck to the towel. Gelila wouldn't want this back anytime soon. Then I held out my right hand to Adrian and sighed in relief as the burning pain faded soon after Adrian coated it with manna.

Gelila stared back and forth between the manna bag and my now-healed hands. "Is that some sort of magic healing paste?"

"Close enough," Adrian replied.

"We need to go to that island," I told Gelila. "Take us there."

"No point. They'll turn you away," she said, still sounding as if she were in shock. "Women aren't allowed on that island."

I let out a short laugh. After all I'd been through to get to this point, I'd be damned if a gender exclusion policy was going to stop me. "They're going to let me on. Trust me."

Gelila shook her head as if the movement would better allow her to clear it, then she looked at me. "It's forbidden. After I transitioned, I wasn't allowed to set foot on that island despite doing so for years beforehand. You can go ashore on one of the other islands—"

"Gelila." Adrian pulled out all our remaining money from the satchel. Her eyes widened at the pile. "This is yours to keep if you stop arguing and take us to that island now."

Her face was very expressive. That was how I knew when her shock lifted and her toughness came through. "Why that island and no other? You intending to do harm to the blokes there?"

"I promise you that we are not," I said, meeting her suspicious stare. Then I took a chance. "You saw how this stick burned me when I touched it, right? But wood doesn't burn unless it's on fire, yet there's no fire here, so how did it burn me?"

"I don't know," she said, staring at the pilum now.

She'd already seen enough to have her previous version of reality shaken. I hoped it would be enough to take her the rest of the way. "It burned me because it's not just a stick. It's one half of a very holy relic. The other half is on that island, and I have to put the two pieces back together. That's why you have to take us there and nowhere else. Do you understand now?"

She let out a laugh that I well recognized. It was one that said *This shit is too crazy to be real.* "I don't understand a bit of it, but if you mean the monks no harm, and if you're able to talk your way onto that island despite no woman ever doing that before...who am I to stop you?"

I flashed a quick smile at her. "Good enough for me."

TANA KIRKOS WAS a long, thin stretch of an island, with a tall ridge of rock jutting through the tops of thick jungle as if the island had a spine. More rocks acted as natural barriers where the island met the water, and I didn't see a dock anywhere. I also didn't see a beach, a single building or really any signs of life. If Gelila hadn't mentioned the monks and the monastery, I would've been sure that it was uninhabited.

Gelila seemed to know where to go, though. As we approached, she cut the engine and allowed the current to drift the boat closer to a lower formation of rocks.

"One of the monks will come out here soon," she stated. "You might not be able to see them, but they can see you."

Well, didn't that have a faintly ominous ring to it? "Why do we have to wait for them?"

She gave me a level look. "If you set foot on this island without their permission, they will forcibly try to remove you. I assume that's the kind of trouble you are looking to avoid?"

It was, but... I cast a glance at the sky. It was still a clear, sunny day, yet the sky had changed from light blue to a deeper, richer shade.

"How long until sundown?" It had taken us a good

two and a half hours on the water to get here, and it had already been around two in the afternoon when we set foot on this boat.

She glanced at her watch. "'Round two hours, but no worries. I have no trouble navigating the boat after dark."

Adrian and I exchanged a glance that I had to look away from, or I'd be swept away by all the emotions roiling right beneath my self-control. I knew for certain that I wasn't coming back, and odds were, neither was he.

"That's fine," I managed to say. "But don't, uh, wait around for us. Once we're on the island, just leave."

Her brows went up and that suspicion was back on her features. I tried to come up with a reason that would keep her safely away from what might be a dangerous situation while also not making her think that we were crazy suicide bombers.

"The monks will have lots of questions about how we came to be in possession of the pilum." Adrian's smooth voice cut through what had quickly become loaded silence. "It's a long story, needless to say, yet we want to be sure to tell it. Come back to get us in the morning, Gelila. We'll be done by then."

Only that last part wasn't a lie. We *would* be done by morning, and probably, much sooner than that.

Gelila shrugged. "You're giving me more than enough for me to make another trip out here, but as I told you, I don't think both of you will get onto that island."

I didn't argue with her about it again. Either she was wrong and the monks would make an exception for me, or we'd get around them by outrunning them. Either way, it was happening.

"Someone's coming," Adrian said.

A flash of orange peeked through the thick brush at the base of the rock, then a robed man appeared, smiling and saying something in an unfamiliar language. I glanced at Adrian, but he shook his head. He knew a lot of languages, but not this one.

Gelila replied in the same language, and the smile wiped from the monk's narrow dark-skinned face, which was the only part of him visible from his head-to-toe robes.

"No," he said in heavily accented English. "I am sorry, but it is forbidden for women to set foot on Tana Kirkos."

I cast another glance at the sky. We didn't have time to break the news gently, so I stood up, held out the pilum that was now vibrating with barely contained energy, and said, "You will let *me* on. I am the last living descendant of King David, and I know that the spearhead of Longinus is here. The base of that ancient weapon is in my hands, and I have come to reunite the two parts."

The monk stared at me with shock. So did Gelila. I hadn't called it the more well-known term of the Holy Lance because I'd tried to be a little vague for her sake, but she clearly knew what I was talking about.

Then the monk recovered from his shock. "Why do you believe the spearhead is here?" he asked, his voice now flintlike.

New rustling in the brush behind him combined with more flashes of orange proved that he hadn't come alone, either, and soon, three more robed monks appeared. The first monk's whole demeanor changed before my eyes. Gone was the kindly half-stooped older man who looked like the most confrontational thing he'd ever done was politely shoo away female tourists. *This* man stood with a soldier's ready-to-charge tenseness, and his newly hardened stare promised that he could kick ass and take names.

I held the pilum higher. "Because this directed me here, as I can prove. No matter where you've hidden the spearhead, no matter how many wards you've put around it so its power can't be felt—and you *had* to have warded it or I'd be a mindless mess right now— the pilum will lead me straight to it."

The monks exchanged quick, measured looks. Then another one came onto the narrow rock ledge. "If what you say is true and you are the last of David's line," this new monk said in much better English, "show us the holy marks on your body."

"You have the stigmata?" Gelila whispered in awe.

Since the monks had demanded that I do the supernatural equivalent of putting my cards on the table, I gave up any attempt at vagueness. "Nope," I said to Gelila. "I have tattoos of ancient hallowed weapons that turn into real ones when demons are present."

Gelila gasped at that, but I was more focused on the monks' faces. Since my hands were full, I nodded at Adrian, who pulled my right sleeve all the way up and then raised the hem of my sweater, revealing my torso from hip bone to bra.

"David's slingshot," I said, wiggling my bared right hand. "And you can only see some of it, but Moses's staff runs from my neck all the way to my foot."

The monks exchanged another look, then more rustling behind them and above them revealed another half dozen monks, all clothed in the same bright orange robes. The monk who'd demanded that I show him the goods said something sharply in their native tongue, then all of them suddenly dropped facefirst to the ground. I dropped down, too, expecting a spray of bullets or other imminent attack.

Adrian didn't move, although he let out a short, humorless laugh. "There's no danger, Ivy. They believe what you are now, so they're throwing themselves prostrate before you."

Oh. I felt foolish and more than a little embarrassed. "Get up," I told the monks, getting up myself. "Believe me, I don't deserve to be worshipped."

Hell, if these monks knew how much I'd bitched about my destiny, let alone all the steps I'd taken to avoid it, they wouldn't bow down to me. They'd throw rotten fruit at me.

"Davidian," the monk with the good English said, his wrinkled features easing into a smile as he got up. "I am Sebhat. Allow me the honor of welcoming you to our island."

One of the other monks began saying something excitedly in their language. They all looked up, including Gelila. I did, too, but didn't see anything aside from a dark spot by the sun.

"The Lord Himself smiles on your visit," Sebhat exclaimed. "Behold, He causes the eclipse to appear a full day early to commemorate it!"

Eclipse? With a sick feeling, I realized what the smaller dark ball by the sun was. The shadow of the moon, which meant that this was a solar eclipse. And that shadow would get big.

"Ivy." Adrian's voice held all the tension that instantly rose in me, too. "Day is about to become night."

"Fuck," I breathed, and got horrified looks from all the monks. If they thought my language was upsetting, wait until they realized it wasn't God causing the early eclipse. He hadn't thrown a sky-altering welcome party for me yet, and I doubted today was the day He was going to start. But demons could manipulate the sky to their advantage, although this was really pulling out all the stops.

Then again, demons could smash dimensions together to create new realms. Speeding up a planetary alignment by only a day shouldn't be too hard, and this was the last play of the game. Whoever won this round won the whole thing.

"We're about to be under attack by demons," Adrian told the monks, grabbing the satchel and jumping onto the rock ledge. I came over to that ledge, then turned my back so he could pick me up by my waist. That way, he didn't have to worry about the pilum accidentally brushing him.

"But demons cannot attack here. This island is holy ground!" the first monk who'd met us protested.

"Every inch of it?" Adrian challenged.

Sebhat gave us a grim look. "No. Not all of it."

"Like I said." Adrian's voice was crisp. "We're about to be under attack."

CHAPTER FORTY-ONE

WE TOLD GELILA to drive her boat away as fast as she could. She'd be far safer on the water than she would be on the island. Then we followed the monks up the steep, rocky terrain. The jungle was so thick around us that I could barely see the ground, let alone the path that the monks traveled with ease. But the possibility of losing my footing was hardly my biggest concern.

"Please tell me you've got lots of guns on this island," Adrian said. "The eclipse won't last long, but while it does, they're going to hit us with everything they've got."

And if we survived that, nightfall wasn't far away, so they'd be back for more. Yeah, lots of guns would help. Bullets couldn't kill demons, but they could kill minions. Besides, pumping demons full of bullets would distract them, and I'd need all the distraction I could get to reach the spearhead, reattach it to the pilum and use it before one of the demons stopped me.

"We have many swords, but only a few guns," Sebhat replied.

Adrian ground out a curse in Demonish. Sebhat looked sharply at him. "How do you know that tongue?"

"Doesn't matter," I said quickly. The last thing we needed was for them to freak out over who Adrian was. "We'll need all of you to arm up with whatever you've got, and if you have any mirrors on the island, they need to be broken. Now."

Sebhat pulled out a satellite phone. I would've been impressed that he had one, except the pilum suddenly yanked me so hard to the right, I almost bashed myself into a tree.

"Ivy!" Adrian tried to help me, but I pulled away, breathing hard. I didn't trust what would happen if he accidentally brushed against the pilum again. Ever since I set foot on this island, it had been powering up, until it felt like it was starting to burn me even through the layers of towel.

"Don't come near me, Adrian," I said tightly. "It's too dangerous. The pilum's power is growing, and it's being pretty specific that it wants me to go to the right, not straight."

Sebhat came closer. The way was so narrow, we'd been walking single file. Adrian's tall, broad shoulders left most of the monk's face hidden, but I could still see some of Sebhat's face, and his expression was reverent.

"The spearhead is to the right as the crow flies, but the climb is too steep and the jungle too dense that way. You must follow us up this path until we reach the clearing."

Adrian glanced up at the sky. What had been a small spot before now stretched to a cone shape, and the sky was darkening by the moment. "Whichever way we go, we need to hurry." To me, he said, "Don't suppose you can use the staff to slow down the onset of the eclipse and buy us more time?"

What was meant as a laugh came out as a gasp as new flares of pain shot up my arms. The towel might keep my hands from erupting in burns on the outside, but the pilum now felt like it was burning me on the inside, too.

"Doubt it." The intensity of the pain made my reply more snippy than I'd intended. "For one, my tats haven't activated because the demons aren't here yet. For another, I might have been able to blast away some clouds, but I don't think I can stall the alignment of the *planets*. Lastly, it's taking everything I have to keep holding on to this pilum, so don't expect more from me, because I'm about done."

The look Adrian gave me briefly made me forget how it felt like fire had replaced my blood in the worst possible way. For a second, all the anguish he'd been hiding came out, and seeing it seared me in ways that my physical pain never could.

"It's okay, Ivy," he rasped. "You're right. You're almost done."

I closed my eyes. I hadn't meant it that way, but he was right. I was almost done, permanently. Yet if I looked at him one more moment, I might throw away the pilum, my destiny and the lives of all those trapped people just to see that awful pain leave his expression. Out of everything I futilely wished I could change, hurting Adrian was at the top of that list.

But I couldn't change that, and no matter how it tore at me, I had to look past it. "Call your people," I said to Sebhat. "Tell them to get their guns and break their mirrors. We're almost out of time."

We started back up the path, and I walked those first few steps with my eyes still closed. Only when I heard Sebhat talking into his phone did I open them. By then, Adrian had turned away, yet the shadows that no one else could see had grown until they rose behind him like a living storm. If I was tempted to throw the pilum away, Adrian had to be fighting every cell of his combined demon and Judian heritage not to yank it from my hands and destroy it.

I couldn't say anything to help him with this fight. This one, he had to do by himself. I knew he was strong enough, but it took only one moment of weakness to ruin everything. So many lives depended on both of us being at our best for just a little bit longer. We couldn't fail. We couldn't.

Adrian's head suddenly whipped around, then he pointed up. "A plane's coming in very low. Is that normal around here?"

Sebhat shaded his eyes with his hand as he looked up. "No," he said in a concerned tone. "Not that type of plane."

We quickened our pace up the steep trail. When we reached a small clearing at the top, the plane flew directly overhead, and a thick white cloud released from the back of it. It landed on the island in a way that reminded me of crop dusting, but there were no fields to fertilize here. When a new, even more intense pain suddenly hit me, I thought I knew what it was.

"Poison gas," I said, covering my nose with my sweater even though I doubted that would help.

"No," Adrian spat. "Something else." He gave a hate-filled look at the pale substance falling all around us like a thicker, sandier version of snow. "The ground has been cursed."

What? "I thought you had to enclose a place in circles made from powerful dark relics to do that, like you did when you held Blinky under the church."

"That's one way." Adrian's tone was as dark as his

shadows. "But if you're in a hurry, you can saturate a place with the ground-up bones of hundreds of minions, and that will turn even hallowed ground into cursed earth."

I looked at the pale substance with a disgusted sort of understanding. Minions, like demons, turned to ash when they died, so they didn't leave behind bones that could be ground up. That meant Demetrius and the other demons would've had to keep the minions alive while they hacked off their limbs in order to harvest their bones. No wonder such heinous torture resulted in cursing the earth of whatever it touched.

The sun was more than half hidden by the shadow of the moon now, and a sudden chill swept through the air as darkness descended. The ground was cursed, the sky was darkened and we all knew what would come next.

Adrian met my eyes, his shadows swirling madly around him, and said, "We're out of time. You have to run, Ivy. Don't wait, don't look back and don't let anything stop you."

I knew he was right, yet I still wanted to say that I loved him, I was so proud of him, and a thousand other things. Instead, I turned and ran in the direction where the pilum was leading me. It took all of my willpower, but I did it.

The attack came ten seconds later.

CHAPTER FORTY-TWO

I HEARD SCREAMS behind me and gunshots ahead of me, yet I didn't slow down and I didn't look back. I wouldn't be able to keep going if I did either, and I had to go on. The demons were here; my tats lighting up and sending new agony through me were proof of that, as if there had been any doubt as to who was behind the sounds of attack. No, they were here, and so was the spearhead. Either I or they would wield it soon, and I had to make sure that it was me.

I ducked when the wide green leaves of whatever vegetation populated this jungle suddenly exploded next to me. More gunfire strafed the brush around me, this time coming from the opposite direction. Great, I was caught in the cross fire between armed bad guys and armed good guys, yet I couldn't leave the path. The brush was too thick, so I ducked as low as I could and hoped that somehow the power of the pilum would make me bulletproof.

It didn't. I knew that when I suddenly stumbled after the next volley of shots even though I hadn't tripped. I hit the hard earth of the well-worn path like a sack of potatoes, although I managed to keep my grip on the pilum. In that dazed moment when I first hit the ground, I decided it was a good thing that the pilum had burned my hands even through the towel. They were probably welded to it now.

I felt blood spill out of me when I stood up, but I didn't look down to see where I'd been shot. I couldn't stop to treat my wound and seeing it would only upset me. Either it was bad enough to kill me, or it wasn't. I was already in so much pain that a little more wouldn't make a difference.

When I was able to run again, I smiled. Those trapped people still had a chance. *Come on*, I urged the pilum. *Give me a little of your energy so I can move faster.*

Whether it did or a new surge of adrenaline hit me, I didn't know. But soon, I was able to move easier. I ran up to a small building with a red roof that must have had monks holed up in it, because gunfire erupted from the windows as I approached. Thankfully, none of it hit me this time. Maybe being the only woman on the island was now an advantage. If the monks could see me, they must be able to figure out *not* to shoot me.

A horrible vibration shook the ground, and the building began to collapse far too quickly to be structural deficiency. By the time I was thirty yards away, it had crushed onto itself in a way that was all too familiar.

Demetrius. Of course he was here, and he couldn't be far behind me if he was doing that. I quickened my pace, ignoring the new tiny, bright specks in my gaze that meant I was in danger of passing out. I couldn't do that. I had to hang on a little longer. The sun was completely blocked by the moon's shadow now, but in a few minutes, the eclipse would be over and the sun would be shining again.

I ran past what looked like a primitive courtyard,

yelling, "Stop the demons behind me!" at the orange-robed monks who looked like they'd taken up tactical positions around it. They couldn't kill Demetrius, of course, but maybe they could slow him down and whoever he'd brought with him. It pained me to realize that even if they did, those monks were as good as dead. So was I, but although none of us could save our own lives, if we fought hard enough, we could save other peoples' lives. All I had to do was make it to the spearhead in time.

The pilum suddenly flared with so much power, the force of it caused me to stumble again. This time, I caught myself and didn't face-plant. Instead, I half staggered, half ran toward a small wood-and-stone structure that I glimpsed through the palm fronds ahead. As if confirming that this was where I needed to go, the pilum shot forward, until it felt less like I was running and more like it was dragging me.

The draw was so potent, I ran right into the door as if I were a cartoon character. Then, head ringing from the impact, I forced the mind-numbing pull of the pilum aside enough to try to turn the small metal doorknob.

It didn't budge. It was locked, and none of the orange-robed monks were inside to let me in, or around it to open the door. Maddened, I kicked the door with all the seething need that the pilum filled me with to reach what was inside. The wooden door flew inward and landed with a thud, but a new rush of liquid made my sweater stick to my stomach and the top of my jeans feel soaked.

I still didn't look down. This time, it wasn't because I knew that seeing the severity of the wound would upset me. It was because whatever warding had been blocking my hallowed sensors from detecting the spearhead was now broken along with the door.

Power slammed into me with the force of an oncoming train. It would have thrown me backward if not for the pilum yanking me forward with equal intensity. Between the two incredible forces, my feet left the ground, and I found myself flying into the small hut much like the door had when I kicked it in.

I landed on the door and immediately shoved it aside. I also shoved aside the brightly colored woven rug that covered most of the floor. The spearhead was beneath the hut's wooden floor. I could feel it, and that wasn't only from all my hallowed sensors exploding within me. Now that it had been released from the muting effect of the wards, the power of the freed spearhead briefly caused the entire hut to shake.

It also filled me with a near-demented need to touch it. I dropped the pilum and started to tear at the floorboards with my bare hands until I realized I needed something stronger. These were thick wood planks at least two layers deep, and I was now bleeding too heavily to be able to smash through them with nothing but my fists.

Shelves filled with various items lined the walls of the hut. Most of the objects on them were useless for my needs, like all the pottery pieces and the strange metal globes hanging from chains in the corner nearest me. But in the other corner, I saw a very large thick metal platter. *That* wouldn't break easily.

I grabbed it and began slamming it against the floorboards. Wooden shards flew in every direction and the planks dented. Encouraged, I started hammering at the boards with even more fervor. After a minute, the first layer broke. I kept slamming the metal platter down, using all my strength, until the area where I knelt became stained red with my blood.

A deafening bang suddenly filled the room, and I was knocked over. I didn't understand what had happened until I looked up and saw Demetrius in the open doorway holding a smoking gun. Either my brain was starved of oxygen due to blood loss, or the parts that were still working were being driven by an insane need to get to the spearhead, because I wasn't at all afraid. Instead, I was furious.

"You *shot* me? That's low even for you!"

Demetrius laughed, a cruelly pleased sound that only pissed me off more. "Are those really what you're choosing for your last words, Davidian?"

He blocked a lot of the doorway and it was still dark from the eclipse, so I didn't see him behind Demetrius at first. I might not have seen him at all, except those twin red orbs stood out against the midnight-blue backdrop of the sky. But those eyes glowed with the same *tapetum lucidum* that caused most animal's eyes to shine, and I knew of only one large, flying creature with eyes that big and red.

Brutus! I had no idea how he'd gotten here, but I couldn't be happier to see him. I also couldn't be sure, but I thought I saw Brutus pull back his lips in a vengeful grin as he soared right toward Demetrius's unsuspecting back. Never let it be said that a gargoyle couldn't hold a grudge with the best of them.

"Why are you smiling?" Demetrius demanded, the smirk wiping from his features.

"You'll see," I said, and flattened myself onto the floor.

Demetrius turned—and Brutus slammed right into him. The momentum from his aerial assault took out most of the small hut, too, as demon and gargoyle plowed right through it. Stone, wood and countless pieces of pottery rained down on me, yet I stayed flattened on the floor until the worst of it stopped.

Even those few seconds felt like too long. The spearhead had me in its thrall, demanding that I free it. I began digging through the debris, heedless that I spilled more of my own blood with every strenuous movement. I found the pilum and tucked it next to me, then shoved enough of the hut's ruined remains aside to find the partial hole I'd dug into the floor. Once I did, I grabbed the heavy metal platter and began slamming it into the floorboards again.

"Ivy!"

I was so engrossed in my task, I barely looked up even though I was surprised to hear Costa's voice. "Good, you can help," I told him. "What are you doing here, anyway?"

I caught Costa's grin out of the corner of my eye. "I came with the gargoyle, of course." Then Costa's smile faded as he got a good look at me. "You have blood all over you."

"I know. Grab something heavy and help me bash into this floor. It's under here. Only one more layer."

He touched my back. "I think you need to—"

"I don't," I interrupted, knowing what he was about to say. "Any second, one of the other demons could come. Demetrius isn't alone—you had to have seen that when Brutus flew you over the island. Stop arguing and help me, or find Adrian and help him."

Costa sifted through the debris until he found a thick

metal rod that could have been one of the hut's former support beams. Then he began slamming it into the wood floor harder than I'd been able to for the past couple minutes. Between both our efforts, we soon broke through the last layer of floorboards. My breath caught as the platter I was using clunked against something long and hard wrapped inside cloths of crimson, purple and gold.

At last, the spearhead! I dropped the platter and reached for it, but Costa grabbed both my hands.

Startled, I looked at him, and a beautiful smile wreathed his features. "Thank you, Davidian."

My last thought before everything went dark was *Demetrius*...

CHAPTER FORTY-THREE

"Oh, you're awake."

I recognized the voice. It was Demetrius's real one, not the very impressive fake he'd used when he'd shape-shifted into an exact replica of Costa. Yeah, I was awake, although I didn't know why. Demetrius had me and he had the spearhead. I should be dead, not waking up. I almost wondered if I *was* dead, except the dead couldn't possibly hurt this much. At least, I hoped not.

"I have to tell you, Davidian, when that gargoyle slammed into me, I wondered if the spearhead wasn't here and this entire thing had been a clever setup."

Demetrius's voice was so cheery, I kept my eyes closed a little longer. The only thing worse than listening to him gloat would be seeing him gloat. But then I heard an extended moan from another familiar voice, and my eyes snapped open.

Adrian was in the corner of whatever room or building we were in. I couldn't tell which because all the windows had been blocked off, and the interior was so plain that it could have been part of the monastery, or it could have been a freestanding hut. Either way, the floor was sprinkled heavily with what I now knew to be ground-up minion bones. The eclipse might be over, but the combination of cursed earth plus shut-tered windows blocking out any remaining sunlight meant that Demetrius had time to gloat. He had all the time in the world.

The bodies of several monks were scattered across the floor, and at least two dozen living minions filled the room, too. It wasn't small, but with all of them in it, it was now standing room only. Of course, they were giving Adrian a wide berth, and for good reason. His shadows were extended as far as they could reach, their tips formed into knifelike points that stabbed at everything around him. Thick metal chains covered his legs and his torso, and he must be injured, because blood seeped out through them. More blood covered his face, and some of it had gotten into his eyes. He'd obviously put up a ferocious fight, but just like me, it hadn't been enough.

"Ivy." His voice was as broken as I felt in that moment. "I am so sorry."

"Don't sound so dejected, my son," Demetrius chided him. "Yes, I had initially intended to kill her right away, but now I've changed my mind. For one, it should be quite fun to let her watch what happens when I transform the spearhead from a hallowed weapon into a cursed one. Who knows? If she's miserable enough, I might even let her live on for years."

Adrian lunged at him, but all those chains must have been anchored to something sturdy, because he made it only about a foot.

"I'll fucking kill you!" he snarled.

Demetrius wagged a finger at him before returning his attention to the items on the table in front of him. They were rubber storage containers, of all things. He popped the lids off while smacking his lips apprecia-

314 THE BRIGHTEST EMBERS

tively. "Do you have *any* idea how long I've been waiting to use what's in these containers?"

"I don't care."

My voice was a whisper, and I hadn't meant it to be.
At last, I looked down and understood why Demetrius
hadn't bothered to tie me up, let alone use the same
overkill restraints he'd used with Adrian. The holes in
my sweater showed me the two places where I'd been
shot. Otherwise, I wouldn't have been able to tell how
many times that had happened. The entire front of my
sweater was soaked through with blood, and when I
tried to move, I couldn't.

But that wasn't what forced a cry from me that I bit
back as soon as I saw the pleasure light Demetrius's
face. It was my right arm. Or, to be more specific, the
bloody, tied-off stump at the end of my elbow where
my right arm *should* have been.

"I couldn't allow you to pull that slingshot out and
ruin my plans, could I?" Demetrius said with vindic-
tive satisfaction. "Don't worry—you'll see your arm
again. I'll retrieve it so I can transform the sling it con-
tains into a cursed weapon, too, after I'm finished with
the spearhead. And then you'll either willingly remove
the staff from your body so I can transform that, too,
or I'll cut it out of you, and that, my dear Davidian,
you would regret."

"You think I want to live to see what you'll do once
you transform that spearhead?" I might be reduced to
whispering from my massive injuries, but not even
that could mask the hatred in my voice. "Kill me. It'll
be far preferable."

Demetrius clucked his tongue. "And murder my own

grandchild along with you? What kind of monster do you think I am?"

He knew. *He knew!*

I'd thought I felt cold before. I hadn't known the meaning of the word. When Adrian's stunned gaze met mine, I couldn't stop the tear that slipped out even though I hated to give Demetrius one more thing to gloat over.

"I didn't realize it until earlier today," I whispered.

"And you didn't tell me?" The hurt in his eyes hit me like a sledgehammer. "How could you not tell me that?"

"I'm sorry, Adrian!" I must've tried moving closer to him, because a fresh spurt of blood leaked out from my sweater. "I couldn't tell you when…when I knew it would only hurt you, considering what was going to happen."

"See? All loved ones lie," Demetrius said, his dark gaze landing on Adrian. "You disowned me and your entire race for lying to you, yet your own wife admits she is no different. Come now, Adrian, stop being petulant. If not for me keeping her from using that spearhead, she'd be dead, as would your unborn child. Can't you see you have no reason to hate me? I am giving you everything you most want!"

"More lies," Adrian spat. "She's bleeding out in front of you, yet you're busy taunting her and playing with your Tupperware. She's probably lost the baby already!"

"She hasn't," Demetrius said, a wave of his hand dismissing the pool of blood around me. "I can still hear its heartbeat. And if she does lose it, I'll raise it back to life. I already brought *you* back from the dead today. How else do you think my minions managed to get you wrapped in those chains without your shadows ripping them to pieces?"

"He was dead?" I was sick at the thought, and sick over feeling grateful to Demetrius for bringing Adrian back.

"Killed him myself," Demetrius replied, and my momentary gratitude vanished. "He had to be shot repeatedly first, of course, which is why I made sure all my men were armed, and—"

"The baby," Adrian suddenly said, his gaze burning as he looked at Demetrius. "That's how you've been able to track us lately. You used to be able to track me through our blood tie before I blocked you by tethering my soul to Ivy's. But the baby isn't tethered to anyone, and it has your blood, too."

I thought I couldn't be shocked by anything else, yet I was wrong as Demetrius's slow smile confirmed Adrian's suspicions.

"Blood calls to blood, son, always. When I heard it again, I thought it was your blood breaking through your tethering to call to me, but it wasn't. I didn't realize that until I was about to break the Davidian's head open, and realized I heard two heartbeats coming from her body instead of one."

Adrian stared at me, and the knives formed by his shadows blunted until they were no more than wisps against the writhing, inky darkness around him. Then he looked at Demetrius.

"You have the spearhead and the other hallowed weapons, so you have everything you want, except for me. But you can have me if you heal Ivy, and leave her and the child alone. Do that, and I swear I will stand by your side for the rest of my life."

"Adrian, don't," I gasped. "You can't!"

"Yes, I can," he said, and didn't look away from Demetrius. "You can punish me as you see fit, and you can direct me to use my shadows as if they were your own. All this I give to you in exchange for the life and safety of Ivy and my child."

"You think your word is sufficient for me to believe you?" Demetrius mocked. But from the sudden gleam in his eyes, he was tempted. Not even he was a good enough actor to hide that.

"You have more than my word," Adrian said, his voice hardening as he ignored my continued pleas for him not to do this. "As long as they are alive, you also have matchless incentive for me to remain loyal to you, because we all know the first thing you'd do if I wasn't."

"I do have a temper," Demetrius agreed.

"So do I," Adrian said, flashing a cruel smile at his father. "And if you think I've caused you problems over the past several years, you don't want to see what I'm capable of if you break this deal. I don't care if you control all the realm gateways and our people crown you king, I will lay waste to your *universe* if you betray me on this."

Demetrius stared at Adrian. Then he began to chuckle in that low, malevolently amused way that was unique to him. Those deep rumbles of mirth soon gave way to full roars of laughter.

"I *knew* you'd come back to me! I didn't expect it to be under these circumstances, but life never fails to surprise, does it? Besides, you are far stronger now than you would have been had you never left. Very well, my vicious, vengeful son. I agree to your terms, with the understanding that if either of us betrays them, countless bodies will drop, starting with hers."

"Agreed," Adrian said even as I screamed, "No!"

At last, Adrian looked at me. "We both gave it our best shot to beat him, Ivy, and we both failed. All we can do now is make the best of what's left."

Tears spilled down my cheeks, and they felt warm against skin that had grown so cold. "I can't let you do this, Adrian."

"Ivy," he said with a sigh. "It's already done."

CHAPTER FORTY-FOUR

DEMETRIUS, OF COURSE, was completely unconcerned with the aftereffects of smashing Adrian's life and our relationship with one blow. "Now that that's settled, back to more important things," he said.

I wanted to continue arguing with Adrian, to find the right words that would somehow stop him from making the worst mistake of his life, but all of a sudden, I was too exhausted to even speak. It shouldn't be a surprise. I didn't know how I was still conscious after all the blood I'd lost, both from my bullet wounds and from getting half my right arm hacked off. If Demetrius or someone else hadn't put a tourniquet on it, I definitely would have bled to death already.

Demetrius returned to carefully emptying the contents of the plastic containers into a huge bowl that was absolutely not plastic. Instead, it shone as brightly as gold, and knowing the demon's avarice, it probably was gold. Adrian gave the sawdust that Demetrius poured into it a knowing look.

"Is that what I think it is?"

"What else?" Demetrius said, then slanted a look at me. "You have no idea, though, do you?"

"I don't care," I said, but Demetrius was in full bragging mode, so he told me anyway.

"This is all that remains of the Tree of the Knowledge of Good and Evil, the very one whose fruit prompted mankind's original sin. Nothing else in all the realms compares to its darkness. Even a sprinkling of this can turn the most hallowed of items into a cursed relic in an instant, but you don't have to believe me. See for yourself. Bring the prisoner!"

The doors opened and four more minions came in. I almost didn't recognize the person they had tied with ropes between them because he was covered in layers of dirt and blood. But when he lifted his head and his long black hair fell back, I recognized him and let out a silent scream.

Not Costa, too!

Adrian also appeared shocked. "What are you doing here?"

"Came with Brutus," Costa mumbled. "Zach said that we hadn't been forbidden from helping like he had, so he sent us."

"And despite my men carelessly killing all the monks, now I have a human to handle the hallowed items that might otherwise kill me or my minions if we touched them," Demetrius said archly.

That was why he'd kept Costa alive. Of course it hadn't been out of any sense of compassion or mercy.

"So, Michael was forbidden from coming?" Demetrius laughed. "I do so love when Archons are required to play by rules that I am free to ignore." Then that coal-colored stare landed on me. "You know this means God wants humanity to suffer. Otherwise, why would He forbid His general from stopping me from reopening the realm gateways?"

I had no idea. It wasn't because I'd be the one to

stop him. I'd given that my best shot and had come up far short.

"Think about it," Demetrius continued. "If God knows everything, then He knew that if you came to this island without Michael, you would fail. Yet He still forbade Michael from coming with you. How does it feel to know despite all your efforts, it was foreordained that you never stood a chance?"

I looked away. I didn't want to admit that Demetrius was right, but at the moment, it was hard to call him wrong. Maybe this had been part of a plan. A huge, humanity's-gonna-get-it plan, with me leading everyone straight into demons' arms.

"Stop baiting Ivy," Adrian said in a flat tone. "Aren't you tens of thousands of years too old to use mere words to wound?"

"I would prefer to use knives, but that would break our agreement," Demetrius said, his brow arching. "But you're right, back to business. Dip the tip of the pilum into the bowl," he ordered Costa, and the minions holding him loosed the ropes from around him and shoved him forward.

That was when I saw that he'd been holding the long stick all along. As Demetrius had pointed out, Costa was a regular guy with no supernatural lineage and no demon-tethering ties like the minions, so the pilum had no effect on him. It didn't even appear to be pulling him toward the spearhead, wherever that was.

Costa cast a grim look at me, then folded his arms around the pilum and didn't move. "I won't do it unless you let me treat Ivy's wounds with manna."

A snort escaped Demetrius. "You are very lucky that my people murdered all the other humans here, or I'd kill you for daring to assume that you could bargain with me."

"Let him do it," Adrian said wearily. "You've already agreed to let Ivy live. Why wait until she dies and you have to drain more of your power to raise her to honor our deal?"

Demetrius sighed. "Because I'd like to see her dead at least once. Still, you're right. Raising people drains me of strength, and I've already depleted a great deal of my power by killing Blinky so he couldn't get to the spearhead before I could, causing the eclipse to come early, and then by raising you, Adrian. Very well." He turned back to Costa. "Give it to her, but first, drop the hallowed weapons right where you stand."

Costa's mouth dipped downward. Seeing it, Demetrius laughed. "You didn't expect me to let you near the Davidian while you were holding them, did you?"

From Costa's expression, he had been hoping Demetrius would be that stupid, but of course, the demon wasn't. Costa dropped the pilum. Then he reached behind him and pulled something from behind his back. When he dropped it and I saw the crimson, purple and gold cloth wrapped around it, I realized he'd been carrying the spearhead with him, too.

It was only twenty feet away. So close, yet also an unbridgeable distance considering my physical condition and being in a room filled with minions and an über-powerful demon.

Then Costa came over to me and knelt next to me, his expression twisting when he looked at my sawed-off arm. His expression grew even darker when he lifted my sweater and saw the bullet holes I still didn't want to look at. Instead, I watched as he pulled a bag of manna from his jeans pocket that was bulging full. He had come to the island prepared.

"You should use some yourself," I said, although it was becoming much harder to talk. "You look awful."

"You first," he said, forcing a smile as he smeared both hands with the sticky substance, then put one over my stump and the other over what was probably the worst of my bullet holes.

I braced for the pain that always came when flesh was forced to rapidly repair itself, yet nothing happened. Costa's expression grew stricken and he grabbed a bigger handful from the bag, then placed the new batch over my stomach.

Nothing. Not even a tingle. When I glanced at my arm, the end still looked open and mangled, too.

"You're not healing," Costa said in anguish.

I wasn't, which meant only one thing. My wounds were mortal. Now all we had was our worst enemy's word that he'd bring me back after I died, which would be very soon.

CHAPTER FORTY-FIVE

ADRIAN'S FACE WAS several degrees past stricken. I had never seen him look so tortured, and his gaze filled with tears.

"No," he whispered.

"Yes!" Demetrius said delightedly. "Looks like I get my wish to see her dead once after all."

If my severed limb had been anywhere nearby and I'd had the strength, I would have thrown it at him. I had resigned myself to dying, but I hadn't wanted it to be like *this*.

"Let me free," Adrian said, twisting against his chains. "I won't let her die alone."

"She's not alone. She's right there," Demetrius said with an exasperated wave in my direction.

Adrian stopped struggling and he lasered a glare at Demetrius. "Once you're done here, I am leaving with you and I'll probably never see her again. You can give me this."

Demetrius sighed. "From admiringly vicious to depressingly sentimental. Very well, since this will indeed be one of your last moments with her, why not?" Then his gaze narrowed. "I don't need to remind you that I am now Ivy's only hope of resurrection, so if you try anything, you will lose her forever. Then, of course,

I'll murder your friend and your gargoyle in ways that will haunt your nightmares for decades to come."

Brutus was alive? Despite my circumstances being as grim as they could get, the thought cheered me. I had feared the worst after realizing that Demetrius had bounced back so quickly after Brutus's attack, not to mention the gargoyle's absence now.

"Understood," Adrian said coldly. "Now release me."

Demetrius nodded at his minions. From their expressions, they didn't want to do this, but since they were standing on the grainy remains of minions who had probably pissed Demetrius off, no one argued. They hurried over and began to unlock and then unwind the chains from around Adrian.

"Now, no more delays. Dip the end of the pilum in the bowl, boy," Demetrius said to Costa.

Costa got up, giving me an apologetic look. Then his face turned to stone as he took the pilum and brought it over to the table. I knew what Demetrius had said about the power of the ground-up remains of that infamous tree, but I still hoped nothing would happen when the end of that long stick touched the sawdust-like contents in the huge golden bowl.

All the air felt like it was sucked out of the room, and the pilum, which had been a deep shade of brown, turned black as pitch before my next blink. I hadn't realized how much energy I'd been siphoning from the pilum until everything that was hallowed about it abruptly vanished. My vision narrowed, my body turned to ice and I might have even briefly passed out, because the next thing I knew, I was gathered in Adrian's arms.

"It's okay," he was crooning, and I realized he was rocking me, only because I saw him moving. I couldn't feel it, nor could I feel his arms around me. I couldn't feel anything anymore.

"Adrian," I whispered. I wanted to say more, but I lacked the ability. Had I died and Demetrius had already brought me back? No. That couldn't be. If he had, I wouldn't still be paralyzed by weakness from my injuries and blood loss.

"Shh," he said, kissing me. "You'll be all right soon."

Here you go lying to me again, I thought, unable to say it out loud. Nothing would be all right soon, least of all me. Even if I were brought back, that would only mean I'd keep living to miss him every day, plus regret how I'd failed all those people in the realms, plus doomed Adrian to their same fate.

"Now the spearhead," I heard Demetrius say, unbridled joy in his tone. "Don't merely dip the end of it in the bowl. Drop the entire spearhead into it."

No wonder the bowl was so big. That was the only way the spearhead could fit inside. And couldn't I at least die before witnessing Demetrius's greatest triumph? Damn that bowl. From my vantage point on the ground, its huge, shiny surface filled much of the space past Adrian's arm, which my head was currently lolled upon. I'd tell Adrian to move himself or his shadows so that he blocked it, but I didn't have the strength to speak.

Besides, *Move a little to the right* would hardly be a good choice for my last words.

Costa picked up the bundle of royal-colored cloths and unwrapped it. With that, I finally saw the ancient relic I'd first tried so hard to find, then tried to convince myself not to find and then finally tried to find again.

It didn't look like the most sought-after weapon in the world. It looked like an extended metal arrow with a triangle point at the tip. It was wider at its base where the pilum would connect and thus triple its overall length. Of course, Demetrius was waiting to reassemble the weapon until after he'd cursed this part of it, too.

"Is that blood?" Costa said, tilting the spearhead.

My vision was dimming too much to tell, but Demetrius didn't have a problem seeing it. He let out a derisive sound.

"So the rumors are true—the blood can't be washed off. Discovering that scared Longinus into abandoning the Roman army after his role in the execution, or so they say."

I silently willed Costa to throw the spearhead at Demetrius instead of putting it in the bowl. Even if Costa didn't impale him with it, maybe getting brushed by the spearhead would kill Demetrius. But Costa didn't, and Adrian didn't break his word by interfering, either. He only kissed my face again.

"I love you, Ivy," he whispered.

I love you, too, I thought as Costa went over and held the spearhead over the golden bowl. Then I closed my eyes.

I didn't want to see Demetrius's face when the spearhead was dropped into the bowl. I didn't want to see what the spearhead looked like after the silvery-colored iron had turned black. Or see Demetrius hold up what had once been the world's most hallowed relic yet was now the world's most evil. I didn't—

An explosion went off. My eyes flew open, yet I didn't see the walls crumbling, the furniture overturning or anything else that would account for the enormity of the shockwave that had just hit me. More confusing, no one else seemed to notice that anything had happened.

Demetrius peered over the edge of the bowl, which hadn't even shifted despite the concussive force that had blasted into me. "Why is nothing happening?"

"How should I know?" Costa said curtly.

How could they think nothing was happening? If they hadn't felt that incredible expulsion of power a moment ago, couldn't they feel its equally thunderous intake *now*, as if the entire island had suddenly sucked in its breath?

"Bury it completely beneath the grains," Demetrius ordered Costa. "Do it!"

Costa said something I didn't catch, but I assume he pushed the spearhead all the way beneath the ground-up remains of the cursed tree, because Demetrius's frown cleared.

"That should do it," the demon muttered. "Now, one of—"

Demetrius didn't get to finish his sentence because the room exploded again. This time, *everyone* felt it.

CHAPTER FORTY-SIX

LIGHT SHOT FROM the bowl, a hundred times brighter than Zach at his most dazzling. The bowl shattered and the ceiling disintegrated the moment the light touched it. Then that light widened and Adrian flung himself over me. Now I couldn't see anything except his chest and part of his shadows, which looked like they tried to cover me, too. But before my gaze, they burned away, until nothing was left of the ones that I could see.

My ears were ringing from the blast, so I didn't hear it at first. Moments later, I realized the other high-pitched sounds partially deafening me were screams coming from every direction, none louder than the one with the voice I most hated.

"No!" Demetrius's shout cut through all the others. *"NO!"*

I couldn't see what had him howling in despair, and I really regretted that. Whatever it was, I loved it.

Suddenly, Adrian was gone and I was back on the floor. I looked up to see Adrian wrestling Demetrius away from me. The demon's eyes were wild from rage, and dark rivulets ran from them, his ears and his nose.

"She did this!" Demetrius howled. "She stopped the spearhead from turning into a cursed object. It has to be her!"

It absolutely wasn't. I couldn't even scoot out of

the way to avoid them, let alone stop a hallowed object from turning dark. Then Demetrius spun Adrian around, and I got my first look at Adrian's back since that light had exploded from the golden bowl. If I'd had enough breath left in me, I would have gasped.

His shadows were completely gone. All that was left to show that they had ever been there were scorch marks on his now-bare back. When the light had burned them away, it had burned them to the point where they'd caught his shirt on fire, too.

It left Adrian with nothing but his strength to fight Demetrius, and the demon was stronger. But he'd expelled a lot of his power earlier, plus been injured by the light explosion, judging from him bleeding out of every hole in his face. Demetrius couldn't summon his minions to help him, either. If the demon looked to be in bad shape, his minions were in far worse.

They were on their knees, that same inky substance shooting from eyes, ears, noses and mouths, but in far greater quantities. It looked as if their bodies were convulsively purging out all the evil that Demetrius had given them when he tethered his soul to theirs and turned them into minions. I wasn't surprised when they started turning into ashes, their bodies unable to handle the effects of the supernatural assault.

"Let go of me, Adrian!" Demetrius shouted. "I tried to spare her for you, but the spearhead didn't transform. It has to be her fault! Can't you see that she must die now and stay dead in order for this to succeed?"

"If she dies forever, then so do you," Adrian snarled, spinning Demetrius around so that the demon was farther away from me. "Costa!" Adrian yelled. "Connect the pilum to the spearhead!"

"No!" Demetrius screamed. "Don't! I'll kill you!"

Costa, who appeared to be the only one uninjured from the massive explosion of light, ran over to the remains of the golden bowl. The only reason he almost fell was because the ground started shaking. Then Costa plunged his hand into the pile of sawdust and withdrew the spearhead. Grains from the cursed tree still fell from it when Costa shoved it onto the top of the pilum.

Another shockwave blasted into me that no one else seemed to feel. It brought back all the pain that had previously dimmed, until my body felt like it was being scalded within and without. The agony was so intense, it cleared the haze from my mind and even brought my vision back to momentary clarity. That was how I was able to see the pilum go from deepest ebony back to its normal brown shade. Attaching the spearhead to the pilum had somehow cleansed it from being a cursed object. Now the pilum was hallowed again, and the fully reassembled, supercharged weapon was only a short distance away.

"Give it to me, Costa!" I shouted, reaching out with the only hand I had left.

I don't know how I had the strength for those words when I couldn't speak before, but I did, and my voice rang out with all the hopeful desperation in me. I even managed to twist myself into a sitting position. I must be siphoning energy from the rejoined hallowed weapon. That was the only explanation.

"No!"

Demetrius's assault became so frenzied that it pushed Adrian back toward Costa. Then he shoved Adrian so hard that Adrian lost his grip on him. But he tangled his feet in Demetrius's at the last second, and both of them ended up tumbling to the floor.

Costa looked at the tangle of bodies in a life-and-death struggle in front of him. They blocked his way to me, and the fighting was so fierce, it could overtake him at any moment.

Costa muttered something in Greek. Then he hurled the reassembled spear at me while yelling, "Catch!"

Who throws a spear at a one-armed dying woman? I thought incredulously. But, as if that single word activated a muscle-memory reaction in me, my left hand shot up and I caught the wooden part of the spear as if I'd been snatching spears out of the air my entire life.

Demetrius met my eyes at that exact moment, and I saw something in his that I had never seen before.

Fear.

Then power crashed into me with the same force that had burned away Adrian's shadows, killed the minions and severely injured Demetrius. I felt it killing me, too, but I felt something else, and it made the indescribable agony of all my blood vessels suddenly bursting worth it.

I felt light blast into every demon realm, blowing them open as easily as that other light had blown the roof off this building. Felt the legions of minions they contained being struck by the same violent, deadly convulsions I'd seen here, and felt the demons recoiling in crippling pain, too. I also felt where those new passageways of light led to: the Archon realms, reminding me that Zach had said every time demons made a new realm, Archons struck back by making one of their own.

More important, like a whisper across my soul, I felt

the same emotion from the countless trapped humans who were finally seeing light after too many years of darkness.

Hope.

Demetrius had often taunted me that I never stood a chance. Too many times, I'd believed that. But the last thing I felt was the knowledge that the power behind the unstoppable third hallowed weapon had never been in danger of being used by demons. Demetrius had been right about one thing: all of this had been planned long in advance. It was he and the other demons who had been doomed from the start.

With that final, satisfying thought, I died.

CHAPTER FORTY-SEVEN

I'D HEARD PEOPLE describe post-death, out-of-body experiences. They talked about floating above a surgical room after their hearts stopped during an operation, or seeing their prone bodies following a car accident. All the ones I'd heard featured people saying they didn't feel any particular attachment to what they were looking at, as if all their normal emotions were too petty once they were outside their bodies.

I didn't have that kind of blasé attitude.

For one, I could have cheered myself hoarse when I saw Adrian take advantage of Demetrius staring at me in fear after I grabbed the spear. While I was being blasted apart internally, Adrian grabbed Demetrius's throat and ripped his heart out of it. Then, while his father's body was still falling to the ground, he flipped Demetrius in an MMA-worthy move that ended with the demon on his back and Adrian's leg around his neck. Adrian then used all his incredible strength to rip Demetrius's head right off.

Cue me doing cartwheels of joy despite not having a body.

Adrian didn't stop there. He also grabbed the biggest piece of the shattered golden bowl, spilling out the remains of the cursed tree that hadn't been enough to overcome the power behind the spearhead. Then

Adrian used that piece to beat Demetrius's decapitated head in. Afterward, Adrian started bashing Demetrius's body to a pulp with that heavy golden remnant. Costa finally stepped in and pulled Adrian off Demetrius, which I understood, although after everything Demetrius had done, I could've stood to see Adrian wail on his crumpled body a little longer.

Adrian's shoulders slumped as he dropped the now heavily dented piece and looked across the room. My body was there, and wow, did I look terrible. It looked like I'd showered in blood. I hadn't, of course, but at some point, I must have rolled around in the puddle my wounds had made, because you couldn't tell what color my hair was anymore. The only thing more jarring was seeing the stump at the end of my right elbow. It looked even more ragged with my new bird's-eye view.

Adrian ignored all of that grossness when he went over, threw his arms around the bloody, mangled mess that was my body and cried. It hurt to watch and not be able to do anything to comfort him. I wanted to tell him it was okay, that we'd done what we'd hoped to do and I wasn't in pain or afraid anymore, but of course, I couldn't say any of that.

Costa knelt next to him. I was touched when I saw his shoulders heave with sobs, too. Then someone appeared behind them, although neither of them noticed.

Zach. He stared at them, his expression showing more empathy than I'd ever seen from the Archon. Wow, he was capable of feeling deep emotion after all. Go figure.

Zach suddenly looked straight up and one eyebrow rose in his usual, challenging way as if to say, *Oh, really?* If I still had eyes, they would have widened in shock. Could he *hear* me?

Zach! I tried screaming, but he only tilted his head down and looked at Adrian and Costa again. That was when Adrian finally noticed him, and he swung around so fast, he was holding on to the hem of Zach's hoodie before Zach could take a step backward.

"Please," Adrian said, his sapphire eyes never more vivid. "I don't care what you were ordered. She did everything you people wanted her to do, even though she was *pregnant*, and she doesn't deserve to have it end like this!"

"As I told you and her many times before, I cannot raise her," Zach began, only to have Adrian shove him away violently. Then, to my anguish, he grabbed the reassembled spear that had fallen a few feet from my body and hugged the length of the weapon to him.

But he didn't drop dead, which was obviously his intention, because he frowned at the weapon, then shook it as if that would make it work. Zach sighed and held out his hand. The spear pulled free of Adrian's grip and zoomed over to Zach, turning itself spearhead-side up before the pilum landed in his hand.

"The power it contained has been used as it was intended," Zach said. "It is now depleted and can do you no harm."

"But you can," Adrian said, and lunged at Zach.

The Archon sidestepped him with a speed I might not have been able to track before. Then he held up his other hand, and Adrian was suddenly frozen in place.

"Let me go," Adrian snarled.

"I know why you're filled with more darkness and rage than you've ever felt before," Zach said with his usual annoying calmness. "Your humanity died when Ivy did. The bond that had tethered your souls together dragged it with her into the grave. You are fully demon now."

Costa looked as stunned as I felt. Zach had previously assured me that Adrian would survive my death because his humanity was the smallest part of his Judian/demon makeup. But he sure hadn't told me that it would result in this.

"Fine." Adrian was the only one who wasn't reacting in shock to this news. "And Archons kill demons, especially the Archon general himself, so do your job, *Michael*."

"I could," Zach agreed coolly. "Or you could use your newfound, fully demon powers to raise her."

Now Adrian looked stunned, and I was so blown away, I couldn't even think straight. "I can do that?" Adrian managed.

"You can now," Zach said, his look turning knowing. "Had Ivy not died, your remaining humanity would have blocked your ability to raise her, but as a full demon, there is nothing stopping you."

"But you said she was forbidden from being raised." Adrian sounded confused, as if he was searching for the catch to this.

Zach's mouth quirked in a hint of a smile. "No, I said that *I* was forbidden from raising her."

"You sneaky Archon," Costa breathed, his expression changing from shock to awe. "You knew all along that it would come to this, didn't you?"

"I knew that it could," Zach said simply. "But only if Ivy fulfilled her destiny while Adrian did not fulfill his."

I still found it hard to believe that I could actually come back. Yes, that was what Zach was saying, but it had been so often stressed to me that if I died, that was it—curtains! Finito! Adios!—that I struggled to comprehend that it wasn't over.

Adrian appeared just as shell-shocked, yet he went over to my body and knelt next to it. "What do I do?"

Zach stayed where he was. "You pour out every last drop of your power into her. Hold nothing back, and understand that when it is over, you will still technically be a demon, but you will have no demonic abilities left."

"How's that?" Costa said, echoing my thought. "Demetrius raised people from the dead, and he still had his abilities afterward."

"Demetrius was older than this world," Zach replied. "His powers had untold ages to strengthen and grow. Adrian's are new, and doing this will deplete all of them."

"I don't need them," Adrian said, taking my left hand and bowing his head over it. "I only need her."

"Then pour your abilities into Ivy," Zach said softly. "To do that, you must first let yourself feel all the pain you're trying not to feel now. Hold none of it back. Then turn that pain into power and fill Ivy with it. Give it all to her, until you have nothing left, and then—" Zach looked up, and it felt like he met my eyes even though I didn't know how that could be possible "—she will return to you."

Adrian dropped my hand and gathered me into his lap, holding me the way he had when I was dying. He even began rocking me again. When he pressed kisses onto my face and told me how much he loved me, every tear that slid down his cheeks felt like a tug on a body that I no longer had anymore.

"You have to come back to me," he whispered. "I can't do this without you, Ivy. Even if I could, I don't want to."

Tug. Tug. Tug. It was the weirdest thing—I could feel it in a tangible way, but I couldn't point to *where* I was feeling it, since my physical body was down there. I didn't know what I had here. Disembodied consciousness, clearly, but was there more? Was Adrian pulling on a thread that reached me even here?

"You're so tough on yourself, but that's because you don't know how amazing you are," Adrian went on. "You try so hard to do the right thing. Even when you tried not to, you still couldn't help yourself." Then his voice became ragged. "I was so angry at you over that. I wanted you to love me more than everyone in this world and all the others, and I didn't care what that meant for the people trapped in the realms. Not until you made me care. From the moment I met you, you made me a better man, even when I didn't want to be. Even when I didn't think it was possible."

Adrian's head dipped and his shoulders began to shake. Costa looked away, as if doing so would give Adrian privacy while he willingly ripped himself open in order to give power to his pain. Zach stood there, a silent sentry, no expression on his face. As an Archon, he was probably used to seeing the deepest, most personal aspects of people's pain.

"You know what? I'm still mad at you."

Adrian's voice was barely comprehensible from how choked it became. At the same time, those invisible tugs I'd felt strengthened, until they felt less like tugs and more like hard, increasing yanks.

"Letting Demetrius trick you by pretending to be Costa? Come on, Ivy! Didn't your tattoos flare up? Didn't he sound different? Or were you too obsessed with getting the spearhead to notice? You were too obsessed to tell me about our baby, and I am pissed as hell about that. You knew I'd tell you to wait, that I'd make you wait if I could, and yeah, you turned out to be right about not waiting to get the spearhead, but I'm still pissed at you. I shouldn't have heard about our baby from Demetrius. I shouldn't have learned that I'm going to be a father *that* way."

Yank. Yank. YANK!

Adrian's face began to blur. So did Costa's, Zach's and even the entire room. Seeing it made me panic, yet I didn't know what to do. Shouldn't they be getting clearer, if I were coming back? What if this wasn't working?

"But you were right again." Adrian's voice was completely broken now, and the sob that heaved out of him made everything vanish. I couldn't see anything anymore. Couldn't feel anything, either, yet I could still hear his voice.

"If I had stopped us from coming to the island—and I would have, we all know that—then Demetrius would've kept chasing you through his link to our child's blood. One day, he would have caught you, and he would have made you find the spearhead for him, either by tormenting you, or by tormenting our child, if it was born by then. Things would have been worse, and it would have been my fault. Now we have another chance, and it's because you were strong when

I would have been selfish again. Even at my best, I'm not like you, but come back to me, Ivy, and I swear I'll try to be…"

Suddenly, I couldn't hear him anymore. I couldn't hear anything! What was happening? I couldn't see, feel, hear or touch. I was supposed to be coming back, not fading away completely. Something was wrong. Something was very wrong! *Zach? Zach? Zach! This isn't working! Don't leave me like this! You have to help—*

"…always," Adrian said, and relief shattered me when I could hear him again. "For you, Ivy. I promise. I love you," he whispered, brushing his lips over mine.

Wait a minute. I felt that. I FELT THAT!

I opened my eyes. At first, all I saw was red and my eyes stung. I tried to wipe the red away, which had to be blood, but I used my right arm out of habit and ended up hitting myself in the face with its stump.

"Ivy?" Adrian's whole body stiffened, then he grabbed me tight enough to hurt and leapt up, swinging me around in a wild embrace. *"Ivy!"*

"I love you, too, Adrian."

My voice wasn't hoarse. I don't know why I thought it would be. Maybe because my arm hadn't magically regrown even though the other wounds in my body had to have supernaturally healed or I'd still be dead. I didn't even hurt anymore, although my arm felt… weird. The skin around it was now smooth and closed over. Not seeing the mangled inside of it anymore was a relief.

"You're back!"

Costa ran over, hugging both of us, since Adrian had

yet to let me go. Not that I wanted him to. I couldn't get enough of feeling his arms around me again.

"You did it," I whispered to Adrian.

He kissed me, so hard and fierce, I wasn't sure if I was tasting old blood from my former wounds, or if my lip had gotten nicked on his teeth. Either way, I didn't care. I didn't even care that my right arm now ended at the elbow. I had never felt more whole in my entire life.

"Your tattoos are gone again," I heard Costa say several moments later.

That caused me to pull back from Adrian's blazing kiss. I looked down. My top was torn enough to see that the staff etching was gone, and the sling hadn't reappeared anywhere else that I could see.

"I hope I don't need them anymore," I said, looking over Adrian's shoulder at Zach. "Right? Am I done with all that now?"

"Yes," Zach said, those tiny lights glowing in his dark eyes. "From now on, the fight belongs to Archons, not humans."

I was so relieved that I sagged in Adrian's arms. He bent to kiss me again and I wanted that kiss, but I turned my head. There was something else I had to know that couldn't wait.

"Zach. Did I…"

I stopped. It was hard to continue on without feeling ungrateful, which couldn't be further from the truth. I was unbelievably happy to be back with Adrian, and beyond thrilled to know that right now, thousands of formerly trapped humans were making their way into the Archon realms. Asking about more felt insanely greedy, but I had to know.

"Did I come back alone?" I finished in a halting voice, my left hand resting over my stomach.

Adrian took it, lacing his fingers through mine. "Either way, I love you, and it's going to be okay, Ivy."

I knew it would, no matter what Zach said. I did. But one way or another, I needed to know the answer.

Zach began to smile. It didn't stop at the barest twitch of his lips, which was his normal version. Instead, it spread out to one of his rare, teeth-showing, full-faced smiles.

"No, you did not come back alone."

I started to cry. Hey, pregnant women do that a lot! Adrian hugged me again, far more gently this time, and through my tears, I saw Costa smile and swipe at his own eyes.

"Enough of that, you two. We still have work to do. Demetrius trapped Brutus in a sinkhole on the island, so we have to get him out. Then you two can break the news to that spoiled gargoyle that he's no longer going to be an only child."

"It's okay," I said, repeating the words I'd heard so often today yet had only believed during the past few minutes. "I know Brutus will make a *wonderful* big brother."

* * * * *

ACKNOWLEDGMENTS

I CRIED WRITING the Acknowledgments page for my last book, since I was giving a tribute to my late mother in it. I don't want to break into tears again, so I'm keeping this one short and sweet. As always, my first thanks go to God. Some days, I still can't believe I have the job that I dreamed about when I was a kid. Of course, I also have to thank my husband, Matthew, for far too many things to list, and my family, for their love and support. Thanks also to my wonderful editor, Allison Carroll, and to my fabulous agent, Nancy Yost. Special thanks also go to dear friends Melissa Marr and Ilona Andrews, who dropped everything to give me notes during a very tight turnaround time. Thanks also to the Harlequin team for all their hard work with this series. Finally, I'd like to send endless gratitude out to the readers of this series, and to readers everywhere. Each time you open a book, you make our stories come alive.

AUTHOR'S NOTE

THE MOST RECENT full solar eclipse occurred in a different month and was visible over a different continent. For the purposes of this story, however, I changed both.

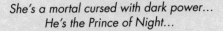

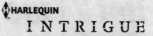

Get 2 Free Books,

HARLEQUIN

ROMANTIC suspense

Plus 2 Free Gifts—
just for trying the Reader Service!